"A wonderful read for anyone who e̶̶̶ characters with larger-than-life per̶s̶onalities. The story ̶u̶̶̶̶ against the background of contemporary life in the American West with an abundance of quirky, modern twists. Filled with humor and heartbreaking insights about loss, love, and deep misunderstandings, Froman gives her readers the gift of a fine book. A good story, well told and enhanced with insights about the value of differences. Definitely a keeper."

—**Anne Hillerman**, New York Times best-selling author of
the Leaphorn-Chee-Manuelito mysteries

"I love a good mystery! When I also learn something new— about 3D printers and drones, in this instance—I know I'm in the hands of a skilled writer. That's why I loved B. K. Froman's *Hardly Any Shooting Stars Left*. A northwest setting, unique characters with struggles we can relate to. Add plot twists and turns and refreshing images and you have one fine, fine story I loved."

—**Jane Kirkpatrick**, New York Times best-selling author of
The Healing of Natalie Curtis

"BK Froman has done it again with a shoot-from-the-hip witty mystery. If the Oregon setting isn't inspiring enough, the story offers quirky entendres, murder, mayhem, and marvelous characters. Froman's clever writing is always a cut above. This one has 'Award Winner' written all over it."

—**Anne Schroeder**, author of *The Caballero's Son*

"Entertaining, page-turning mystery of twists and secrets. Kudos to Froman for capturing a young woman's struggle to find both her place and a killer in a small town of odd and strangely endearing characters."

—**Linda Ulleseit**, author of *Aloha Spirit*

"Froman gives us a heroine of humor and courage who can face a murderer, high-tension, and the ghosts of her own past while navigating the old and new West."

—**Lynn Downey**, author of *Dudes Rush In*

"Funny and moving, told in clear-eyed, good-hearted style."

—**Patricia Lichen**, author of *Kidnapping the Wild One*

"A page-turning tale of old wounds and long-buried tension in the new West."

—**Helen Wand**, author of *Echoes of Forgotten Places*

"*Hardly Any Shooting Stars Left* melds mystery and technology into a tantalizing whodunit. Lexi Depriest strives to introduce reluctant ranchers to modern technology. When her boyfriend is found murdered at her 3D print shop, Lexi becomes entangled in a web of intrigue that threatens everyone and everything she loves."

—**Candace Simar**, award-winning author of the Abercrombie Trail Series, *Shelterbelts*, and *Escape to Fort Abercrombie*

HARDLY ANY

SHOOTING

STARS

LEFT

B.K. FROMAN

IRON
STREAM
FICTION

Birmingham, Alabama

Hardly Any Shooting Stars Left

Iron Stream Fiction
An imprint of Iron Stream Media
100 Missionary Ridge
Birmingham, AL 35242
IronStreamMedia.com

Library of Congress Control Number: 2021950069

Cover design by Hannah Linder Designs

ISBN: 978-1-64526-372-2 (paperback)

ISBN: 978-1-64526-373-9 (ebook)

1 2 3 4 5—25 24 23 22 21 22

MANUFACTURED IN THE UNITED STATES OF AMERICA

To Amy S., Linda W., Anne S.
Thanks for lifting me up when I forget how to fly.

1.

Lexi Depriest spit into the sink, then rinsed her toothbrush. A high-pitched wail cut through the silence of her house. The shriek of the drone's stability alarm made her drop her toothbrush and dash for the monitor in the den.

"No, no, no!" Grabbing the controller, she thumbed the left stick sideways while flicking the right stick forward. "Come on, get out of there."

On screen, images of pasture and black cattle wobbled and turned. She thumbed harder, yelling as though she could push her will through the controls. The view twisted in circles, each slanted spin showing it neared the pond, the sun glinting off ripples on the surface. "C'mon, lift. Lift!"

The view jolted and stopped moving. The drone's front-mount camera cast a cock-eyed image across mud and water, gazing toward the barn. Like a slow-moving train wreck, Lexi watched the view slowly tilt, panning upward until the camera faced the crisp, blue morning sky. Grumbling, she tapped buttons on her keyboard, saving the video images the drone had broadcast to the computer as it flew over the cattle.

"Six a.m. Time to go fishin'," sang the rubber fish on the wall, a clock-face in its belly.

"Oh, shut up." She threw the controller onto the desk, knocking over a framed photo. *Sorry, Dad.*

She grimaced, hurrying to her bedroom, cursing her crappy luck. She'd already dressed for her presentation at Rotary. Shucking out of her blue slacks and the maroon silk shirt, she

1

laid them in assembly-line order on the foot of the bed. At least they'd be ready for her quick-change when she came back.

On her way out the door, still buttoning her jeans, she passed the monitor. The screen image, spattered with mud, showed a cow snuffling and stringing slobber across the lens.

Great! Her luck was still crappy.

Grumbling, she trotted to the barn. Bigger than the house, the three-story white structure with its craftsmanship of dove-tailed joints and stone-laid foundation showed it was the pride of whoever had built it. Stalls lined half of the bottom floor. Well-worn ladders led to hay lofts, grain storage, and cobwebs in the upper stories.

The old ATV sat in a stall with buckets, tubs, and tarps piled on it. Lexi arm-swept them off, coughing from the dust. She kicked open a swath in front of the vehicle.

The key dangled from the ignition where her dad had left it. A quick twist. Nothing happened. A few more torques and the engine still didn't turn over.

"Figures." It hadn't been used since he'd died thirteen months ago. "Aaaargh!" She pounded the steering wheel.

Jumping off, she grabbed an empty gunny sack and jogged through the backdoor of the barn. With two fingers circled in her mouth, she gave a two-note whistle. The paint horse lifted her head and ambled from the pasture. Lexi grabbed a halter and ran to Molly, giving the blaze on her forehead a quick rub when they met.

"Hey, girl."

Still clutching the gunny sack, Lexi put both hands on the mare's back and jumped, rising to her chest before sliding back down.

Molly U-ed her neck and watched.

"I'm out of practice, okay?" Lexi jumped again. This time she managed to drape herself over the horse's back like a wet string. But before she could pull herself into a sitting position,

Molly began walking, snorting, and sawing her head. Lexi slid back to the ground.

"I don't have time for this. Stand still." She grabbed a handful of mane, then sprang up. Teetering on top like a seesaw, she swung a leg over the horse's back and squeezed her legs. Molly took off, the gunny sack flapping in the breeze.

It had been a while—a long while. Lexi kept her eyes open and one hand buried in the mane, remembering her twelve-year-old self riding with eyes closed, arms wide, embracing the wind.

Above her, the sun owned the heavens, drying the pastures from the thunderstorm several nights ago. The clean scent of new-washed earth clung to the morning, dewy grass muffling the beat of Molly's hooves.

Clusters of Black Angus, with numbers freeze-branded on their flanks, looked up or skittered aside as she passed. Without thinking, she scanned the animals, just as the drone had been doing. Number 717 hung its head too low as though it were ill. She'd check it against the video footage from the past two days. See if it had a worsening condition.

Her dad's voice echoed in her mind. "Robo-beef. It's no way to ranch."

"It's either them or you," she'd told him when she began using drones. "I can't take care of both. Which do you want?"

"There's never time enough to do it all." He'd given her a half-smile, then looked out the window, his tubes and hoses lying against weather-creased skin that should have been out in the sun.

Lexi hated those last mental pictures. Him wishing he could be outside. Her wishing she could be in her shop.

Each morning, she sent a drone to programmed waypoints over the pastures, recording their cattle. Later, she reviewed the videos. The drone had eased her chores—until today.

"Whoa." Lexi shifted her weight back, signaling the horse, then slid off before Molly had fully stopped. At the edge of the pond, five steers circled the two-foot-wide drone. Her boots sank into the muck, making squelching sounds with each step.

"Move!" She slapped hindquarters, working her way between cattle. Elbowing their heads out of the way, she carefully pulled the device from hoof-pocked manure and mud.

A frown crossed her face. A propeller arm should've protruded from the four corners of the drone, but now there were only three. Plunging her hand in sludge, she noodled for the missing piece. Nothing. Several steers left, their hooves splattering her as she held up the device, mud falling in chunks as she inspected it. One of the corner booms was gone, as though it had been chewed off. She ran her finger over the rough, jagged plastic. A lead pellet fell into her palm.

Her glare snapped toward the good-neighbor gate separating her property from the next ranch several acres away. No one was in the pasture, but a trail in the dew showed someone had been there.

"You hateful old coot!" Sure he was watching from his house, she held up the drone, shaking it, flinging mud around her. Molly sidestepped a few feet away. "You're gonna pay for this!"

Stuffing the muddy drone in the gunny sack, she mounted— after three tries—and kneed the horse into a gallop, thundering back to her barn.

※

At the back of the property, a skinny young man stepped from behind a tree. He resettled his hat from its pushed-back position. Man. Why should a young woman have such a temper? Usually it was old, dried-up, bossy women who were so bitter. It wasn't right for a young gal to flare up like that. Her red hair might account for some of her peevishness, but still … some guy oughta teach her to calm down.

4

His eyes followed the horse and rider across the pasture, the hoofbeats fading into the barn. He looked around. It was a pretty place. Lotta work. He shook his head, pushing away the idea teasing his mind. He didn't have time to get involved. He had work to do, and it meant a lot of money.

He might even have to kill some fool to make his plan work. His mouth tensed. That young woman and her temper could get in his way. He hoped not. But he understood how to make his intentions work. He could be patient.

Staring at the open door of the barn where horse and rider had disappeared, he decided he'd get what he wanted. All of it. He shouldered his shotgun, turned, and stepped back into the woods.

2.

Lexi rushed into the house and back to her bedroom. The slacks she'd neatly laid on the bed were now on the floor with the dog nesting on top of them.

"Chicken! What have you done?" She pulled the pants from under him, gave them a sniff, then a shake. "Aaargh!" Hair floated in the air.

Chicken lay flat, looking up at her. "I'm so sorry, boy." Unsteady on one foot, she tried to pat his head as she slipped a leg into her trousers. "I know you're bored, ol' fella, and I can't do anything about it right now. We'll do belly-rubs tonight."

Pulling her bedcover partially onto the floor, her toe tapped it as her foot emerged from the other trouser leg. "Nap on that. I'll see you in a few hours." She stepped into her shoes and put on her silk blouse, buttoning it as she walked out the door. Her clothes felt heavy with guilt. She paused, listening for the dog. Not a whimper or whine, only her silent regret.

She drove like Batman, gravel flying behind her F-150 for the seven miles to the fizzled-out burg of Telos, Oregon.

The truck skidded to a stop in front of BrainSmith Printing. At seven-thirty in the morning only one figure stood on Main Street. She hopped out, yelling, "Hi, Rick. Gotta grab my laptop." Before the young man could answer, she'd unlocked her shop door and dashed inside.

Rick stopped brooming water across the sidewalk to watch her. He was Vietnamese, but language wasn't the reason he wasn't quick to answer. They'd gone to school together, same grade, but Rick had special help to get through classes. His face sometimes wore a grin as though he reveled in the happy music of life that the rest of world couldn't hear.

The shop's door slammed behind Lexi and she ran to her truck. Rick gave her a two-fingered salute. "All is well."

"Good job." She returned the salute, their usual morning exchange. "Can't talk. I've got to make a speech." She hopped into her Ford F-150, but as she started driving, she saw Rick framed in her rearview mirror, pointing at her, his face dimming.

Throwing the truck into reverse, she gunned it backward, the tires sliding as she braked. She rolled down the window. "Whatsa matter?"

"You have hair on you."

"Oh, yeah, the dog—" She waved. "I'll tell you later. Thanks." The tires squealed as she took off. In the mirror, Rick's grin spread ear to ear.

It took five seconds to drive one block to the Crusty Biscuit. With one hand on the steering wheel, she beat at her slacks. Hair floated throughout the cab and settled back on her.

She snagged the last spot in the diner's parking lot, got out, and rushed inside. With the laptop clutched to her chest and a large canvas tote swinging from her shoulder, she nodded to folks, mumbling, "Hi," as she threaded through tables, moving toward the back room where the Rotary held its meetings.

"Slow down, Shorty, before you tip the cart," Sull Wixly called out as she squeezed past his chair.

"You! You destructive ol' coot." She eyed her neighbor. "I'm pressing charges. Be ready to pull out your wallet and pay for my drone." She glared at the crease-faced old man, his white hair sticking out beneath a well-worn, GI-issued boonie hat.

He lifted bushy eyebrows and grinned at the men at his table. "Bzzzzz. Bzzzzzz."

"You can't shoot people's property out of the air. Vietnam is over," she said.

He mumbled a comment she didn't hear. Giving him a burning look, she headed toward the back room. Laughter followed her.

As she slipped through the swinging door, the president, Bill Brandt, pointed to an empty seat. "We started without you. We're concluding new business." He nodded toward twelve people eating breakfast.

"Go ahead. Sorry, I'm late. I had to take care of a piece of vandalized equipment. I'll set up while you finish eating." Lexi connected her laptop to the projector and surveyed her audience. She'd wished more people had come. There were several ranchers and local business people, including a realtor. But no big businesses. She'd hoped the manager of the plastic manufacturing plant in La Grande would be here. That would be a bread-and-butter account, paying the rent for months.

As the waitress cleared the dirty dishes, Bill stood. "I'm sure many of you have known Lexi Depriest since she was in 4-H and a champion rider. But now she's a businesswoman helping to rejuvenate our town by dragging us into the twenty-first century. She's here today to talk about her shop, BrainSmith Printing."

Lexi resisted pulling down her shirt or smoothing her slacks as she stood and cleared her throat. "When you tell your family or friends about this presentation—and I hope you *will* tell them—this is the point I want you to remember. It's not a question of *if* you'll ever use a 3D printer. It's a question of *when* you'll use a 3D printer. This is the appliance of the future."

She showed the video of the printers in her shop laying down thin strips of plastic, creating wrenches, vases, and statues. "Any tool, mechanical part, or thingamajig you can think of, I can design a computer program which instructs the printers how to create it. The possibilities are endless.

"For instance, my dad's tailgate wouldn't open. We took it apart and discovered the plastic lever that fit in the ratchet had broken. Rather than try to find a place that still stocked parts, I made one in less than an hour and fixed the tailgate."

Lexi surveyed the group. At least no one had pulled out their phones yet. "Currently, I print for hospitals in two counties, as well as a security firm, a power boat manufacturer, and an architect. Just last week, the high school ordered twenty-five of these for the senior class." She held up a small white tiger head. "Students stick it on a wall or the inside their locker and this mascot holds their headphones or jackets. So ... not to be outdone ..."

Lexi set small hawks in various colors across the table, their talons reaching forward, ready to hold a device. "The Joseph Booster Club ordered these little eagle mascots to prop up a phone while watching video." She slid her phone in one to demonstrate.

"For permanent advertising, you could give your associates and customers a branded item such as ..." She handed out bottle openers, custom hinges, and converters to adapt AA batteries to C-battery appliances. "And these are made at a fraction of the cost you'd pay at retail."

That's usually when she lost listeners, and this time was no different. They wanted to play with the gadgets. She concluded her speech by talking about 3D construction, adding, "In Dubai, Amsterdam, even Austin and New York, they're using 3D printers to lay down concrete to create small houses. Someday you might live in a 3D home." Several people had questions and she finally wrapped up the session, delighting her listeners by offering them any freebies on the table.

A half-hour later, she packed up her laptop. Several people had made appointments to watch the printers in action, which usually ended with orders.

As she walked from the back room, Bill called, "Wait." In his late forties, his hair was thinning on top, but his affable smile and a quiet manner made him successful selling policies against disasters. Lexi gripped her laptop and braced herself, suspecting what he was going to ask.

He looked around the diner. Several tables were still occupied. Bill lowered his voice. "Have you thought any more about selling your ranch?"

And there it was, the dark question she'd been asking herself for months. She looked at the floor and let out a breath. "I definitely did this morning! But I'm afraid if I sell, Dad will roar down from heaven and chain his ghost to me."

"I understand." He squeezed her arm. "It's a hard decision. Just promise you'll talk to me first whenever you're ready." He looked across the room as he spoke. Lexi followed his gaze. It landed on the face of Sull Wixly, who stared back.

Lexi nodded a goodbye and worked her way through the diner, heading toward the exit. Sull's voice rose and his gestures became more animated as she passed his table. "That gal was a bitty thing. Only eight or nine."

Without intending to, her steps slowed.

With a sly grin at Lexi, Sull continued, "Kept trying to jump on that horse, bareback. Bounced off like a tiddlywink. That's how she got her name. But you kept trying, didn't you, Shorty?"

He was the only one who called her that—and it had been years since that incident. She fixed him with an acid stare. "My name is Lexi. You'll soon be calling yourself names when a thousand dollars for the drone you shot down comes out of your pocket."

"Not sure what you're goin' on about," Sull said. "With my bad arm, I'd have a hard time keepin' a gun aimed that high." He hinged his elbow up and down with a grimace. "But I'll tell you somethin'. The buzz-buzz of your thing scares the cows."

"The cattle have seen a drone so many times, they don't pay attention unless I drop it right above their heads. The backwash from the rotors is what makes them move. It wasn't even on your property, you jackwagon. It uses GPS to fly pre-set waypoints."

"Tain't right, Shorty. Your dad didn't like it either. And if he could hear the way you talk right now, he'd tan you till you couldn't sit."

Lexi let out a breath through clenched teeth. "You need to move on, *Coot*. Stop living in the past." She took a step toward the door, then turned back. "You understand that at one time, even barbwire was new technology." She strode away, her eyes on the exit. Just a few feet to the cool breeze outside. To her truck. To drive away from these technophobic fossils.

"Just like her mom. All hiss and ice," one of the men said loud enough for her to hear.

She stopped short of the front door. Her eyes closed as a red heat exploded in her chest. The noise of the diner went silent in her head. An image of herself turning around, spraying curses like flames grew in her mind, her words scorching the old geezers till their skin blackened and blew away.

A hand touched her shoulder, shattering her thoughts. "Lexi D?" Rosalee Starr stood beside her, searching her face. "Hon," the waitress's voice rasped with years of cigarettes, "I didn't get to serve you any breakfast. Each time I went in that room you were busy. Let me get you something to eat. A cinnamon roll to go?" She patted Lexi's back, her face wrinkling as she pulled her hand away. "Good heavens. You've got a lotta hair stuck on you. Are you okay?""

The fire in Lexi's eyes went cold like yesterday's cigarette butt in the street. She let out a long breath. Great. She'd pitched her business while looking like a Yeti.

She glanced at Rosalee. No need letting the waitress know something dark and raging smoldered deep in her gut. It waited. It made her anxious, dreading the moment an accusing word or a misplaced insult would set it loose. No sense letting the world know that secret.

"Thanks for the offer, Rosalee. I'm fine," she said and left.

3.

Lexi picked up bakery treats from the Latte-Da II, and parked in front of the hardware/feedstore across the street from her shop. She rolled down the window, allowing a breeze to drift through the cab and cool off her anger. She surveyed her hometown. Telos had been built with hope. In 1908, on the whispered promise of extending the railroad line, the founding fathers had platted lots and laid out streets on the eastern Oregon prairie. Investors helped Deerheart Brewery build a long red brick building on the north side of Main. Soon thereafter, clapboard-front stores and granite-hewn buildings populated the south side of the street.

As often happened, politics diverted the rails to a burg fifteen miles away. There were lawsuits and accusations of payoffs, but Telos withered like the meaning of its unfortunate name: the ultimate end.

In the following years, economic booms caused the old buildings to refill with folks who harbored hope and had always wanted to start a business: a barbershop, an antique store, a bar, even a small-screen movie house. Then markets turned lazy again, as they always did. Sole proprietors locked their doors and moved away, returning the area to cows and grizzled ranchers.

In the latest financial uptick, the old brewery had been divided into leased spaces. BrainSmith Printing occupied the location next to the Pizza Shop. Paul's Welding rented the remaining leases, cluttering the spaces with sculptures, and stacking rebar and rusty sheets of metal in the back lot.

Her temper once more in check, she left her truck and entered her shop. "Hello? I stopped at Latte-Da II and got muffins," she called out. No one answered. She yelled louder, "Hello? Any calls this morning?"

Nine 3D printers of varying sizes sat silent in the cavernous work area. Three smaller rooms had been partitioned in the corners of the gaping space: a bathroom, a storage closet, and an area they referred to as The Other Room.

"I'm not your secretary, taking your messages." Mrs. Shirley Blackburn emerged from The Other Room. "I have my own business to run. You need to be here to care for your own concerns."

Lexi waved a hand, dismissing Mrs. Blackburn's comment. "I've been busy. Do you know the sheriff's phone number?"

The gray-haired widow frowned. She'd spent twenty-two years as administrative assistant at the high school. She'd heard every excuse known to teens or parents, and she didn't let anyone slide without a tongue-lashing. When one of her eyebrows arched and her mouth flatlined, it was time to shut up and cringe. At the present, her expression was solemn. "These are ready to be mailed." Straight-armed, she held two small packages in front of her. "And why do you need the sheriff?"

Before Lexi could answer, a baby goat the size of a large kitten nosed through The Other Room's door and bounded toward her like a four-legged pogo stick.

The little Nubian wore an aqua sweater accented with blue triangles. The sleeves covered his front legs and the bodice reached to his belly. A disposable diaper wrapped his back half.

"PeeWit! You little bonker." Lexi kneeled, offering him a piece of muffin. He bounced past her hand, butting her calf, knocking her off balance. She rolled backward; he jumped on her stomach, two-stepping right and left.

"You want to be changing diapers all day?" Mrs. Blackburn bent and snatched the muffin from Lexi's fingers. "He can't have sugary dross. Now, what's with you and the sheriff?"

13

Lexi lay on her back. It felt like the first solid footing she'd had all day. And PeeWit's attempts to chew her shirt buttons tickled and cheered her. She grabbed his tiny head with both hands and scratched behind his ears. The goat tap-danced side to side as Lexi described the morning's drone sabotage.

"A fat lot of good the Young County sheriff will do you." Mrs. Blackburn looked at her wristwatch; her mouth puckered as though the mention of him left a sour taste. "You'll have to buttonhole him and demand action if you need help. Maybe he's finished collecting freebies from the diner and made it to his office by now." She pulled a small pink paper from her sweater pocket. "And you did have a phone call."

Lexi hid a smile. The older woman couldn't let a ringing phone go unanswered. "Who was it?"

"Gavin Ceely again. He said he'd wire the barn this afternoon. Isn't he a customer? The Celesto Company?" She handed Lexi the note scribbled with the number. "Are you adding something to your barn?"

"I can't decide between a treadmill for my horse or a whisky distillery. I hate it when booze stinks up the kitchen," Lexi said. The skinny old woman gave her a sharp glare. Lexi answered with a shrug.

"Don't be smart-mouthed, and get off the floor. Look at you. Why do you have hair all over you? It's not PeeWit's." Mrs. Blackburn's eyes narrowed. "You didn't go to a business meeting looking like that, did you?"

"Why would I?"

Mrs. Blackburn's gray eyebrows arched and her mouth went stick-straight. The goat stopped wiggling and pulled from Lexi's grasp.

"I'm only your renter, and even though most of my orders come from the internet, I still consider this my place of business. You have clients. Try to act with some decorum and be professional. Treat this like a workplace. Get off the floor." She turned to leave, adding, "And I don't take messages."

I should get a medal for the things I don't *say*. Lexi watched Mrs. Blackburn walk back to The Other Room, wondering how many professionals brought their goat to work. PeeWit trailed behind the old woman, his hooves *tick-tick*ing on the floor.

⅋

Sheriff Cal LaCott had the weekly *Young County Register* open across his desk when Lexi entered the office. A barrel-shaped man, the sheriff filled out his dark-brown uniform to the point of straining the buttons with a tiny triangle of white undershirt showing at the collar.

Lexi introduced herself, adding, "Darron Depriest's daughter, sir," as a reference.

The sheriff didn't look up. "I know who you are."

Lexi waited, thinking he'd get to a stopping point in his reading and give her his full attention. After a minute, when he didn't, she cleared her throat. "Sir, I'm sorry to interrupt, but I want to file charges against Sullivan Wixly. He shot down my drone this morning."

The sheriff kept his eyes on the newsprint. "Heard about it. Got any proof?"

Lexi gave an indignant grunt. "He's over at Crusty's bragging to the old soldier's club."

"I just came from there. Wixly's spinning his usual war stories and ranting about technology. Never a word about taking a bead on your drone." He glanced at her. "Is it even legal for you to fly that thing?"

"It's registered," she said louder than she'd intended. "I've got a UAV—unmanned aerial vehicle license—and have been checked out by the Traffic and Safety Administration. Why are you questioning *me*? It's that geezer who's the problem."

"You got proof he fired at your drone?"

She searched his face. Was he serious? The community jokes about the sheriff's laid-back policing methods flashed through her mind. "I've got a propeller arm that's been chewed off by buckshot. How do you explain that, sir?" Her voice had risen again, changing her words into an accusation rather than a question. "A trail in the dew leads back to his place. He destroyed my drone, and it wasn't even over his land. I have it on a GPS-programmed route to stay on my property."

"So you saw him shoot it?" LaCott turned a page, the paper rustling beneath his matter-of-fact tone. "You watched him flee the scene?"

"No. An alarm alerted me that something had knocked the drone off its course. I had a heck of a time flying it to keep it from hitting the pond."

His head popped up. "I thought you said it only traveled a programmed route. You were flying it manually?"

Lexi bit her bottom lip, weighing whether she still needed to be civil. Her good nature said to keep a veneer of politeness, but it lost the battle. "I can't tell if you're yanking my chain or just naturally thick. It was blasted off course. I had to manually save it."

"I see."

"Are you going to do something about it?"

He smoothed the newspaper with his palms. When it was perfectly flat, he leaned back in his chair and looked at her. "Lemme see. It's been a busy morning. I've got reports of a thief breaking into the weld shop and some yahoo burning rubber along Main Street early this morning." He fixed Lexi with a hard stare. "The description sounded like your truck. You know anything about that?"

"Oh, good grief!" Lexi threw her hands in the air. "I'm right in front of you, trying to file a complaint." She leaned forward, tapping his desk, emphasizing each word with her finger. "Drone. Investigation. Charges."

"Okie doke. I'll put your complaint with the others in the VIP file." He picked up his newspaper. "If you find any proof, you let me know."

Lexi glared at the paper blocking his face, then turned and left. "What an unbelievable fugspot. No wonder Dad never voted for you."

⁂

Lexi spent the rest of the day cleaning the 3D printers and filling orders. She took off at four and drove to the ranch, letting the clean scent of the wind whip through the truck's windows. Winter still clung to the surrounding foothills above the valley. Far away, a few patches of snow dotted the ridgeline of the Blue Mountains. She pulled into her long, graveled driveway. Gavin Ceely's green Subaru Outback was parked next to the barn.

Butterflies emptied into her stomach. Not wishing to appear too eager to see him, she parked and banged through the side-screen door into the house instead of going to the barn. "Chicken, where are you?"

The border collie lay on a waterproof pad in the front room next to the window. Hearing his name, his black-and-white faced pinched into a sorrowful frown. He scooched his nose between his paws. Only his eyes moved, watching Lexi through her bedroom doorway as she changed into jeans, a black t-shirt, and a red quilted vest.

She came from her room, kneeling, running her hand over him, inspecting him. "You okay, buddy? You're a good dog, but stay off of my clothes." His dismal look didn't go away. She stroked his head. It was challenging having a dog that could solve problems, understand sentences, and lived to please its master—who had been her dad.

Pushing one of Chicken's pills to the back of his tongue, she kept her hand around his graying muzzle until he swallowed.

"Let's clean you up a little." He licked her cheek as she hefted him outside and set him on the front porch.

She brushed him, throwing frequent glances toward the barn. Filaments of hair drifted in the sunlight, floating from the dog like pieces of his past. After fourteen years of gathering cattle, his shoulders had broken down and his spine hurt from spurs. He'd put hundreds of miles on his body, running through forested hills and across acres of pasture, then he'd chase the ATV home, begging for something else to do. Now it hurt him to stand or walk. He mostly crawled.

Figuring a few victories over age and arthritis would be satisfying, Lexi helped the dog stand and pee against a tree.

"Lexi D. You need any help?"

"Hey there." Lexi flashed Gavin Ceely a smile as he walked from the barn. Specks of wood shavings stuck to his black-rimmed glasses and short beard that always looked like it was two days old. He had nice features, but it was his hands that she'd memorized—mostly because she hadn't allowed herself to stare at his face while they were working on circuit board designs in college.

"Would you hold his shoulders? He's mortified I'm assisting him when his job has always been to help me. It's some kind of alpha thing. He likes men best, but somehow we make it work." She nodded toward the barn. "Can I put out grain for my horse now?"

"You bet." When Chicken finished his business, Gavin picked him up. "You need a little field trip, don'tcha, fella?" He carried him into the barn and placed the dog on a tarp, Lexi trailing after them.

Hands on her hips, she stood in the front section of the barn, leaning back to look at the roof three stories above her. "I don't see any cameras."

"Wait a second. I want to do another perimeter check." Gavin stepped outside and tossed a small customized drone into the air. She shook her head and rolled her eyes, but aerial security was his passion. He'd finished his degree and started Celesto with two friends while she'd left a year before graduation to take care of her dad. He'd kept in touch with notes and phone calls, and used her print shop to create specialized UAVs for companies throughout the world. In some small, indirect way, it made her feel she contributed more to society than just growing hamburger or printing plastic parts. And it allowed her to keep in touch with Gavin.

"All clear," he said as he walked in, closed the door, and flicked the light switch.

"I would've helped you install the cameras. I could've used the lesson."

"You already understand wiring, and you're doing more than you know by letting us use this place." Her gave her a hug and kiss the top of her head. That giddy feeling fluttered in Lexi's stomach again.

"The only other spot with enough room was the high school gym—too many people hanging around there. This testing facility won't draw attention." He opened his laptop. A grid appeared on the screen showing ten different areas.

"Seems weird. A barn isn't the same as the International Space Station," she said.

"Air density inside the ISS is the same."

"What about gravity? Our drones only go up. Gravity makes them come down."

"Space drones are fitted with reversible fans on all sides, allowing movement in any direction. The rest of the modifications are closely guarded secrets." He leaned next to her ear, whispering, "And I won't divulge our innovations no matter how much you tempt me."

"Guess I'll have to keep trying." She kissed him, a quick peck on the lips, then chided herself for going too far.

He blinked, then leaned back with a smile. "Miss, I protest your sly methods—but not too much." He stepped away, shaking his head as though clearing it, then tapped the keys of his computer. "It's not the ISS, but as close to the passageways as I could replicate. Watch the monitor." He set a fan-studded drone, no bigger than a Frisbee, on a barrel and tapped the arrow keys. "Sky3 is just a little test model. Tell me if you lose sight of it or the screen image gets too dark. I think we'll need a few mobile lights to brighten the upper floors."

The drone rose and he threaded it through what he called Course A—over and under rafters. With a prepare-to-be-amazed smile, he fanned his hand toward an X chalked on the floor. The drone plummeted thirty feet toward the cement. Several feet before impact, he reversed its rotors, letting it hover a few inches above the X.

"Show-off." Lexi made a face. "But that's nothing. This morning I screamed at a drone so loud, it evaded a water slam."

Gavin didn't respond as he slowly moved the unit toward the horse stalls. "I'm expecting problems with Course B. The actual drone will have to follow a person through narrow passageways, carrying a payload."

Lexi watched the device rise beside a ladder and pass through a hatch in the loft to access the second floor. He flew it through loops of rope and edged it over partitions. Along the route, Lexi pointed out where more lighting was needed to record its movements.

He turned the unit, allowing its side rotors to push the drone up a wall to the third floor. It bumped through the opening in the floor, bounced into the area, finally coming to rest on a metal tape marked in millimeters.

He groaned, then removed his glasses and rubbed his eyes. "TETT is twice as big as this drone and has to crawl at least three meters. Joe's still designing the collapsible legs, which will make it even bigger. This means our body design has to be reworked—again."

"TETT?"

"Two Eggs and Two Tacos. It was late. We were hungry and exhausted when we filled out the NASA paperwork for the competition. We made up some technical name for the acronym, but that's what it really stands for."

Letting out a long breath, he flew the drone to the rafters above them. Holding out his hand, he let Sky3 freefall again. This time he grabbed it when it hit his palm.

She rolled her eyes. "You know what would be more impressive than your fancy flying? A drone that could carry feed sacks and pound fence posts."

"After this competition is over, I'll get right on that." He placed the drone in a padded case along with the controls. "I'll even gift you the schematic for it." He gave her a half-grin. "Though I'm sure you'll never need to print parts because you'll never crash it or break anything."

"Well"—she winced—"speaking of fixing things … my crotch-headed neighbor shot down my SX2 this morning. I printed new parts. Would you mind starting on the reassembly while I grill steaks?" She smiled, tilting her head. "I've got beer in the fridge."

⁂

They sat on the front porch in wooden chairs, their plates empty except for the bones. The sun had slipped behind the hills. Plumes of gold streaked a purple sky. Chicken lay near them, his bowl between his paws as he licked steak drippings off his kibble.

Gavin had that thousand-yard stare engineers often wore. Lexi was sure he was deep inside a physics equation and didn't see the black-barreled cows dotting the pasture, their heads down, chewing green sprigs in front of him. "Hey!" she repeated several times, finally poking his arm.

"Sorry." He blinked, refocusing around him. "Did you have a hired man working today?"

"I have an old dog and a sassy horse. That's all the help I have."

He looked toward the barn. "I thought I saw …"

"An old white-haired guy?" she finished his sentence. "If that old coot is snooping around, we're going to his house and have it out right now. Where was he?" She stood.

Gavin waved her back into her chair. "I already looked for footprints. I didn't mean to rile you up."

"Old wound." Her mouth tightened in a grimace as she sat down, staring across the pasture toward Wixly's place. "Years ago, my dad asked him for help on the farm. That old codger was a real jerk about it. When Dad and Mom split, my kid-brain assumed if the ol' coot had helped Dad, then things would've been better around here." She drew a breath. "And Mom would've stayed. Sounds silly. But I needed somebody to blame."

"Your mom left for the old guy?"

"No." Lexi made a disgusted face. "He's ancient. A grizzly guy full war stories. Who knows why Mom left? Dad never said. Wixly stays on his side of the fence and I stay on mine, until today when he shot down my drone."

"Sorry. I didn't know you had a Hatfield-McCoy thing going on," Gavin said. "When I came up the driveway, I thought I saw movement next to your shed. I sent up a drone, but didn't spot anything. I probably imagined it." He leaned forward, a scowl overtaking his face. "I'm edgy. This project is highly competitive. It's a lucrative contract. The technology has multiple applications. It could make or break our company. I feel like my career and life are on a cliff ready to fly or dive. A thousand things can go wrong. That's why Celesto needs a big test space and *absolute* privacy."

"You're at the right place. Relax." She gave him a flat look, smacking his arm. "You're in the hinterlands, you townie, or is there something you haven't told me about this project?"

He smoothed the crewcut stubble at the back of his head. "You know what? I really need to go work on a few problems I saw today."

"We could work together," she suggested.

"It'll have to be another day." He stood, staring into the dusk spreading between the buildings.

Lexi frowned, feeling the light go out of both the sky and their conversation.

She walked him to his car, cursing her ineptitude at relationships. She'd skipped boys in high school because they mainly seemed determined to out-drink each other. College offered a wider selection, but Gavin was the only one not cowed by her intelligence and blunt remarks. They'd become good friends and it seemed to be moving toward intimacy. Surely, there was a flowchart of procedures concerning how to tell if the guy you liked felt the same way. She'd have to google that. For the moment, perhaps treating him like her horse was the best solution: Give him some space. He'd come around.

Neither of them spoke as he got in his car. She tried to think of something to say, confused thoughts tying her tongue. "Stay!" she blurted out, then lowered her voice. "I'd like for you to stay. I don't know how to do this, but you're the only guy I've felt this way about. It's like wiring a circuit board and when you connect it, it actually—"

"Works," he finished her sentence. "The light comes on inside."

She nodded.

"C'mere." She bent to his window. "I love your mind and the fact you don't play games, Lex. We have a special relationship, and I'm not going to ruin it by rushing. We're growing it steady and sure." He leaned partway out the window and gave her a quick, gentle kiss. "I can't stay tonight. But there'll be other times to talk about this. You understand, don't you? My company is depending on this project."

"Unfortunately, I get it. I'm also a bit obsessed when I have a problem to solve."

"I know." He gave her a single nod.

She frowned, the butterflies in her stomach frozen in mid-flutter. Did that mean he thought she was clingy? But his tires were already crunching down the gravel driveway. She stood listening until the sound of his engine faded into the night.

A few frogs awakening from their winter sleep chirruped into the silence. A chilled sensation grew in her stomach. She'd blown it. She'd acted like a fool. She'd spoken her thoughts out loud, and it felt like a public performance, rather than a quiet talk between two friends. Rubbing her gut, she gazed at the inky darkness around her. It unsettled her as though eyes were watching, like the whole world was a stage—watching her. "Oh, Chicken, I'm such an idiot. Another successful foot-in-mouth experience, huh?"

From the porch, Chicken's tail thumped twice.

She walked to him and scooped him up. "Let's get inside." The dirty dishes could stay on the porch and wait until morning. The darkness did not feel friendly tonight.

4.

The new moon had set, leaving the night to the stars. The dew beaded heavily on the grass and would be dripping off bushes by morning.

He paused at the screen door and raked the bottom of his shoe across the boot scraper. He took a raggedy towel off the hook by the door and wiped his tennis shoes. He'd prefer to traipse through the pasture in boots, but Bullet had once told him if he was going to do something iffy, always wear different shoes nobody had seen.

One time, he'd tracked footprints inside and had to wipe up the mess. He'd learned his lesson and now took care to have dry soles before entering.

Slowly, he pulled on the screen door as though he were extracting glass from a wound. It didn't creak. The oil he'd put on the hinges earlier had worked its magic.

Once inside, he drew in a lungful of air. Boots, shoes, and Crocs were scattered around, scenting the mudroom with dirt and manure. Moving into the main part of the house, he sniffed again. It smelled better in the dining room, where she often lit candles to cover the dog smell. Not that it worked.

One night, he'd found a candle still burning on the dining room table. Three wicks fluttered an apple cobbler aroma from an amber glass container. He'd blown it out. Thank you very much for saving the house. Why not He'd be living here someday.

She wasn't a neat housekeeper, but it wasn't hard to get around in the dark. LED lights glowed from the fridge and microwave. Even the fish clock had a green eye that lit the dial. Two o'clock.

Dishes heaped in the sink. Clothes piled on the furniture. He lifted papers on her desk and opened drawers, but nothing caught his attention. On silent feet, he crossed the room and eased into a dining room chair. From here, he could watch both outside and into her bedroom.

The night was dark. A cool breeze rolled down from the hillsides and shook a few pine needles from the trees. All was quiet. He could just make out her form under the bedcovers, her back to him and the old hound snoozing beside her.

Tools and drone parts littered the dining room table. He hated those things. This afternoon, a nerd had flown a silent one above the buildings. Ducking into the defunct chicken shed, he'd remained hidden for hours. Mama hadn't raised a turnip-brain. The crack by the door hinge didn't give much of a view on what was happening or when it was safe to beat a path back through the pasture. He'd waited so long, he'd had to take a leak on a crate of rusty mole traps. Served her right for jamming him up in there while the man outside played with toys.

On his way in tonight, he'd scouted the barn where the nerd had been going in and out. Nothing strange there, except it had been cleaned up since the last time he'd looked. Floors cleared of tubs. Feed bags stacked. Blankets and ropes hung on rafters. Was she hiring help? Most likely the city goof was trying to look good so he could get in her pants. Get in line, buddy.

Now, he'd picked up a piece of plastic from the table without thinking, turning it between his callused fingers, wondering what it did. Bullet's advice rang in his mind, "Never touch anything unless you're wearing gloves." He stuck the drone part in his pocket. That should put a dent in this project, like losing a piece of a jigsaw puzzle. Using his shirttail, he placed another piece on the floor next to the dog's feeding bowl. Blame it all on the mutt.

The bed creaked. His eyes darted to her room. Lexi had turned over. He stood.

On the balls of his feet, he crept to the doorway. Specks of light from a smartphone, Fitbit and tablet cast light into the room, but the clock on the nightstand illuminated her best feature. Her face shone under its blue light.

She looked like a queen with her smooth skin and aura of holiness. Her hair gleamed as it fanned across the pillow and draped onto her bare shoulder.

His thumb rubbed a circle against his index finger, aching to touch her skin. It would feel like silk as he slid his fingers along her delicate jaw, dropping to her shoulder, then dipping down her chest.

He took a small step inside her room. Standing motionless, he listened and was rewarded with a new sensation. Soft little huffs like a baby bird alone in the nest as she breathed in and out, steady and sure. He pulled her scent deep into his body, and it came back out in an *aaaaaaah,* whispered like the wind.

⁊ᴇ

The noise in Lexi's dream began like cardboard ripping apart, a slow tearing across corrugated pieces. Her body rocked in a galloping rhythm as she rode Molly. She'd given the mare her head, and the paint horse bounded across the field. The ripping noise chased them.

She heeled Molly's ribs and the paint ran faster, the green pasture fading with each hoofbeat. Finally, they streamed through a gray-humped barren land. The roar caught up to her. A rasping, loud, guttural sound next to her ear. She turned to look at it. Her stomach clenched.

Layers of sleep jetted away. She shot upward, breaking the surface of blackness. She jerked upright in bed with a gasp. A chain-saw growl hummed from Chicken's throat.

She reached for him, gaping around her. His paws hung over the bed's edge, his *gnarr* vibrating the blanket under him. He edged toward the floor as though judging the distance.

"Chicken!" She grabbed a fistful of his hair. He whipped his head toward her, still growling. "What is it?"

She held her breath, waiting, listening. High-pitched howls of coyotes came from the north. She flipped back the sheets and got up, padding through the house in the dark, peering into rooms and out windows that never had curtains. Why would they? The nearest neighbor was an old man a half mile to the south.

Slipping through the screen door at the side of the house, she stood on the concrete steps. The yips and howls were louder and closer than she'd thought. She squinted into the barnyard shadows until her feet got too cold to stand on the concrete. Nothing had moved.

What was the matter with her? She'd lived here most of her life. Nothing was ever stolen. No one had wandered around the property. They'd never locked the doors. Gavin's paranoia had tweaked her nerves.

A breeze rustled the weeds in the flowerbed. The yips and howls parading through the foothills moved on, the hunt songs fading to the west now. She drew a breath of cool air and went inside.

The screen door thudded softly behind her. She paused. Had she heard that sound when she woke? Had it been part of her dream? Chicken, still lying on the bed, whimpered.

"It was coyotes, Chicken." She climbed under the sheets and flopped onto the pillow. "You chased them away. You're doing a good job. Good boy."

He whimpered several times, looking from her to the door. "What'sa the matter? Is it the medicine?" She patted his hind leg. Hair coated her fingers. She looked at the clock. "C'mere." She patted the mattress closer to her. "Nothing ever happens at two-thirty."

Chicken didn't move.

Over the roof, a breeze sighed and passed into the tops of the pines. The compressor on the refrigerator kicked on, sending a hum through the rooms. Her pats became further apart until her fingers lay still on his foot.

Chicken finally lowered his head, his stare never wavering from the doorway.

5.

Gray morning light filtered through the window as Lexi lay in bed, staring at the ceiling. She'd slept poorly as though trying to scratch her way out of a deep well. In her mind, she'd replayed her supper with Gavin, wondering if he would call today. Each rewind and review improved the memory—not of her actions, she'd been embarrassingly awkward—but Gavin had been his patient, logical self. He'd call. He was that kind of guy.

She rose before the alarm went off, made a cup of coffee, and sat at the dining room table to finish the drone reassembly. Halfway through the process, she couldn't find one of the landing legs and a sensor. She moved pieces, looking beneath them before searching the floor. The avoidance sensor lay next to Chicken's feeding station. "How did you knock this off, and what have you done with the rest of it?" Chicken only sniffed one of the dining room chairs.

Again, she scanned plastic parts scattered over the tabletop and did one more visual sweep of the area around the room, deciding it would be easier to make another part than clean the house looking for it. She pushed Chicken's snout away as he nosed along the leg of her chair. "Okay, if you want attention, how 'bout we go check cows and water tanks?"

Hefting the dog to the barn, she loaded him in the cart on the back of the ATV. "Sorry, you just have to endure this," she said as she noodled his front legs through an old barn jacket and zipped it closed. Snugging a beanie over his head, she laughed at the tips of his ears hanging out. He tried to lift a paw to rake it off.

"Leave it! You get cold nowadays."

Chicken sat still, but refused to look at her.

The sky had lightened to pink-blue, waiting for the sun to crest the mountains on the far horizon. She pulled the truck into the barn and jump-started the ATV. Twisting the three-wheeler's throttle, she took off with a jerk, making her grab and steady Chicken.

The cool air in their faces carried the scent of damp dirt, new flowers, and dew flinging off the tires behind them. Chicken rode with his tongue out, head swiveling side to side. The paint trotted to them and the dog greeted Molly with a *woof*.

When his front paws made anxious steps like an excited child, Lexi veered the ATV toward the cattle. They circled the group, checking for whatever bothered him: A calf too far from its mother, a limping heifer, any general slowness in the herd. They buzzed through pastures, Molly loping after them, and finally racing past them.

In the back of the south pasture, Lexi stopped at the top of the ridge. Scrubby trees and dense thickets of Rabbit brush covered the sharp slant below her to the creek. "Stay," she told Chicken. "I'll check the cattle down there."

On foot, she made her way down the steep hill, using narrow cow paths through the bushes, pines and crooked oaks, the tips of their branches swollen with green buds. A few cattle moved between tree boles. The chirps and trill of a song sparrow filtered from the trees.

The creek at the bottom was no wider than a sixth-grader's broad jump, but had once been the gateway to the universe for Lexi. Kneeling by water riffling through the creek bed, she set a leaf boat on the clear surface, watching it glide over the pebbles. A hobo spider darted from the edge of the bank.

She liked the small and harmless hoboes. She'd found one in her fourth-grade classroom, secretly capturing it in a plastic sandwich bag. At recess, she carried it outside, holding it up, studying its little brown legs. The spider had no idea what was happening. Or why it had broken any rule of a world it didn't know existed. For some unexplainable reason, it was being thrown into a new wet, cold environment. It was part of a system it couldn't fathom, and she didn't know why she was crying.

She didn't see Kyle Krucker approach. He grabbed the bag, smacking it between his palms with a sneer and the taunt of "Crybaby." That had been the moment she learned to keep her emotions hidden.

On the creek bank, Lexi watched the hobo scrabble beneath a leaf. "Hide, little guy, hide," she whispered. "We're in a world we can't understand."

Behind her, a stick broke and several rocks rolled down the hill. Recognizing Molly's approach, Lexi didn't look up. The paint soon hung her head over Lexi's shoulder.

Wiping away a tear, Lexi murmured, "Life used to be easier, didn't it, girl?" She launched another leaf to a faraway dream land.

The paint stepped around Lexi into the middle of the stream, splashing the leaf to the bank, lowering her head to drink. Lexi let out a long breath and gazed at the treetops, searching for the sparrow serenading them.

Movement gave away its location. Its streaky brown head turned side to side until suddenly it lifted off, tail pumping downward and snatched an insect. The bird returned to the same branch, and repeated the scenario. Lexi noted it always returned to the same branch. It always claimed a familiar spot in a world it couldn't truly fathom.

She knew the colors and wingbars of all the birds in this forest. This was her place. She and Molly had spent hours here making up their own world, trying to forget the other one where all girls had mothers who sent them to school with perfectly braided hair and taught them to cross their legs at the ankle and how to fit in.

Chicken whimpered from the ATV, nosing the air, then looking from side to side as though calculating the pain of jumping down. "Hold up! We're coming." Lexi hiked back up the hill, the night's tension easing from her shoulders.

The sun broke the horizon as she topped the ridge, out of breath. "Do you need to wet down a tree?" The border collie jutted his nose toward a scrubby oak, sniffing the air. Lexi set him next to the tree. He snuffled the trunk, looking from her to the ground. "You want a different tree? Good grief." The paint sauntered over and joined them, nosing the tree bole at hand height, then both animals stared at her.

"I hate it when you two treat me like a dummy. Why doesn't somebody invent—" Her words stuttered to a halt as she stared at the footprint in the dirt beside the tree. She looked around as if the owner of the tennis shoe with a zigzag tread would appear and greet her.

"Is this what you were growling about? Get 'em." Grabbing the dog in her arms, she bent, holding his nose to the ground every few feet as Chicken wiggled to get loose. The horse clumped beside or in front of them and sometimes on top of the scent trail, bringing a *woof* from Chicken. Behind them, a calf followed, and its mama trailed behind it.

They moved downhill again, then across the creek and finally stopped at the fence separating her land from a two-lane dirt road heading north.

"Does it end here?" Lexi asked. "You guys are the noses. It's all pine duff and dead leaves to me." She tried to hold Chicken's head over the fence to help him catch a scent, but he stared up at birds, now bored with the game. She scanned the road, but didn't see any tire tracks.

"So that sneaky old coot must've hiked down the road, came up the back of the property, and shot the drone. He probably didn't want to hike back down again, so he took off across the pasture, not caring whether I knew because I can't prove he did it. He won't get away with it."

She grumbled curses at her neighbor then hitched Chicken higher in her grasp. Her cheeks puffed, slowly releasing air as she looked at the hill rising above her. "Okay." She hooked a thumb at the trees. "Molly, would you consider letting Chicken ride you?" The dog and horse stared at her. "The ATV's back up there, and I'm tired. I know you both understand that sentence."

The paint walked away. Lexi followed, toting the dog, planning what she would do to Coot, how she could embarrass him, get even—make him pay. By the time she'd huffed halfway up the hill, she'd tossed away her ideas as petty and overdone. That was her trademark, wasn't it? Her hot-headedness always got her. Anger and energy drained from her. She grabbed Molly's tail, getting a tow. The horse kept climbing without a nip or a kick. For that, Lexi was thankful.

6.

Her phone rang multiple times during Tuesday morning errands. She answered two of those calls from customers. When she finally entered BrainSmith Printing, she yelled, "It's Chocolate-Bourbon Cupcake Day at Latte-Da II." Looking inside the white bakery sack, she inhaled the chocolate scent. No response from Mrs. Blackburn. "And I found a strange footprint at my place." That should draw the old gal out.

Mrs. Blackburn's voice preceded her, even before the door flung open. "Where have you been? I need this by tomorrow. Full size." She thrust a photo of a human skull at Lexi. "I've already downloaded the file. You need to slice it and get it printing."

Lexi studied the photo. "That's going to take eighteen or more hours."

"Why do you think I've been calling you? If you're going to operate a business, you need to answer your phone. And you need to keep regular business hours. You can't expect …"

Lexi tuned her out. She'd pushed the old woman's calls to messaging because she hadn't been in the mood to be chewed out this morning. She only tolerated the old gal because she needed the rent from subletting The Other Room to her. Lexi interrupted the lecture. "How smooth does the surface of your skull have to be?"

Mrs. Blackburn huffed a breath. "Very. It's a *Cinco de Mayo* piece of art."

"Then you've got plenty of time. That's not till May." The look on the old woman's face would singe hair off a poodle.

"You want it now. Okay, I get it, but I've got a chair leg to print for Mrs. Pone. Her husband sat on a corner-chair, one of those antiques at her house that nobody is supposed to sit in. I told her I'd print a new leg, sturdier than the original, and you'd paint it to match the others. She wants it by Friday. Company's coming."

"I doubt that very much. On Fridays, her only company is the mailman, who stops at her house for a long lunch." She gave Lexi a knowing look as she peeled the paper off a muffin. "You didn't get coffee?"

"You didn't make any?" Lexi glanced toward the dusty coffee pot.

"I'm not your secretary."

"No one's saying you are. Hey! I found a footprint in the woods—it's Coot's, the old trigger-happy warrior."

"Coot? Is that what you're calling Sull Wixly?" Her eyes narrowed. "That's gracious. And your footprint isn't earthshaking. It could be anybody's. People walk pastures looking for cattle, chasing coyotes, poaching mushrooms. Why don't you quit frittering away your mornings? You'd get more production from this place if you were actually here." She turned, calling over her shoulder, "Now, get moving on my skull. Tick tock. The machines will be running late as it is."

Lexi tossed the photo of the skull next to her computer and dropped heavily onto her chair. While running errands, she'd told folks about the footprint. No one was interested. She glanced at The Other Room—not even the nosiest woman she knew.

⁊�፨

By two, Lexi had four printers extruding layers of plastic onto their heated platforms. With clicking sounds, the hot ends slid back and forth, their movement controlled by computer software, keeping the nozzles .5 millimeter above the build surfaces. Fans hummed, cooling sections of the machines. Filament inched off the spools. Every fifteen minutes, Lexi left her work desk, a sheet of plywood on sawhorses, and eyeballed the temperatures and the builds, before making minor adjustments on the printers.

A couple of hours later, four high-school girls came through the door. A stout girl named Carla wore destroyed jeans, a Tigers booster t-shirt, and carried an unmoving PeeWit.

"Is he okay?" Lexi rose.

"Yeah, yeah." Carla glanced at the kid's head asleep on her shoulder. "He's worn out. I had to carry him around all day. In health class, we're studying reproduction and family. Mrs. B. made the arrangements for me to take him, and lemme tell you, he's a lot more exhausting than carrying around an egg like everybody else did. They just pretended to feed their egg. Every four hours, I had to actually bottle-feed him and clean the bottles. And he's into everything. I *never* want children." She let a large diaper bag of goat supplies slide off her shoulder and *thud* onto the floor.

PeeWit's upper torso was covered by navy-blue fleece pajamas. Spaceships dotted the fabric. His front legs poked through sleeves with the body cape snugging his stomach.

"He's so cute," crooned Janice, bending to look at his sleeping face. She stuck a finger into the waistband of his diaper and sniffed. "He needs a change."

"Get away." Carla slapped her friend's hand. "Why's everybody telling me how to raise a kid?"

Janice rapped twice at The Other Room's door. "Mrs. B., we're here."

Mrs. Blackburn opened it and waved them in, their chatter about raising children following them.

The teens worked on different projects as a kind of after-school club. Rather than naming it after their activities— knitting, painting, coloring, and web designing—they called it the Club Club. Mrs. Blackburn always kept the door open when she had teens in her room, and their muffled voices filtered through the shop.

Lexi worked at her desk, and when their high-pitched laughter rang from the room, she wished she could hear their encounters with bullies, hunky guys, and awkward moments. Mrs. Blackburn seemed more patient with the girls than she'd ever been with her.

A tap on her shoulder startled her. Haisley, a shy girl with curly black hair and uneven teeth, stood behind her.

"Um … you got a lamp?" The teen looked at Lexi's monitor image of a horse overlaid with thousands of tiny triangles storing data about locations, angles, and orientation. "Is that a CAD program?"

Lexi nodded. "I'll use the data to create a file that instructs the printers how to move. You know Davina Duff, the welder down the street?" The girl nodded, her eyes squinting at the screen. "I always make a 3D model before she starts welding an art piece. It helps her plan it out. Are you interested in computer-assisted design?"

"Yeah, but the program is only on one computer at school, and the teacher doesn't let anyone else use it."

"What?" Lexi frowned at her.

"I guess there's not enough money to go around, and he doesn't want the program wrecked. I'd like to learn this stuff. Do you need help here?"

Lexi shook her head. "I can't afford to hire anyone else right now."

"Oh." Haisley looked down. Lexi recognized that kicked-in look. "A lamp?" Haisley mumbled. "We're doing a photo shoot." She followed Lexi to the storeroom. Shelves stacked with spools of filaments lined the walls in gold and silver metallics, bright solids in rainbow hues, and glittery transparents. Lexi pulled an ancient gooseneck lamp from a box and handed it to the girl.

"I'm not creative." Haisley wrapped the electric cord around her hand. "I'm kind of searching for somewhere to fit in. You wanna see what I did?"

"Sure." Lexi followed her back to The Other Room where the teen had arranged Mrs. Blackburn's hand-painted miniatures into dioramas. Tiny sets of furniture decorated doll houses, gnomes and ferns created fairy gardens, ghouls lurked in Halloween street scenes, and the Astra Imperial Guard surrounded the rotting demon of Forgeworld.

Mrs. Blackburn painted a Warhammer guard figurine, a pair of jeweler's loupes over her eyes. Her brushes, fine detail cutters, and drills lay beside her in organized rows like a surgeon's tray. Two hundred miniature paint pots sat in a turntable rack on the other side of her.

In the corner, Carla rocked a sleeping PeeWit. The other girls critiqued the photos they'd taken of the dioramas. A redhead named Gina posted them on social media and the Club Club's Etsy page.

"You know what?" Lexi told Haisley after looking at the activity in the room. "I need to change filament. Maybe you'd like to watch?" It was small atonement for shutting the girl out earlier, but at least it was a little bit of attention. Haisley shoved the lamp in Gina's hands and hurried after Lexi.

An inch of the skull was visible on the build plate. "It doesn't look like much. You have to know what it is to determine what it will be, but so far, I'm pleased with it." Lexi pointed. "Perfectly even base layers are the secret to all good 3D objects. It's far enough along I don't have to check every few minutes now. Do you like math?"

"It's all right, I guess."

"You can learn the CAD program, but the better you are at math, the better designer you'll be."

As Lexi walked Haisley through changing the spools, the front door opened. Rick Pham ambled in wearing his trademark baggy sweatshirt and jeans. "That's my job," he said, his forehead creasing as he pulled a red rubber band from the pocket of his jeans.

"Haisley, this is a good friend of mine, Rick Pham." Lexi, her hands lifting a spool, chin-pointed at Rick. "You probably know him from the Pizza Shop, but he also keeps things working here on nights when there's a project with a long run time."

"Really?" Haisley's voice was full of doubt.

Rick nodded, snapping the rubber band between his fingers. Lexi looked at Rick. "Haisley just wants to see how it works."

"I work here," Rick said. "I take out the trash and change the filament and watch for problems." He looped the rubber band around his wrist, took the spool from Lexi's hands, and finished threading it into the machine as both women watched.

"Thanks, Rick," Lexi said. "Will you be able to work your pizza deliveries between checking on the printers? These builds will go until eleven tomorrow unless there's a problem."

Rick nodded, then focused on the floor. "The machines are hot. Nozzles get clogged. The place could burn. I check them." He pointed at Haisley, still not giving her eye contact. "You can't chew gum, use tobacco, or stick magnets on the printers."

"I don't have any magnets." She looked at him owl-eyed.

Lexi put her hand on Haisley's back. "Thanks, Rick. We'll get out of your way."

Once they were in The Other Room, Haisley mumbled, "He's weird."

Lexi clicked the door shut. "Rick has had a neurodevelopmental disability since birth. He's high-functioning on the autism spectrum. He's clever, intensely interested in computers, and puts a spider outside if he catches one, but people don't know that because they don't know him."

"The kids on our bus call him Broom Boy," Haisley said. "He's always sweeping the sidewalk when we pass in the morning."

"Do you know why he does it?" Lexi asked. The girl shook her head. "Because every morning, Rick's father used to toss a couple handfuls of grain onto the sidewalk and watch two mallard ducks, a male and a female, fly in and gobble it up. Then one day some jerk complained there was duck muck on the sidewalk and the grain might attract rats.

"So now each day, Rick washes the sidewalk and sweeps it clean. It lets his father remember his wife and Rick remember his mother and the time when they fed the ducks as a family back in Vietnam."

"Some of the high-school guys throw things at him when they drive by," Janice said.

"He's been my friend since first grade. We dodged a lot of flying objects in high school. I've seen him go through bullying that would make you weep. And yet, he's not bitter. He treats people better than they treat him."

"Why's he do that thing with his hand?" Carla asked.

"He snaps a rubber band to burn off worry," Lexi said.

"No, I mean this." Carla held up her arm, wrist cocked, fingers together in the shape of a cobra.

Mrs. Blackburn took off her loupes and looked at Lexi. Neither woman said anything. The older woman then examined the figurine she was painting. "I haven't seen him do that in a long time. It's something he does when he's nervous—like you crossing your arms over your chest."

"I saw him do it once to that guy who sits in front of the feedstore store looking for work," Janice said.

Mrs. Blackburn's eyes caught Lexi's again, then she quickly held up the tiny figurine in her hand. It had been 3D printed with gray PLA filament. Mrs. Blackburn had painted it into a lifelike, red-corseted warrior woman, eternally frozen in a jump-attack, swinging knives and whips. The scabbard and fold of the fabric were shaded as though the warrior were running toward a light. "Thirty bucks, girls, for doing something I love. Let's get back to work. How's our sell page looking, Gina?"

Lexi left the room, a small ember of anger smoldering in her chest. Rick had returned to the Pizza Shop, leaving her with the printers. How had he turned out to be so gentle? She'd been bullied and made fun of for being his friend but, unlike Rick, the offense and unfairness lived under her skin. A scratch was all it took to bring it out. Maybe she would've been more patient if she'd had a group or a mentor when she was young. All she had was a horse.

A burst of laughter traveled through the doorway. The ember sparked again. She shook off the silly idea it was jealousy. She was a grown woman. She didn't need bosom buddies. Quickly, she walked to the printers to check them. The dentures were slowly forming on the skull. For a long while she watched the hot end move back and forth, making the teeth appear in a vacant grin. She understood a little of what it might be like to be Rick.

To be left out again.

7.

Wednesday morning the war within Lexi continued as she rode Molly through the pasture. Chicken had had another bad night. It must have been torture for the dog to be inside when he'd been active all of his life. She should have put him down, but he was the last piece of her father. And so was this ranch. She wasn't ready to lose either of them. But she wasn't sure it was right to keep Chicken living this way. She blinked back the wetness in her eyes and strong-armed those thoughts into one of the manholes in her mind, dropping an iron lid on it.

She slid off the horse, her feet hitting the ground with a *thud*. She bent over, looking for more footprints at the forest's edge. Molly nipped green shoots as crows flew from the woods, catcalling at them.

Finding nothing suspicious, Lexi remounted and rode the fence line, stopping at the neighbor-gate. The passing years had made it sag slightly on its hinges. The wooden cross timbers had grayed and weathered. It wasn't chained, but she'd never seen it open.

"Folks who lived here long before us used it," her father had said. "The women had nobody to talk to but kids and chickens. They'd shortcut across pastures, visiting each other or leaving jam, eggs, or sugar in the wooden box on the hinge post. Their husbands or sons collected whatever was inside when they checked the cattle. Folks didn't run to town if they needed something like they do now."

"Did Mom feel alone here?" Lexi had asked, but her dad hadn't answered.

Not long after her mom had left, Lexi had put blue wildflowers in the box still affixed to the post to see what would happen. They lay there a year, fading from blue to beige, losing their petals. On the day of her eleventh birthday, she made a wish—a sign that somewhere out there, somebody thought of her. She lifted the wooden flap. The dried stems flew out like wheat straw, cartwheeling in the wind across the pasture. Today, she peeked inside, not really expecting anything. She wasn't disappointed. The box only contained a spider, which scurried across its web. She let the lid smack shut.

Pulling a small drone from the leather scabbard laced to her saddle, she unfolded its propeller arms. It was the loudest of all the drones Gavin had given her. Several times she'd refused to accept it, but he'd insisted because she let him use her printers for free.

She didn't want their relationship to be a balance sheet. He'd spent so much time teaching her skills, answering her questions, standing close with that affirming smile of his. Then he insisted on giving her his experimental designs. "You're my special beta tester." He'd slipped his arm around her and kissed the top of her head.

With a sigh, she tossed the drone into the air. It hovered a couple of seconds. The paint goggle-eyed and sidestepped at the whirr, but the drone was soon away.

With her phone attached to the controls, Lexi watched the screen as the UAV lifted 100 feet into dawning sky. The 360-degree aerial view showed pastures turning green, broken by patches of forests. Occasional houses, outbuildings, and lone pines dotted the landscape. Clumps of black cattle grazed in fields. To the northwest, the jagged line of mountains edged the horizon.

She flew the drone slowly over her cattle and fences. Then it was time for Operation Good Morning, Vietnam.

Her conscience kicked her, but she continued to maneuver the drone to Coot's back door. With a smirk, she buzzed the drone back and forth in front of curtain-covered windows too dirty to offer a peek inside.

Coot appeared in Lexi's monitor, coming out the door in heavy green work pants, white short-sleeve t-shirt, and a thundercloud on his face. He grabbed the handrail with his left hand as he tottered down the steps, watching his feet as though they would betray him and send him sprawling into the gravel drive.

Lexi maneuvered the drone over the house like a UFO zipping away in a movie. The last view she had of the old cuss was of him stiffly twisting, turning, and searching the sky. She landed the drone at her feet, her laughter erupting, her conscience slumping back into the manhole beside her guilt.

⁊ₑ

Rick was washing the sidewalk as she parked in front of her shop. In his bright-green hoodie and black sweat pants, he stopped and saluted her. "All is well. I checked through the night. Nothing jammed. That stick with the flowers on it is finished. The skull is still running. It looks weird though."

Lexi frowned. "I'll check it. Thanks."

"You're not gonna fire me, are you?"

"Do I need to?"

He shook his head quickly. "You need me tonight?"

"We'll see. Get some sleep." She walked in, wondering what melted-plastic horror she'd find.

The chair leg was perfect and the skull looked fine. The plastic columns in front of the eye sockets had probably confused Rick, but they were needed to support the overhang of the brow or it would sag into a droopy-looking Neanderthal.

By noon, the skull had cooled. Lexi broke away the support columns and sanded the rough spots. A full-sized skull. She admired its smooth-looking creepiness. To celebrate a job well done, she called Crusty's, ordered steak fingers to-go, and left to pick them up.

Outside, gray clouds had moved in. The wind felt damp as it tumbled a paper cup along the street. Lexi chased it in a stomp-dance toward the diner. It brought back memories. She'd often been ordered to pick up trash. The former sheriff thought such punishment would deter underage drinking, mailbox bashing, or any high-school prank. She caught up to the cup with a final stomp.

An uneasiness, as if someone watched her, settled on her. Gazing around, she spotted a hound sprawled in front of the hardware/feedstore. Next to him sat a man, leaning back in a chair, the front legs off the ground, his hand patting the dog.

Recognition dawned. Embarrassed to be caught chasing a cup, she gave her former classmate the barest of courtesies. "Ash," she said, adding a micro-nod. He gave her a casual hey-there wave with two fingers, then refocused his stare over the top of the old brewery. She picked up the cup under her boot and hurried on her way.

The smells of fried chicken, bacon, and cinnamon rolls escaped as she opened the door to Crusty's. Coot sat at a table, but Lexi ignored him, picking up her to-go order as Rosalee's cigarette-rasped voice croaked. "Sure you don't want some peach cobbler? Osiah just took it out of the oven. I been standing back there with a spoon, bugging him to cut into it."

"Sounds great, but no thanks." Lexi hesitated, considering what a pitiful creature she must be if she could heed the diet police in her head, but ignore her conscience hollering that she should hurry out the door. Now!

Instead, she crossed the diner's tiled floor and stood beside the corner table, directing a smirk at the seventy-five-year-old man. "Buzz-buzz, Coot. I wanted to wish you good morning."

His eyes stared from beneath his boonie hat. His callused finger pointed at her. "Tweren't funny, Shorty." Her conscience thorned her again for picking on a wounded vet, but he was picking on her.

"You can shoot my drones, but you can't stop someone who can print new drone parts every day. Welcome to the future, Coot."

"Why would I shoot your eye-in-the-sky, Shorty? And I'm here to warn ya, the future doesn't always work out."

"What does that even mean?" Her forehead furrowed. "Never mind. I don't want to hear the loose gears rattling in your head. Just remember, they couldn't stop the stagecoaches and trains from reaching here. You can't stop progress." She walked toward the door.

"Progress comes and goes, Shorty. None of those conveyances you just mentioned are around anymore," he called to her back.

With a shrug she walked away. Two minutes later, she sat at her computer, dipping a steak finger into ranch sauce, thinking about the restaurant encounter. It became less satisfying with each replay. Mrs. Blackburn would've gladly told her why. Thank heavens, the old matron wasn't around today, though it'd be nice to see PeeWit.

Her cell phone buzzed, showing a photo of Gavin.

"Lexi D," he said brightly when she answered. "I'm at your house. Did you know that any pirate, felon, or art thief can drive in and walk through your house—which is what Joe did because he had to use the bathroom."

"That's okay. Why are you and Joe there?"

"Steve is here, too. We're running a simulation."

"Today?" She frowned.

"Yeah, the clock is ticking, and we were excited about the improvements we'd made. Gotta try 'em out. I wanted to let you know we were here."

"I can be there in ten minutes," she said.

"No, it's a closed session. Security. Confidentiality. Stuff like that. We won't be here long. Just wanted you to know. Oh, and I'm sending you an app to put on your phone."

"What for?"

"I installed a solar-powered device on your gate. Anytime the gate's opened, it'll send the app a notice. Then you'll know when someone's driving in."

"I don't need it. The gate's never closed."

"Yeah, I figured you'd say that, but it's closed right now. And I only installed the infrared device so it would trigger an alarm. You can activate the camera later if you want to see who's passing through."

"Look. That's nice of you, but I don't need all this—"

"Sorry. Joe's starting the run. I'll try to call you later."

The connection went dead. Lexi stared at the black screen mirroring her face. She reminded herself not to make fun of his suspicious, we're-all-prey attitude like she had last night. The gate alarm was his way of saying he cared about her and wanted to protect her. Or maybe it was only security for his experiment.

Still, it was irritating. He should've asked her permission before installing it. It was also annoying he'd shown up at her house without calling first; he always called before stopping by the shop. But she had to admit these were small, insignificant grievances. All of them sprouting because she couldn't deny the hurt. She'd been shut out as though she weren't trustworthy.

8.

As the afternoon wore on, her thoughts simmered down and soon faded with bookkeeping and viewing the ranch drone videos she'd let pile up. Then she viewed last night's recordings from the cameras inside the shop.

Rick had entered five times to check the printers. On the first trip, he'd collected the trash and looked at the drawings on her drafting table. On his final entrance, he ran through the shop with a nerf gun, shooting at a fat rodent racing across the floor.

In his rat pursuit, he'd knocked over a box of screw-top containers Rosalee had ordered for her homemade honey hand cream. Rick disappeared from the screen, then came back with a push broom. Probably the same one he used to scrub duck crap off the street. Lexi scribbled a reminder to check the containers before delivering them to Rosalee.

She went to the whiteboard on the wall and added to the list:

*Don't FOUL up a Run!!
*No Magnets! No Chewing gum! No tobacco!
*DON'T TOUCH 3D objects, unless you have permission.
She added
*NO RAT CHASING.

At five o'clock, she left a message with Rick's father, saying she wanted to talk to Rick about workplace behavior. That would set him into a tailspin. For the next two weeks she'd have to listen to him worry she was going to fire him.

The bell tied to the door jangled. She turned to see Gavin entering. Several straws of hay stuck to his charcoal sweater and red twill shirt. The knees of his khaki chinos had smudges of dirt.

"Just a warning," she called out. "It's been a crummy day, and I'm ticked at you."

"How can I fix that?" He set his messenger bag on her work area and slipped an arm around her shoulders. "And in the spirit of transparency, I'll add that my day sucked too."

"Because?"

"The prototype didn't perform as well as we'd hoped, but I think we've solved the problem. It'll require a few new parts. Is it okay to use your MAX machine?"

"Okay. Send me the file. I'll check it."

"Uhhh … there's the rub." He gave her a pained smile as he pulled his laptop from his leather bag. "I need to tweak the design, then run it myself. It's proprietary information."

"Who's the proprietor?"

"Celesto."

"That's only you and your two business partners. Tell them to let me check the file, or it won't be running on my machines."

"You know I won't mess anything up." He took a step closer, leaning over, whispering into her ear. "Trust me. It's just the way we handle security on designs we don't have trademarked."

She stared at him. "Why are you whispering? You think this place is bugged?"

"No." He stepped back, a flush rising on his cheeks. "I was … trying to be suave and romantic like … James Bond."

"Oh." Lexi blinked. "Sorry. I missed that. I appreciate it, but I'm still peeved you barred me from my barn and installed a gate-guard I didn't want. It's a sore spot, people leaving me out of decisions. I don't want to be a hard nose, but I'm setting boundaries. It's my printer. My rules. That's *my* security." Lexi crossed her arms over her chest.

They stared at each other before a smile touched the corner of his mouth. "I suppose I deserve that. Okay." He nodded. "I, of all people, need to respect your right to security measures. Wait a minute. Let me do some calculations." He tapped keys on his laptop before handing her a zip drive. "You hold my future in your hands, my dear."

She held up the small beaver wearing an orange Oregon State University shirt with a USB connector protruding from its removable tail. "Cute."

He shrugged.

She plugged it into a port, keyed a few buttons, then read her screen. "Okay. I only checked for viruses. And in deference to your privacy, I didn't download it or look at the splicing—that's how much I trust you. I hope you did the math correctly." She paused, waiting to see if he wanted to check it again. He circled his finger in a *let's-go* signal. "All right, I'm sending it to the printer. Go ahead. You can adjust the settings." He began fiddling with the knob and leveling the build plate. "How long will it take?" she asked.

"It'll be a while. There's no need for you to wait. I'll clean up and shut off the machine. I promise I'll be careful and not burn the place down."

She smiled and pooled all the courage she could muster. "We could try the romantic Bond-thing again." When he looked at her quizzically, she stepped closer and whispered. "You don't have to drive all the way back tonight. Why don't you stay at my place? We could throw your clothes in the laundry. I have a bed or couch—whatever you prefer."

"What I prefer, huh?" He smiled. "It may be late. I might have to tweak this and run it again."

"Then I'll leave a light on for you."

He wrapped her in a hug, leaned down, and softly kissed her. Lexi's heart beat in her ears. Her mind fogged. She could barely focus on what he was saying about overstepping boundaries. "… and I'll remove the gate alarm if you don't want it. I really can't thank you enough for all you're doing to help me with this project."

She put her arms around his waist and closed her eyes, her cheek against his chest. Finally. Tonight. This would be their night.

※

By six p.m., Lexi had finished picking up the mess around the house. She called Rick. "Hey, I don't need you at the shop tonight."

"I went to see you," Rick said, agitation in his voice, "but there's a strange guy over there. Am I fired?"

"No. I have a friend who's using a printer. He knows how to run it. Just let him do his project. Don't bother him."

Rick didn't reply.

"And one more thing …"

"Yeah?"

"No more shooting varmints with a nerf gun. You got that?"

"It was a rat. Dad says they can't be here. The city will close his business."

"If the rodents can't get to any food, they won't hang around. Oh … darn. Listen, I left some french fries in the wastebasket by the door. Could you empty my trash? Just don't bother Gavin."

"Okay."

She hung up, knowing he'd bug Gavin anyway. But Gavin was a good guy. The kind of guy who wouldn't hurt a spider. He'd visit with Rick and get his project done.

At eight o'clock she ate, then put Gavin's bowl of chili in the fridge. She had hoped it wouldn't take him this long, but she didn't get a good look at the entire file so wasn't sure how large or how many pieces he was running. She wished he'd get here.

She settled at the dining room table and assembled her drone. When she finished, she turned on the TV and flopped onto the couch to wait.

It was after eleven when she awakened. She clicked off the TV and looked around. Gavin still wasn't there. Good grief. He must've messed something up and had to do a re-run. Picking up the phone she tapped in three numbers, then stopped. How far could she push? She didn't want to appear needy.

Maybe Rick could check on Gavin. She called the Pizza Shop. "Mr. Pham?" she said when Rick's dad answered. "This is Lexi. I know you're cleaning and closing, but is Rick still there?"

In a moment, Rick's tenor voice came through the phone. "Yeah?"

"The guy I left at the shop, what's he doing?"

"I don't know."

"Well, yes, I don't know what he's printing either, but can you peek inside without him noticing and see if it looks like he's finishing?"

"No."

At the abrupt answer, Lexi frowned. "Why not?"

"I emptied the trash right after you told me to. I don't think he saw me. His back was to me, and he was busy working. About ten thirty, I took a pizza to the Lost Nickel. As I passed your shop, I pulled on the door to peek in. It was locked. I didn't have my keys with me. I knocked but the guy didn't answer. When I came back to the shop, I found my keys and checked if he'd turned off the light. The place was dark. Nobody was there."

"Oh. Okay. Thanks."

"Am I in trouble?" he said.

"No, thanks for making sure the lights were off and the shop was locked up tight."

Lexi hung up, looking out the window. A single moth circled the yellow porch light, avoiding broken strands of cobweb waving in the breeze. She smacked the light switch with more force than necessary, flipping it off. She stared into the blackness, anger beating a wild rhythm in her head, her teeth clenched. Her thoughts wrapped her in a hard silence.

At some point she felt a chill and glanced around, having no idea how long she'd sat there. It was late, very late. It felt like her heart had detached and fallen into her stomach. Clutching her gut, she went to bed feeling nauseous and cold and empty from inside her chest to her toes.

9.

The sky was steel-gray and the birds hadn't begun to sing when Lexi's phone vibrated on her bedside table. In the blue light of the clock, Chicken stared at a glass of water on the nightstand, its contents quivering from the phone's shimmy. It was enough to rouse Lexi from a fitful sleep, but not enough to make her check who was calling. She told herself probably one of those cursed spam calls.

It stopped. One minute passed and the phone began vibrating again. The universal code for answer-your-phone.

"Uggh!" Lexi picked it up, blinking at the screen. The lock screen read 5:00 a.m., S. Blackburn

"Why are you bugging me before dawn?"

"Get to the shop immediately!" Mrs. Blackburn snapped.

Her sharp tone jolted Lexi wide awake. "Are you all right?"

"Just get here. Now." Mrs. Blackburn's stone-cold voice mentally took Lexi back to high school when the former secretary had called a student to the office.

"I've got chores. I'll be there in about—"

"You'll be here in ten minutes. Park behind Davina's shop. I'll make coffee." The phone went to black screen.

❧

A narrow dirt passageway ran behind the old brewery. The county commissioners called it a service road, while the shopkeepers called it an alley. Lexi drove her truck along the two-track path until reaching the turn-around at the end.

Davina waited by the wide, tall gate covered with welded profiles of eagles. The fifty-year-old woman wore a black plaid jacket and wide-brimmed hat, beckoning the truck forward as she held open one side of the gate. As soon as Lexi drove through, Davina pulled the panel partially closed.

Lexi glared at the Cadillac XT4 parked on the other side of the lot next to a rack of rebar. "What's *she* doing here?"

Davina waved her hand, her voice a whisper. "Hush. On with you. Take the alley to your shop. Go in the back door."

"I don't have a key to the back door." Lexi didn't take her eyes off the Caddy. "It's been locked since I rented the place."

"Mrs. Blackburn has one. She'll let you in," Davina said.

"Why doesn't that surprise me?" Lexi's eyes narrowed. "What's going on?"

"Go!"

"Remember the last time you ladies tried to set me on the right track? It backfired." Lexi's finger pecked the air accusingly. "If this is another intervention attempt, I'll rip each of you until you wish you had earplugs and a helmet."

"Oh, get on with you, numptie." Davina pushed her through the gate-gap, closing it behind her.

Bulging clouds hung low in the sky, making the air damp. In scuffed boots, ripped jeans, and brown flannel shirt, Lexi plodded along the alley, kicking at weeds beside the dirt tracks.

Mrs. Blackburn must've deemed another come-to-Jesus meeting necessary. Davina would also be at the shop in a few minutes, and they'd gang up on her, intervening because she'd stepped over their imaginary lines of conduct—again. Bless their meddling souls. Maybe Mrs. Blackburn was riled because she'd often arrived at work late, but with a ranch to run and a business to grow there was too much to take care of. And so what if she'd stirred the hornet's nest more than usual by harassing Coot—in public?

The back door opened before she could rap on it. Lexi stepped inside, scowling at Mrs. Blackburn. "Why do you have a key to this door?"

"The same key fits the front as the back."

"Oh. I've never tried it."

"Obviously."

"I'll warn you, this isn't going to be a civil conversation. I'm not putting up with being told what to do. If that bothers you, leave now."

Mrs. Blackburn exhaled a frustrated huff of air. "Put a cork in it and go through."

The woman standing next to the desk held the 3D skull in her hand, inspecting the teeth. She wore an aqua-colored suit with an orange silk blouse and a floral scarf that tied both colors together. Lexi crossed the cement floor. The woman looked up and spoke in the quiet solemn voice that came with her vocation. "Alexandra."

Lexi plucked the skull from her hands and set it on the desk, replying in the same bland tone. "Mother."

In public, their paths rarely crossed. Catharine Stewart directed the Stewart Funeral Home in La Grande, Oregon, the legacy of Lexi's grandfather. When both women happened to attend the same event, a fundraiser, Elks meeting, or the Salt-lick Art Contest, they exchanged a simple nod and tried to stay on opposite sides of the room.

Catharine's eyes ran from Lexi's unbrushed red hair to her manure-speckled boots and finally locked onto her daughter's face. Lexi crossed her arms over her chest and stared back.

Beckoning with one finger, Catharine walked away. Lexi trailed behind, feeling seven years old and trying not to *clop* as she walked.

Her mother had always moved with light-footed grace, her A-line skirt swaying side to side. Unlike Lexi, the woman barely made a sound in voice or motion, but when she focused on a person, boundaries crumbled.

"If I came in and rearranged the shop," her mother said, "you would explode like Vesuvius. So, do you notice anything that has changed?"

"What'd you do?"

"Look around you."

Lexi gave her surroundings a glance. Nothing seemed different. "I don't wanna play this game. Just tell me."

"I didn't do anything. I only wanted you to look now with a neutral attitude rather than later. See if you notice anything out of place." She continued walking. Lexi followed, her mouth wrinkling in a sneer. In the back of the shop, Catharine turned and faced her daughter. "What do you know about this?" She twisted the knob of the storage room door.

As it opened, Lexi noticed her mother had donned beige latex gloves. A man lay in the closet on the floor, not moving. It took only a second for Lexi to recognize him.

"Gavin!" Lexi started forward.

Her mother grabbed her arm. "Who is he?"

"Did you call an ambulance? Is he okay?"

"He's dead."

"And *this* is how you tell me?" Deep lines furrowed Lexi's forehead. "What's the matter with you?" She yanked away from her mom's grip, rushing into the narrow room.

"Don't touch anything." Catharine's voice lost its serenity.

Lexi stood above Gavin, her eyes locked on his face, her breath damming up in her throat.

Dark bruises collared his neck, his eyes fixed on the ceiling in an eternal stare.

"So you know nothing about this?"

"What?" Lexi whirled toward her mother, who already had both hands up in a calming gesture.

Catharine said quietly. "Come out of there. There's nothing you can do for him."

"Except call an ambulance. Maybe he's not completely dead." Lexi put a fingertip to his neck. Her diagnosis registered across her face. "Call the sheriff."

"Mrs. Blackburn found the body. She should be the one to call." Her mother paused, her expression darkening. "However, I happened to notice he was garroted. With your plastic line."

Lexi winced, her brain fogging. The icy, brackish feeling clutching her gut last night had returned. "What are you talking about?"

Her mother gave her an oh-please look. "Is the spool just inside the door usually wound like that?"

It took Lexi several moments to focus her attention to where her mother was pointing. It took even longer for her to see the plastic line was garbled around the spool, not wrapped neatly like the spools on the shelves. Her mother was right.

"But that means …"

Catharine ignored her words. "It appears he fought his attacker. There's a faint bruise beginning to appear on his cheek and his shirt is torn."

At the clinical tone in her mother's voice, something inside Lexi snapped. "His *name* was Gavin Ceely. He was …" Lexi's voice came low from her throat. "Just leave, Mother. You have the sensitivity of a jar of nails. Always have. I don't know how you've stayed in business."

"Believe it or not, I'm trying to help you." Her mother laid a hand on Lexi's arm, which Lexi shook off.

"I'm only pointing this out because if you don't present the murder weapon, they'll confiscate every piece of filament in this shop. You'll be shut down for weeks. Probably longer, considering this sheriff. Can you afford that?"

"Get out of here!" Lexi turned on her, fists clenched. "I don't need you!"

Catharine gave Mrs. Blackburn a look encrypted with messages, then walked away. When the backdoor clicked shut, Lexi went to the desk phone and picked up the receiver. "What's the sheriff's number?"

Mrs. Blackburn, trailing behind her, put her finger on the cradle switch. "We wait ten minutes."

"Why?"

"To give your mother time to leave town. She and the sheriff don't always get along."

"Why?" Lexi's voice pitched higher. "Why did you call her in the first place?"

"My dear, someday you'll understand, but that's a story for later." Mrs. Blackburn's face softened as she took the receiver from Lexi's hand. "Justice may be blind, but here in Young County, it's also deaf and dumb. Do not expect competence, fairness, or a quick resolution. This very well could be the end of your business. Your mother is only trying to help."

"How? I don't understand any of this." Icy fingers clutched her stomach. Gavin hadn't stood her up last night. He was gone. Dead in her shop. Murdered, if her mother could be believed. She glanced at Mrs. Blackburn. "And what's wrong with me? I don't feel anything but selfish and sick to my stomach."

"That's shock." Mrs. Blackburn followed Lexi as she paced. "Grief will come in its own way, at its own time."

"We've got to do something. We can't just stand here." Lexi's eyes moved in frantic jerks, scanning the area in front of the large printers. "Look, most of the shop isn't visible from back there. Maybe someone came through without being noticed." She hurried to the MAX printer. "Gavin was using this machine. Now it's turned off. Would a killer do that?" She bent over, examining the build plate, her fingers skimming the surface. "It's clean. No scratches. No residue. His piece was expertly removed. Either Gavin finished and cleaned up or his murderer knew 3D printing.

"And look …" Her words picked up speed, running together as she checked out the nearest machine. "The build plate isn't level. The control box is wonky. It's been bumped."

An angry ember flared in her chest. Her mother had been right—it appeared there had been a struggle. Why was that witch always right?

Lexi stepped inside the storage closet, trying not to look at Gavin's face.

"What are you doing?"

"Checking the filament Gavin used yesterday."

"You're in panic mode," Mrs. Blackburn said. "Don't mess anything up. We're about to call the sheriff—"

"I need to check this for myself before they come in and take over," Lexi said.

Mrs. Blackburn dug in her pocket. "Then use my painting gloves, but hurry."

"My fingerprints are supposed to be here." Lexi glared at her. "This is *my* place."

"Put them on *anyway*." Mrs. Blackburn's hard-chiseled stare indicated she would tolerate no back talk as she shoved the gloves against Lexi's chest.

Lexi snapped on the gloves and turned her attention to the filament. "Gavin wouldn't have set this spool on the floor." She lifted it, checking the mis-wound coils. Mrs. Blackburn gave her a questioning look.

"There are two types of plastic," Lexi explained. "They look the same but have different qualities. The ABS filament goes on the shelves. That was what Gavin used." Lexi pointed to a spool on the shelf. "See. It's neatly coiled and ready to use. He must've finished his project and cleaned up."

"Okay. Come out." Mrs. Blackburn beckoned. "You need to save your energy for what the sheriff will put you through."

"But see, this isn't right." Lexi lifted the spool of gray PLA filament on the floor, next to the doorframe. It uncoiled like a line spinning from a fishing reel. A piece about four feet long popped away from the loops and fell on the floor. The women stared at it.

Mrs. Blackburn's face wrinkled. "That's probably the murder weapon." Then she shook her head. "You're done now. Leave it. Hurry up. Put the spool down."

"We use a sprue cutter," Lexi said, examining the end. "This has been chopped with a knife. See the way the plastic is mashed."

"Stop touching things!" Mrs. Blackburn had her arm extended, her finger jabbing the air toward the exit.

Lexi left the piece on the floor, stowed the spool, and emerged from the room, pausing by the MAX printer. Mrs. Blackburn bumped into her, but Lexi managed to keep her balance.

"If Gavin was bent over, cleaning the build plate, someone could've easily slipped by him."

"Was the front door locked?" Mrs. Blackburn asked.

Lexi looked at the door, searching her memory. "I assume it was … but I don't remember locking it." She glanced at the small room. "If Gavin finished, he would've taken the spool to the storage room. Someone could've stepped behind him and twisted … ." Her face pinched. The cold ache rose higher in her chest. Her manic drive to do something, solve something slowed like a machine creaking and contracting, cooling after a hot run. "Why hide the weapon back on a spool?"

"Why not? Gavin looks like a good-size man." Mrs. Blackburn urged her away from the printer. "Maybe the perpetrator had too much to carry without including the garrote?"

Lexi flung her hands up, eyes wide, her mouth agape. "Wait a minute, where's Gavin's laptop or his messenger bag and the piece he printed?"

"Come on." Mrs. Blackburn herded her toward the back door. "Some questions the sheriff will have to figure out for himself, though I have little hope in his abilities or success."

But Lexi stopped in the middle of her shop, gazing around her, blinking back tears. A numbing feeling rolled through her head. She wished the day had never begun. Her voice cracked with the same lost confusion she remembered as a ten-year-old child. "What am I supposed to do now?"

"Where are your keys?" Mrs. Blackburn said quietly. Lexi wriggled them from her jeans, holding them up. "Good. Move your truck to the front of the shop. When you come through the door again, that's the time you officially arrived."

Lexi coughed, easing the tightness in her throat. "Why? What do you know about this?"

"Nothing. But I know it's important to try to make this day as normal as possible, and you always park in front, not in the welding yard."

"But nothing about this is normal."

Mrs. Blackburn grasped Lexi's hand. "I know you're in shock. You want answers right now, but it's going to take time to unravel this. Breathe. Be patient. Look at me." She waited until Lexi focused her gaze. "Listen. Your mother was never here. Understand?"

"No. Why not? I don't get any of this." Lexi's eyebrows pinched together. "This is like an out-of-body experience. Why are *you* so calm?"

Mrs. Blackburn's face darkened, then the heaviness disappeared as she straightened her shoulders and spine. "I've dealt with catastrophe and the dead before. I found my Mike after he fell off the roof. Now go. Move your truck. Hurry. The clock is ticking."

"Whose clock? Why did I have to park at Davina's? Did my mother have something to do with Gavin's murder?"

"Oh, Lexi," Mrs. Blackburn groaned. "Grow up. I'll make coffee. We're going to have lots of people in here today."

Lexi squinted at her. "You making coffee *is not* normal. Why is this happening?"

"I don't know." Mrs. Blackburn shook her head, exhaling a loud sigh. "But I can honestly say you're your own worst enemy. Right now all of your energy and attention *must* be in minding your mouth when you talk to the sheriff. *Think* before you speak each word. Now go! Tick tock." She gave her a little push. "Don't make things worse."

"Worse!" Lexi spit out the word as she went through the back door. "How could I make this any worse?"

10.

Lexi studied the dull, gray light sifting from the old brewery's narrow hopper windows near the rafters. She tried to pay attention to Mrs. Blackburn, who was prepping her for the arrival of law enforcement, but her mind was screaming that the world had once again become a place she couldn't fathom. Her eyes searched the rafters, looking for a hobo spider.

The door of the shop slammed open, making Lexi jump.

"Heavens! That was fast," Mrs. Blackburn exclaimed as a bulky man entered the building.

"I was at the diner, waiting for it to open. Heard the call and got here before you messed up the crime scene more than you already have." Sheriff Cal LaCott scanned the area without looking at either woman. Mrs. Blackburn shot Lexi a narrow, watch-yourself glance.

"Tape off the door," LaCott called to the deputy trailing behind him. He headed toward the printers, grunting, "Where?"

"Where what?" Mrs. Blackburn said. "The coffee? Duct tape for taping the door? It's always best to be specific."

LaCott turned and gave her a flint-eyed look. "You called about a body. You want me to look at it or not?"

"That would be helpful, but if you'd prefer to go to breakfast first, that's up to you." She clasped her hands together, her mouth pursing into a button.

LaCott hawk-eyed Lexi. "You gonna be of more help?"

"This way." Lexi walked past him, swallowing to loosen the tightness in her throat.

The sheriff followed her. "Whatta *you* doin' here? Early for you, isn't it?"

She took a half-step, anger, sparking, rising, seeking a way through her thin skin. It wasn't his business what time she came or went. She continued walking. "It's my shop. Why wouldn't I be here?"

When they reached the storage room, LaCott put his hands on both sides of the doorframe and leaned inward, gazing at the corpse. Lexi stayed back, not wanting to see Gavin's body again.

"Who was he?" The sheriff finally asked.

Thoughts ran rapid-fire in her brain. Images of conversations with Gavin and their times together flickered, swirled, and faded. Finally, she simply said, "A friend. A customer. Gavin Ceely."

"What was he doin' here?"

"When I left last night, he was working on a project." She bit her bottom lip. Maybe if she had stayed—Focus! Do what Mrs. Blackburn said. Answer only what's asked.

"What time was that?"

"Around five."

"What project was he working on?"

Gavin's face, lined with worry, floated into her mind. He'd asked for absolute privacy. "I don't know," she said. "Something customized for a client. He was in the security business."

The sheriff eyed her long enough to make her uncomfortable. "You often let customers have run of the place?"

"No, but—" she hesitated. Mrs. Blackburn stood behind LaCott, her eyes burning with the unmistakable stare teachers give students to shut them up. Lexi instead shook her head, saying nothing.

"Is this how you found him?"

"*I* found him, *Mr.* LaCott." Mrs. Blackburn's sharp voice drew the sheriff's attention from Lexi. "He was positioned just as you see him."

LaCott half-turned, looking down at the small woman. "You call anybody else this morning?"

"She called me," Lexi said, frowning. "Should I have called Gavin's relatives? I don't really know—"

"Darrel will handle that," LaCott said.

"I called the *Young County Register*," Mrs. Blackburn said, her face not entirely innocent. "My nephew is a stringer. Always looking for news. I help him any way I can."

The sheriff's focus switched to the floor, his lips pressed against his teeth, the muscle along his jaw pulling tight. "Course you did. Thanks. What a bustard buster," he muttered.

"I think someone snuck in," Lexi said. "They either knew how to 3D print or waited until Gavin finished because—"

"All right, Miss Depriest. I'll do the investigating," LaCott said.

"If that's what you want to call it," Mrs. Blackburn mumbled.

LaCott's gaze landed on the deputy. "Get these women outta here so we can work. Take 'em to the office."

※

When they stepped outside, Lexi noticed the sun was just now breaking through the sky-gap of the distant mountains. *Good grief. It feels like a day has passed since I got out of bed.* Gray clouds banked high above them. The cool air promised rain.

"Sorry about this," the deputy said as he ushered Lexi and Mrs. Blackburn toward his cruiser. "LaCott's in a mood 'cause he didn't get breakfast."

"Lexi and I haven't eaten either." Mrs. Blackburn paused, grabbing the chain looped through the door handles of the old movie theater. She steadied herself, blinking. "My head is light. I guess it's the shock."

"Do you need to sit, ma'am?" The deputy grasped her arm.

"You always were a polite young man, Darrel. It's good to see you still are, even though your boss has the gentility of a neurotic monkey. My blood sugar is terribly low. Please, I need food. Lexi will help me to the diner. They're open by now. We'll wait for you there."

"I don't know." The deputy looked back at BrainSmith Printing. "LaCott said to take you to the station."

Lexi put her arm around the old woman's shoulders, giving the deputy a black look. "What's the matter with you? She can't answer questions if she's unconscious. Do you think we're going to do a runner across county lines?" She leaned toward him. "You're looking at a lawsuit for inhumane treatment."

"All right, settle down." Mrs. Blackburn patted Lexi's arm. "You're a bit manic with shock. I'm sure Darrel will let us take care of ourselves. He understands we've just discovered a murder."

Darrel nodded. "Maybe it would be better for you to wait at the diner."

They walked on the opposite side of the street of BrainSmith Printing. Lexi peered at the open door of her business. One end of the yellow police tape had already come loose, fluttering from the doorframe like a homecoming decoration.

No one was around them on the street yet. They walked under the watchful eyes of Davina's rusty metal bird statues sitting on the roof in front of each shop. A welded crow perched on top of BrainSmith Printing. An owl sat sentry over the Pizza Shop. An iron eagle stared down from the welding shop.

Davina frequently had to repair her metal sculptures because teens, drunks, or jerks shot at them. The accumulated fixes and increased armor had left the birds with ever-threatening features. Lexi thought of them as gargoyles warning the populace below. If only they had deterred whoever had come to murder Gavin.

Darrel deposited them at Crusty's. Mrs. Blackburn admonished, "You go back and get LaCott calmed down. The sooner your boss finishes looking around, the sooner this atrocity will be over, and we can pick up our lives. I made a pot of coffee there. Help yourselves."

"Thank you, ma'am. I'll try to hurry him along."

The older woman chose a booth in the far corner of the diner. Lexi settled across from her. "Okay, Mrs. Methuselah, *what* are you doing? What's with the frail act? You don't eat breakfast. Why are you treating the sheriff like crap, then acting like Sister Theresa to the deputy?"

"In spite of all your juvenile antics growing up," said Mrs. Blackburn, "you still haven't learned there's a hard way and an easy way to accomplish your goals. You're like a bird that keeps flying into a window, beating yourself up to make your point. Someday you'll wise up. In the meantime, I have a plan if you think you can cooperate."

"What is it?" Lexi leaned forward. This was a side of Mrs. Blackburn she'd never experienced.

"Order your breakfast first."

Rosalee appeared at their table the moment they set their menus down. "What's going on?" she whispered out the side of her mouth. "Why was Darrel escorting you? And why's your nephew here?" She wagged her head toward the door where a gangly young man was quickly heading toward them, waving his camera.

Lexi gasped, her eyes widening. "Seeing your nephew made me think of something." She lurched out of the booth, bumping Rosalee aside.

"No, you don't." Mrs. Blackburn grabbed for her.

But Lexi twisted out of reach. "I'm so stupid. I haven't been thinking straight. I can solve this right now. Be back in a few minutes."

11.

When Lexi slipped through the door of BrainSmith Printing, she spotted LaCott at the back of the shop near the printers, crawling on his hands and knees between the work tables. She wondered if he'd find any nerf darts from Rick's rat-chasing spree.

"What are you looking for?" She trotted to her computer and pressed the button to wake it.

"Why aren't you at the station?" He grunted as he pushed to his feet.

"According to my civil rights professor in college, I don't have to be there unless you arrest me."

"I can arrange that." The sheriff scowled at his deputy, who had peeked his head out of The Other Room. "Great job securing the witnesses, Darrel! What's in there?"

"Weird stuff." The deputy held a mini Christmas tree in one hand and an ugly Warhammer Gorebeast figurine in the other.

"Leave Mrs. Blackburn's projects alone!" Lexi called as she sat in front of her keyboard. "Why does everyone have to handle the 3D sculptures?" Without waiting for an answer, she pointed at five small black domes mounted on the rafters. "Look. Those are cameras. I spaced out with the shock of … Well, as soon as I can access the recordings, we can figure out what happened last night." She tapped her fingers against her thigh, waiting for the operating system to flash its opening load screen.

"Just what is it you do here?" The sheriff reached for the skull in the middle of the table.

"No. No. NO! Move!" Lexi elbowed him aside and bent to examine the hard drive. Cursing, she stared at a blank monitor. "Those cameras would've captured everything." She unplugged and replugged the cords on the back of the tower and the monitor. Everything was in its proper place, solidly connected. This couldn't be happening. Her movements became faster, her mumbling more frantic. "No. Please, no."

"Somethin' the matter?" The sheriff sidestepped her as she yanked a stepladder from the corner. It banged to the floor as she tried to pry it open.

Darrel came from The Other Room. "You need help? Where do you want it?" The deputy opened the twelve-foot ladder as Lexi pointed, ignored his questions, and scurried to the top, her heart hammering in her chest.

Knocking away cobwebs, she inspected the modem and router sitting on a metal plate hanging from the ceiling. She checked the cords. Pushing reset buttons, she watched the sequence of green lights blink across the face of the router. It shouldn't have made any difference, but she'd try anything. She jumped to the floor, skipping the bottom steps of the ladder.

At her computer, she tapped the keyboard, then punched the keys harder, making the plastic creak and the keyboard scoot forward. No images appeared. The screen remained a constant frustrating blue. Both hands went to her head, grabbing fistfuls of hair. "No, no." Her words faded into a groan.

"I take it there's a problem," the sheriff said.

"I think my computer's been wiped." Lexi began typing again. "Maybe I can reinstall. This is going to cause so much hassle, but I might be able to recover some of the data."

LaCott laid his hand across her fingers, stopping their movement. "Who knew you had cameras in here?"

"Everyone. It's posted somewhere." She waved in a circular motion toward the walls.

"Get your hands off that keyboard. C'mon. Move."

Raising her hands, Lexi groaned. "I don't get it. A man has been murdered. A good, kind man. There was no need to hurt him. And why ruin my computer? They could've simply covered the cameras."

"Maybe they thought you had something important on there. Did you?"

"My designs. Work records. Only things I'd be interested in." She gave the blue monitor a forlorn look.

"Darrel, bag the computer," the sheriff said. "We'll dust it for fingerprints."

"NO!" Lexi rolled her chair in front of the tower. "I need this for work. The BIOS might still function. If it's not ruined, I can reload the operating system and data from backup."

"Darrel, call Judge Tempan for a warrant." LaCott turned to Lexi. "We'll include that backup in the warrant too."

Lexi crossed her arms. Idiot. If she had kept her trap shut, she could've reloaded everything onto the hard drive and been back in business in a couple of hours. *Why didn't I listen to Mrs. Blackburn?*

"And this backup will show the murderer?" LaCott asked.

Lexi stared at the cameras on the rafters, breathed a long sigh, and closed her eyes.

"Well?"

The impatience in the sheriff's voice failed to draw her ire for once. "I guess not. It might restore my computer, but not the surveillance. Nothing has ever happened since I've rented the place, so to save storage, the video archives weekly—on Friday." She swallowed the thought if she hadn't been so chintzy on storage, she might have recorded Gavin's killers.

"Sounds like we got bupkes. Move outta the deputy's way, Miss Depriest. We'll see what the state boys can do with the computer." LaCott pointed at the whiteboard on the wall. "Not too smart to advertise how to foul you up."

"You think a list of 'No cussing, smoking, sticky notes, or magnets' would shut down my shop?" She gave a mirthless laugh, unable to take her eyes off the cursor blinking white on the blue screen. "That reminder was for Rick, telling him not to post notes on the machines. It's a fire hazard. Sometimes he doesn't think. He once used the fire extinguisher to shoo the goat from behind a printer."

"The Pham kid, next door? What's he do in here?"

"He works for me. Cleans. Helps when the printers run all night. He …" Lexi broke her stare-off with the monitor and glanced at the sheriff.

"He have a key to this place?" LaCott cocked his head.

Lexi forced herself to think quickly. "Lots of people have keys. I doubt if the locks have been changed since this place was built."

With a single nod, LaCott pulled her chair, with her in it, away from the desk. He tossed a notepad and pencil in her lap. "Make a list of who you know has a key."

He picked up papers and designs lying on the plywood, inspecting each one, tossing it to the center, clearing the space around the keyboard and screen. "Just take the computer, Darrel. We don't need this other stuff. Then find that Pham kid. He's probably washing duck crap off the sidewalk next door."

"Rick couldn't have done this," Lexi protested. Surely the sheriff wouldn't bring up that old mishap.

LaCott gave her a sharp look. "Sounds like he understands 3D printing, and he's tried to kill someone before."

12.

LaCott sat in Lexi's chair at BrainSmith Printing, asking her questions while she stood in front of him, feeling like an unruly student in the principal's office. Her mind had trouble focusing, switching between the image of Gavin's body on the floor and how she'd put suspicion onto Rick.

And why was *she* being grilled? Today had been horrific enough without adding an inquisition. Enough of this. She dragged a tan folding chair from its spot against the wall and opened it, purposely too close to LaCott. Facing him, she sat down, hoping it made him as uncomfortable as she was. He rolled his chair back a few inches and continued his questions concerning Rick.

"I told you he does cleanup for me," she said. "I'm the only one who'll hire him. I suspect it has more to do with his being Vietnamese than his history or his developmental challenges. He's conscientious and trustworthy. I don't like this line of questioning."

"I don't give a pig's fart what you like. What did the Pham kid know about the guy using the copier?"

"Rick is twenty-six, same as I am, so he's not a kid. And it's a 3D printer, not a copier."

LaCott gave her a watch-your-smart-mouth look.

Lexi ignored it, her mind churning. Mrs. Blackburn was right—LaCott would pin this on the first plausible suspect he could find. He acted like a tea kettle, intermittently rattling and making sounds as if he were actually doing something. And she'd said too much already. Each time he asked another question, she gave him a blank look.

"Okay. Be like that, princess. Darrel, take some of these print machines to the lab as well."

"If you disturb them, you'll have a lawsuit on your hands." Lexi razored him with her glare. "They're sensitive, delicate pieces of equipment and require being balanced each time they're moved. The cost of their reinstallation will assure the county that *you* are an expendable money pit."

Her spiel stopped Darrel. LaCott gave his deputy a disgusted look, then extended it to Lexi. "Then you'd better start cooperating. What else do I need to know about the victim?"

Lexi shrugged. "I've told you all I can. I guess you'll have to do some actual investigation to find out."

The sheriff's voice sharpened. "Did he come in here with a briefcase or anything?"

Lexi's eyes flicked away from the sheriff, then refocused on his square jaw, jutting at her with his arrogant expression. "Wish I could help, but I didn't see Gavin come in. All I know is that it was a custom design. He probably got his plans from his car after I left."

"You're the worst liar I've ever seen."

"Then maybe you should look in a mirror and ask, 'Am I really doing my job or just driving around the county with the lights blinking?'"

"I can make this better or worse. It's up to you."

She tapped the side of her boot against her chair leg.

After several moments the sheriff said, "Okay, did he have a car or a truck? If so, where is it?"

Lexi looked to the spot she'd last seen Gavin alive. In her mind's eye, he was bent over the printer, fiddling with the controls, intensely focused like he always was in the middle of a project. No longer would he be around to tell a nerdy joke or answer questions about circuitry or programming. His recommendations had snagged her two hospital accounts. Every drone she flew had been designed by him. Their relationship was just starting to … what, she didn't know, but had been eager to find out.

She took a breath and let it out, steadying herself. "He drove a green Subaru SUV. I don't know the year." She paused. "And now that I think about it, it's not out front. Where is it?"

"Okay. You're as helpful as squat at the moment. Get outta here." LaCott used the tone most folks had when they chased raccoons from their trash cans. He hooked a thumb toward the door. "Tell Birddog to come over."

"Who?" She squinted.

"In high school, that's what we called Shirley Blackburn. The ol' hound could sniff a lie before it left our lips."

"You're *so* professional." Lexi stood.

"It's just us mavericks here." He gave her a closed-mouth smile. "You don't like her either, I can tell."

"Your rebel-in-arms act isn't going to make us friends. How about doing your job? Did you talk to Sull Wixly about shooting my drone?"

"Yeah, I can be just as cooperative as you." He leaned back, making the chair creak as he closed his eyes and rubbed his forehead. "I told him to shoot another one."

❧

As Lexi crossed the street, she pulled her phone from her pocket to call Mrs. Blackburn, but when she saw Ash Felway in front of the hardware/feedstore, she stowed the device. She'd call when no one could overhear her conversation.

"Everything all right over there?" he said.

"No, Ash, it isn't. But I really don't want to talk about it."

"Anything I can do for you?" He dropped his chair onto all four legs and leaned forward. "You look like you're kinda hurting."

She shook her head. "Thanks. I'll muddle through, but I appreciate you asking." With a wave, she slipped around the corner of the building and walked to the back. George, the owner, stacked bags of fertilizer against the wall of the loading dock. Not wanting more conversation, she stayed out of sight until he went inside, then sat on feed sacks under the covered loading area. She dialed Mrs. Blackburn.

"It's your turn for questioning."

"How are you holding up?" The older woman didn't sound the least bit nervous about LaCott wanting to interrogate her.

"Okay, you?"

"I interviewed the diners at Crusty's. Nobody saw anything strange. What did you say to LaCott?"

"You found a body. Called me. I came in. We called the department. He's asking if Gavin had anything with him when he came in. I told him the color of his Subaru. The rest I don't know."

"I can't see your face but it sounds like you're leaving something out." The woman cleared her throat with a harrumph. "For a part-time hooligan, you're a terrible liar."

"Why do people keep saying that? According to this community, I have only two redeeming qualities—I'm hotheaded and rotten at lying."

The older woman sighed. "Don't be sensitive. You have other traits. You're … enthusiastic and loyal."

"About the loyal …" Lexi picked at the stitching on the feed bag, choosing her words. "I mentioned Rick having access to the shop, and LaCott started asking a lot of questions about him."

"I warned you about giving excess info. If you're going to throw LaCott a bone, make it somebody you hate. You didn't say anything concerning your mother or me, did you?"

"No." Lexi let disgust force the word out, knowing she sounded like a twelve-year-old. "And I don't *hate* you. It's more like no-love-lost."

"That's heartwarming. Where are you going now?"

"Home. I ticked LaCott off. He suggested he might keep me from doing business for a while. If I can't work at the shop, I'll get my mind off it by catching up at the ranch."

"That's the first intelligent thing you've said in a week."

"I live to please others," Lexi said.

"Stay at your house. Don't answer the phone. Don't talk to anybody. My nephew says it was 1953 the last time anyone was murdered here. This is TV-camera news. Do you want PeeWit and me to come stay with you?"

"No." It came out louder than she'd meant. "Sorry."

"It's fine. I had the same feeling."

Lexi propped her heels on the bottom of a feed bag as she scanned the stormy sky. "Well, you'd better get over there, LaCott's waiting. Oh"—Lexi ignored the voice in her head telling her to shut up—"LaCott calls you Birddog. Something about sniffing out his lies when he was in high school."

"Does he? How juvenile." Mrs. Blackburn disconnected.

Lexi climbed into her truck and headed for the ranch. The clouds seemed to be waiting, their dark bulbous undersides heavy with water. It felt as though any flutter in the universe would cause them to dump their load: a one-degree shift in temperature, a slamming door, a high-pitched squeal, a shouting voice.

Three miles from home, the sky opened. Water cascaded in white sheets, blotting out the gravel road. She pulled the truck over and parked, leaving the lights on but turning off the wipers, which had become as helpful as a sponge in a hurricane. The downpour beat the metal cab like angry fists.

This rip in the heavens had surely been caused by her actions. Mrs. Blackburn must be in that interview by now. The bossy woman would be barking orders, her stone-cold voice tearing into LaCott for his general crudeness and calling her Birddog. Lexi wore a half smirk. The old woman had counseled not to toss the sheriff a bone unless it accused someone she hated. But Lexi had given the advice a slight twist. In this case, the bone was LaCott and she'd sicced Mrs. Blackburn onto *him.*

"And so it begins," Lexi murmured.

But her voice was lost in the roar of the rain.

13.

Mist trailed the passing deluge, softening Lexi's view of her pastures. She drove through the gate, stopped, and got out. Water beaded on her hair and clothes. For the first time in her life, she shut the ranch gate. Wiping her wet hands on the back of her jeans, she watched rills of dirty water run down the gravel drive toward the house. The bar ditches on either side gurgled with runoff.

She tapped on the solar panel Gavin had mounted to the hinge-post. How sad that he was the one who had installed it, and his death was now the reason she was using it. She waved at the button-size camera. A *ding* sounded from her phone. He'd set the panel to alert her phone and home computer. She slid the gate latch into its catch with a resolute *clang*.

Charcoal-colored clouds still blanketed the sky. A cool scent of wet grass and dirt rose from the ground. She got in the truck, peering at the closed gate in her rearview mirror. Secured gates hadn't helped Gavin in a world where no one could fathom all that might happen. She felt bad for razzing him about keeping the world out.

As she came through the back door, the house phone trilled. She turned it off without answering. When her cell buzzed, she turned it off too.

Tossing a blanket on the living room floor next to the dog, she flopped onto her stomach, resting her chin on her fist. Her gaze traveled through the floor-to-ceiling window without seeing anything, her thoughts roiling about death and the purpose of life.

For a long time, she barely moved, watching two storm systems blow through. The cows stood unmoving, huddled in clumps. On the horizon another bank of steel-gray clouds appeared.

"So, this is how your day goes, huh, Chicken?"

She stayed at the window with the old hound, staring at nothing until Molly ambled into the side lot, her blue plastic tub clenched between her teeth. The paint horse hung her head over the wooden fence, staring at the house, lifting and lowering the tub in a wave.

"If I have to go out there, so do you," Lexi told the dog. As she gathered him up, he whimpered. She readjusted her grip, trying to be gentle.

On the way to the barn, he stuck his black-and-white nose in the air, snapping at raindrops. They didn't quite make it through the door before the clouds dropped another waterfall. Carefully, she placed him on a horse blanket, making him wince once. Maybe it would be better to put him out of his misery. Was it right to keep him hanging on? Molly bumped her in the back with the tub. Lexi put her arms around the horse, resting her cheek against the paint's neck.

"I'm a coward," she whispered. "I'm such a coward."

⅔

Lexi moped for two days before venturing off the ranch. On one of those days, a white van with a TV station's letters on the side stopped in front of the gate. She'd seen it from the pasture as she repaired a water hose. The distance made it doubtful they could spot her among the cows, but she'd still slunk down behind the water tank until the van drove away.

By Saturday, she'd checked off most of the jobs on her list, using the front-end loader on the tractor for heavy scutwork. She'd need to hire help to do the rest. That afternoon, she called customers who had print orders waiting and explained the situation.

On Sunday morning, Lexi stood on the front porch, surveying another gray day. She texted Davina Duff, the welder near her shop.

Got to talk to somebody.

There was no answer. She drove to Telos anyway. Davina's back gate was locked.

Where r you? she texted. *I'm behind your shop.*

Still no answer. Lexi walked along the alley to her own place. She expected empty boxes to be in her way when she opened the backdoor. Mrs. Blackburn had placed them as a barricade making it appear the door was never used, but the cartons lay scattered. Inside, the shop looked like a free-for-all after a protest rally, with bins and boxes opened and overturned. Her phone buzzed.

Davina had replied: *At church. Can't leave w/o drawing attn. 15 min. Will pick up Shirley.*

Lexi eyeballed the room, her legs feeling weak as though the locking pins had been removed and she would fold into a heap, joining the debris strewn everywhere. *Where do I even start?* Each piece of paper inside her lone filing cabinet had been dumped onto the plywood table. Her keyboard and monitor sat on the desk, minus the computer tower. All signs, placards, and cartoons had been taken down and leaned against the walls or heaped in a pile. The ladder stood in the middle of the shop. A push broom hung above it, lodged sideways in the open rafters.

The printers appeared untouched. Lexi hurried to the storage closet, sure the filaments would be unwound, coiling and snaking together like a giant pile of colored spaghetti. But the spools sat in leaning columns outside the closet, still wound. Cartons had been emptied; the tool chest had been dumped, wrenches littering the floor.

She breathed several curses. Stepping over a trash can and chair lying on their sides, she found herself hurrying to The Other Room. Flinging open the door, her breath caught in her throat.

The room held only table and chairs, but no miniatures, paints, or displays. *Mrs. Blackburn will have a seismic fit.*

Lexi slumped to the floor, rubbing her chest and looking around. A few shelves appeared untouched. That must've been where Darrel searched, she thought. Other shelves had been swiped empty. Books lay open, boot prints across the pages. Her two small air plants had been mushed into the floor.

She assumed LaCott had done the worst of the chaos. When the mountain on her desk had grown too large, the floor had become his repository for paper clips, vectored drawings, sample figurines—even her jar of jelly beans had been sprinkled over the rubble. With a curse, she pushed to her feet, walked to the center of the shop, and began taking pictures with her phone. When she finished, she smacked a trash can upright, then began sorting and hurling papers at it.

"Lexi?" Davina stood in the back doorway wearing a floral dress topped by a red sweater. "Come away, girl. If LaCott thinks you've straightened things, he'll only put it to mess again, and it'll be days getting your shop back."

Lexi ignored her, picking up documents and shoving them into file folders.

"Shirley's back at the shop waitin' for us. Give over, now. You need to leave 'fore you're seen." Davina beckoned as though fanning a hot pie.

Lexi's hand fell to her side, her jaw tightened as she stared around her. The papers dropped from her fingers. She boot-kicked the trashcan, sending it arcing through the room, banging on the concrete, end-over-end, trash splaying across the floor.

As they left, she tried to slam the backdoor behind her, but Davina caught it, shaking her head, and shut it with a *click*. The two women walked down the alley without speaking.

Mr. Pham stepped from his shop, a bulging black trash bag in each hand. Davina held a finger to her lips. Lexi gave him a single nod. He nodded back, then walked to the dumpster, slinging the Pizza Shop trash inside. By the time he'd closed the lid, the women had disappeared through the eagle-festooned gate.

Davina Duff had turned a tiny room of Paul's welding shop into a cozy place to take a break. She called it *olde hame*. Mismatched coverlets hid the threadbare arm rests of an overstuffed couch. A leather-bottomed rocking chair and ottoman sat beside it. The rug's maroon flowers and curling edges covered the cracked concrete floor. A fake window frame hung on the wall with eyelet curtains and no glass. Behind it was a large photo of the Cairngorm Mountains, encouraging viewers to believe they were looking out on Scotland.

While Shirley Blackburn inspected the mugs, looking for three clean ones, Davina fed a couple of logs into the black iron firebox and stirred the coals. "We'll get a little heat under the kettle." She swirled the pot to be sure there was enough water inside.

Lexi sat with a *plop*, her body splayed like a rag doll. "All your stuff is gone," she said to Mrs. Blackburn.

"No. I removed it from the shop. I didn't trust what would happen to it." The older woman cast a scolding look at her. "You should've answered your phone."

Lexi's body seemed to shrink into the couch. "I see. Well, it's okay that you didn't include me in saving any of my stuff," she said peevishly. "I'm used to fending for myself. Because—as you like to point out—I was raised by horses and don't have the sense to answer a phone."

"No—"

"Okay. Don't you two start." Davina held up a hand then looked at Mrs. Blackburn. "I'll allow you to break the kid rule. Mind, only this once."

Mrs. Blackburn nodded and left. In a moment, the baby goat bounded into the room wearing a green and yellow argyle sweater.

Lexi grabbed PeeWit, gathering him into a hug, all four of his legs sticking out, pedaling like pistons.

She pulled the kid's sweater off, murmuring, "You poor thing. Let's get this stupid getup off." She folded his hairy legs beneath his body and snugged him close to her.

Mrs. Blackburn's eyebrows arched. Her mouth flatlined. "The coverings keep him warm and healthy, so he doesn't get chilled. Now, if you are quite settled, I need to say that I didn't abandon you. When I told you not to answer your phone, I didn't mean you should ignore *my* calls."

"My shop looks like a dumpster."

"So, we need to make a plan. All of us, working together." Mrs. Blackburn nodded toward Davina.

After they had recounted what had happened, they sat in silence. Then Davina asked, "Could Gavin have been killed for something he was working on?"

"Maybe, but who would've known what he was doing here in the hinterlands? That was partly the reason he was working out here." Lexi looked at her empty cup. "I haven't told anyone what his project was, not even LaCott."

"Is Gavin's secret going to help him now?" Davina poured more tea, adding a spot of milk whether Lexi wanted it or not.

"His company was in a design competition. They were building a drone that could fly, crawl, and carry items throughout the International Space Station. It was highly competitive. They tested a prototype in my barn, but I wasn't allowed to be there. I thought they were being paranoid because they were security gurus. Gavin insisted on privacy. That's why he was in my shop alone Wednesday night."

"Who knew he'd be there?" Mrs. Blackburn asked.

Lexi shrugged. "*I* didn't even know he was coming. He seemed excited and preoccupied."

85

"Maybe a partner did him in," Davina said.

"Could be, but why?" Lexi shrugged. "That would ruin their chances for a lucrative contract."

"Maybe one of them was going independent? Where's this thingabob he printed?" Davina said.

"I didn't see any printed objects, and I can't check the run. My computer's hard drive has been wiped clean. I suppose it was to get rid of the surveillance video."

"Who around here would know how to do that?" Mrs. Blackburn said.

"Anyone who looks at YouTube. LaCott thinks someone slapped magnets on it. The moron will probably do a house-to-house search for anyone with two thousand magnets on their fridge."

"I've got a grand magnet that'll lift six hundred pounds." Davina said. "Actually, I have two."

Lexi scowled. "Why would you have those? They're dangerous."

"They're switch magnets. They turn off and on. I use them to hold metal plates so I can assemble my sculptures. If I try to weld next to one, the arc will bend away. The magnetic field would probably affect a computer. They mess up my TV if they get close to it."

"Where do you keep them?" Lexi struggled to get up, holding the goat.

"Just sit. I'll get 'em. They're only as big as your fist." Davina went out the door.

Lexi scratched PeeWit's neck; his eyes closed and head leaned back. "Gavin swore me to secrecy about his project. Do you think I should tell the sheriff? I'm afraid LaCott would blab it to the paper and ruin any chance Gavin's partners have to salvage their entry."

Mrs. Blackburn studied her tea as though an answer was written in the bottom of her cup. "During my interrogation, the only pertinent thing LaCott asked was 'If all you do is paint toys, why don't you work from home? Why rent space from Miss Depriest?'"

"Because you enjoy bossing me around?" Lexi shot her a flat look.

The older woman didn't respond right away. "You provide internet hookup and computer support. All I do is step out the door and ask you to fix my laptop when it acts up. You print and mail my work. You provide storage. Someday I'll say more, but for now I'll just say I like getting out of the house. I enjoy the company. You and the high school girls keep me involved. I haven't abandoned the shop."

"Really? Because it looks like it."

"Of course, I didn't tell LaCott any of that. The less one says to him, the better. So, no, I don't think you should tell him about Gavin's project. What I told him was, 'Lexi prints. I paint. It's called teamwork. A skill you've never developed.'"

"So, it wasn't just me who twisted him up and set him loose on the shop?"

"I may have incited him a bit. I'm sorry. I wasn't going to tell you this, but you'll discover it soon enough. LaCott thinks there's no reason for you to have a 3D print shop here in the boonies unless you're doing something that needs to be hidden, like terrorism or money-laundering or printing guns. That's what he's insinuating to my nephew at the newspaper."

"Moron. That's the most ignorant thing—"

"I told you he twists everything to make himself appear bigger. You'll hear all of this again when we get closer to elections."

Davina entered, looking as though she'd been in the wars. Black grit smudged her dress, her hands grime-covered like she'd been working. She held a metal block as big as her fist with a T-shaped knob on top of it. "I had two of these. I've looked behind everything. One is missing."

"Since when?" Lexi took the magnet from her, hefting its eight-pound weight in her hand.

"It must've been nicked when they took copper pipes a week ago. I keep the magnets tucked in a wood box and haven't needed them lately."

"Do you have to plug that in?" Mrs. Blackburn asked.

"No, the power comes from alignment of the magnets inside it," Davina said.

Lexi held it against the iron firebox and turned the knob.

"Now, try to pull it off," Davina said. "Don't yank the stove from the wall."

"Yeeaaah," Lexi groaned tugging at the magnet, trying not to wake the goat in her lap. "This would wipe a computer." A banging noise echoed through the cavernous shop. The women looked at each other.

"Somebody's at the front." Davina turned toward the door.

"Wait." Mrs. Blackburn put her hand on Davina's arm. "You're not open on Sundays. Everybody knows that. Don't answer it. I don't care who it is." Davina rolled her eyes and left to answer the door. Mrs. Blackburn got up and stood, her head partway into the hall, listening.

Lexi turned off the magnet and tossed it in a chair. "My shop is a mess. My computer is a brick. I've got angry customers. I don't know when I can get back to work. I don't have any answers. And I've been abandoned." She shot the older woman a challenging look that went unanswered.

"Ladies …" Davina walked back into the room, making Mrs. Blackburn move out of the doorway. Mr. Pham followed her, waving his hands, speaking fast, partially in Vietnamese, partially in English, and partially in a dialect none of them could decipher. The only thing Lexi understood was, "LaCott has Rick."

14.

"This is my fault," Lexi said after Mr. Pham left. "I told LaCott Rick worked for me. With Rick's past ..."

"Nonsense." Mrs. Blackburn paced behind the couch. "LaCott's a lazy butt who latched onto an easy target. I can hear his nasal tones now. 'If Rick didn't do it, then it'll all come out in court.' Unfortunately, a few lamebrains in this town will actually applaud the arrest."

"Does Rick have a previous record?" Davina asked.

"Yes. It happened before you came here." Mrs. Blackburn emptied the rest of the teapot into her cup. "Ten years ago, but it's hard to erase memories in a small community."

"I testified for Rick." Lexi stared into nothingness. "It was more than bullying. Rick was tortured in high school. Every day. There were the usual stupid pranks like stealing his clothes while he was at gym or catching him in the hall and yanking down his pants. Three guys were the main jerks. One time, they caught Rick walking home alone. They tied him to a swing in the Davis's backyard and left him hanging belly down on a swing seat, pants pulled down around his ankles, his bottom exposed."

"Oh, mercy." Davina shook her head.

"The ropes cut into Rick as he thrashed around, trying to free himself. It was his OCD and hyper focus that helped him calm down. He said he passed the hours by counting the ants crawling under the swing until George Davis got home from the mill after work," Lexi said.

"So, what happened?" Davina asked.

Mrs. Blackburn and Lexi traded a glance, then Lexi looked away first. "It's a black scab on our community. Rick's father didn't want to make trouble. Mr. Pham wanted everyone to come to his Pizza Shop. The rest of us …" Lexi shook her head.

Mrs. Blackburn said, "The group got expelled from school. Dave Criel was sheriff back then and gave the boys a talking to—"

"Which only made them sneakier." Lexi's face twisted with the memory. "When Rick ate lunch in the cafeteria, he'd get hit with a milk carton or someone would knock his tray to the floor. I sat with him, but I got beaned too. He couldn't stand that, so he started hiding in the bathroom to eat. If the jerks found him in a stall, they'd barricade him inside and throw water, grape juice, even turds over the top."

"He could've had an aide with him because of his special needs," Mrs. Blackburn said. "But he refused."

Lexi gave her a hard look. "He's high-functioning. He wants to be seen and treated as typical."

"And everyone simply let this go on?" Davina glanced from one woman to the other.

Lexi shook her head. "Rick put a stop to it. He developed 'snake-hands.'" She bent her elbow ninety degrees and pointed her fingers like a python's head. "He jabbed bullies with his fingers if they got too close. He ended up walking around with two snake-hands up, always on alert. You can imagine how well *that* went over in school. He was mocked even more.

"One day I was behind the Lost Nickel, picking up trash—a little juvie punishment for littering with beer cans"—Lexie rolled her eyes—"when the jerk-trio dragged Rick back there. They were taking turns punching him."

Davina's eyes widened.

Lexi steeled herself to continue. "I was calling 911 when Ed Fissel knocked my cell from my hand and pinned me against the building. Rick went berserk. It was like a switch clicked. He punted Ed hard in the crotch. When Ed let go of me, Rick rammed a knee into his face. Then Chet Gould made a wild grab for Rick, but Rick spun and stabbed Chet in the eyes with a snake-hand. Chet couldn't see but kept swinging wildly. Rick's field-goal kick caught Chet in the gut."

Lexi drew in a shaky breath, visions of Rick's ferocious defense reeling through her mind. "Ash was one of the three left standing. He yelled at Rick, 'Whatsa matter with you? You don't hit people in the face! We never did that to you.'"

"Did Rick stop?" Davina asked.

"Rick clocked him right in the throat with pointed fingers," Lexi said. "Ash grabbed his neck and started gagging. Rick kicked Ash's knees from under him, and when Ash hit the gravel, Rick was on top of him, jabbing like a jackhammer, jamming his hand at Ash's throat. All the fight left Ash. He screamed like a little kid, choking and covering his neck with his hands."

Lexi looked down at her palms. "I couldn't pull Rick off. It was like he was in a trance. So I slammed myself on top of Ash's head. I'm pretty sure I felt the cartilage in his nose give way as I landed on him. At least that's what I told Sheriff Criel. It was a mess."

"Were the other boys hurt?" Davina said.

Silence hung in the air. Mrs. Blackburn finally said, "One of the boys stumbled into the bar, alerting everyone, then he hobbled home. There were closed hearings and lawsuits. I'd have to say when all the abuse came to light, people were ashamed at how much bullying Rick had endured. Part of it we didn't realize. Part of it folks didn't want to accept that we had bigoted attitudes about outsiders living here. And a few people overlooked the violence with a 'boys will be boys' mindset. All four guys served time in detention and mandated therapy. Two of them moved away as soon as they'd completed their programs."

"And the other two?" Davina said.

"Ash and Rick. They're still here, keeping on opposite sides of the street," Mrs. Blackburn said.

"It sounds like Rick snapped when he thought they were hurting you." Davina looked at Lexi.

Lexi's words came slowly as she stared at the floor. "I asked him why he did it. He said he had to end the constant harassment. He'd been watching kung fu videos and realized that these jerks never ended a fight by killing him, therefore they must be letting him survive so they could keep coming after him, again and again. Torturing him. He was fed up. He decided to stop it. He figured the only way to end all the fighting and teasing and bullying was to strike a deadly blow. That way they could never hurt him or me again."

Wood crackled in the firebox. Lexi watched the goat in her arms sleep. Beside her, the rocker creaked as Davina shifted, smoothing her dress over her knees. "Was there any reason," she said softly, "Rick might be jealous of Gavin?"

Lexi didn't answer. Since grade school she'd been Rick's protector. It had shocked her that day behind the Lost Nickel to realize that Rick felt it his job to take care of her. But he wouldn't have done anything to Gavin. Couldn't have. Why would he? She closed her eyes and swallowed.

"Could he have thought he was protecting you, and—" Davina pressed.

"No," Mrs. Blackburn interrupted.

"Then, that's it." Davina sighed. "We'll not let the past repeat by doing nothing." She stood, pulling her sweater closed and buttoning it. "Many's the time I got Paul out of jail. Let's go."

❧

The women drove to Mr. Pham's, picked him up, and arrived at the Young County jail, only to find Sheriff LaCott had gone home and Rick would be held for twenty-four hours.

Mr. Pham looked at Lexi. "You talk better than me." He stepped aside and pointed at the front desk.

"Can we see him?" Lexi asked the officer sitting there.

"Nope." He drummed his pencil against his logbook. "Sheriff said, 'No visitors.'"

"That's not legal," Lexi growled. "We'll have attorneys down here and you'll be part of the—"

"Sir?" Davina shouldered Lexi out of the way. "Rick is in fragile health. I'm sure you wouldn't want to be responsible for anything happening to him overnight."

"Nothin's gonna happen." He tapped his pencil faster.

"His father is worried he might become so frustrated, he'll hurt himself."

While Davina continued talking, using one argument after another, Mr. Pham slipped a red rubber band into Lexi's hand. "Please? You try."

Lexi elbowed Davina aside. "Please, Rick needs this." She dropped the rubber band in front of the deputy. He held up the thick three-inch loop of red rubber, inspecting it. "It'll calm him," Lexi said. "Just like that pencil you're tapping on the desk calms you."

The deputy frowned, dropping both the pencil and the rubber band. He shook his head.

With a *bang*, Lexi smacked her palms on either side of the logbook, her face inches from the officer. "None of this is Rick's fault! He doesn't know why he's in there. It isn't fair that trouble drops out of nowhere on him like bird crap. If you have any decency, give that rubber band to Rick!" She punctuated her message by quickly flat-smacking the desk three times.

"You're not helping by yelling," Davina scolded, taking Lexi by one arm. Mrs. Blackburn took the other. Together they tugged her toward the door, the older woman hissing, "You're letting your temper bake your brains. Get yourself under control."

93

Ignoring the advice, Lexi shouted over her shoulder, "If the sheriff has ever treated you like a four-year-old, then get even by giving Rick the rubber band. It's a small kindness. It won't hurt anybody, but it'll help him."

The women pushed her through the door and outside the station. Lexi paced back and forth in the late afternoon sunlight, pulling in lungfuls of cool air. She let her breath blubber out through closed lips, like a noisy animal.

Davina shook her head. "It's true what Shirley says, isn't it? You really were raised by horses, weren't you?"

"Horses don't abandon you." Lexi scowled at Mrs. Blackburn.

"But they'll put distance between you," Davina said, "when you start acting loco."

15.

On Monday morning when Lexi came in from chores, straw and cold air still clung to her flannel shirt. She turned on her phone and counted. Five quiet seconds ticked by before the ringing began.

"What?" she barked into the receiver like a woman disturbed by too many kids.

"The sheriff wants to see you before he'll release Rick." Mrs. Blackburn sounded neutral and efficient.

"Why? I don't have to see him because he wants to see me." Childish, maybe, but Lexi didn't care. "Tell him I'll text him a photo of me giving him a dead-man's stare because that's exactly how the interview would go."

"That's what you need, isn't it? He'd give your sneering photo to the newspaper along with the tagline, *Miss-Jekyll-won't-cooperate*. This is about Rick, not a contest of wills with LaCott. Get yourself to the jail, and lose the attitude on the way." The line went dead.

"Aaaaaargh." Lexi shook the receiver, then slammed it onto the cradle. "Why am I supposed to drop everything and be supremely happy about answering LaCott's stupid questions *again*?" she asked Chicken. The dog stared at her.

She grabbed a dirty dish on the desk. Shriveled Cheerios stuck in the dried milk at the bottom. She hurled it, along with her frustrations, at the desk chair.

The ceramic bowl ricocheted off the armrest and smashed into her father's clock on the wall. The bass turned tail up, gills down, and made a deep dive toward the floor.

"No! No! No!" She flung herself over the desk, trying to catch it, knocking another dish over the edge. But her reach didn't extend long enough. Pieces of plastic clock scattered across the floor, along with shards of bowl. The clock's battery rolled under her chair.

She tried to calm her breathing, head bowed, eyes closed, clenching her fists, her fingernails cutting into her palms. Without warning, the yell started in her gut, rasped upward through her throat, and exploded from her mouth, loud and long. Chicken joined with a howl.

æ

She arrived at the jail wearing black slacks—with most of the dog hair Scotch-taped off—and a soft gold blouse, accented with a purple scarf. She'd pulled her red hair into a bun at the nape of her neck. In her anger, perhaps she'd pulled a little too tight—her roots were giving her a headache.

Mrs. Blackburn gave her a once-over, then nodded. Mr. Pham gave her a small bow. "LaCott's in there." Mrs. Blackburn pointed toward an office.

"That chunkhead can wait," Lexi snapped. "I'll see Rick first."

A deputy got on the phone, and soon escorted her into the basement. A myriad of LED lights overhead lit the cells. A damp, sour smell, redolent of clothes left in a washing machine for a week, permeated the underground. Their footsteps echoed along the corridor between two rows of cells. "Is it always this bright in here?" Lexi squinted.

"We gotta see what they're doing at all times." The deputy stopped in front of a cell with an open door.

"You could do surgery under these lights." Lexi held a hand above her eyes, shading them. The deputy waved her inside, then left.

On the steel-platform bed attached to the wall, a mound lay beneath a blanket. "Rick," she whispered, "are you asleep?"

"No." The word sounded distant as though spoken from beneath a mountain.

"Can I sit on the edge of your bed?"

He didn't answer. Lexi sat. Minutes passed. "Did you notice the hairline cracks in the floor?"

"They look like Cow Creek on a map of the Blue Mountains," he mumbled.

Lexi's heart ached, sure Rick also knew the number of vertical bars in the jail. He'd probably calculated how far they'd reach if he put them end to end. He would've noticed the cell's asymmetry with corners not precisely ninety-degree angles. Maybe distracting him with comments on the shoddy workmanship would make him talk. "There's something here on the wall." She palmed the concrete.

"Feel the words with your fingers," he mumbled. "It says, *free my mind*. They tried to plaster over the scratches."

Lexi touched the patched area. "Have they hurt you?"

His hand shot out from under the blanket, tweezing one end of the broken red rubber band between his fingers. "They cut it. I tied it together. Doesn't feel right."

"Way to go, Rick. They give you a lemon—you make lemonade."

"You need sugar and water for lemonade. Maybe ice. I only have a mutilated band."

"Yes, okay, it's just a saying. Your dad and Mrs. Blackburn are outside, waiting. We're going to get you out of here, but I need to know if you're all right. You can keep the blanket over your head like Emperor Palpatine in *Star Wars*."

Slowly Rick pushed out of his fetal position and lowered his legs to the floor. "The door was open, but I didn't leave. I didn't want to get into trouble. Will they put me in detention like last time?"

"Is there a reason they should?"

He didn't answer.

"Can I see your face?" Lexi pulled at the blanket mounded over him. It slipped off. His arms snapped up into snake-hands.

"No." Lexi jerked back. Slowly she placed her hands on each of his and weighted them down to his lap. Dark shadows underlined his eyes, huge in his pale face. "Don't do snake-hands," she whispered. "They'll think you're dangerous."

"I *am* dangerous. No one will hurt me anymore. Nobody will hurt you."

"Okay. Thank you." Lexi patted his arm, scanning the ceiling. She didn't see any cameras, but from the deputy's comment about the lighting, she was sure there had to be some. "Let's get the blanket covering you." She stood and pulled it over him, her hand grazing his head. "Is this blood?" She rubbed her fingertips together.

"I pulled my hair."

"Oh, Rick." Lexi inspected the back of his head. Only a small patch was missing, but it made her want to cry. "You won't let others hurt you, but you hurt yourself. I know it helps distract you, but … people pay to have thick beautiful hair like yours."

"I'd give it to them."

"I know you would, but please wait until you're very old and it falls out naturally."

"I saw you kiss him," Rick said. "That fellow didn't—"

Lexi's hand flew up, fingers spread. "We're not talking about that now." She scanned the ceiling again. "Did you tell Sheriff LaCott about the kiss?"

⚜

"Hold on." Lexi looked around LaCott's office. "You know, even prisoners get to sit during an interrogation, so unless you plan on waterboarding me, I'd like a chair."

"Drag one in from the hallway." He pointed at the door. "I read in one of those management magazines, if people have to stand, they'll take up less of your time."

"You read, huh? I think you need different magazines." The folding chair competed with her voice as she rattled it across the tiled floor and thudded it in front of his desk.

"It seems you weren't forthcoming about your relationship with the deceased," LaCott said. "Nor were you forthcoming about your employee stalking you."

"You didn't ask about my relationship with Gavin. And the only stalker I've ever had was Giles Jones in fourth grade. But he was after the apple in my lunch."

"The Pham kid told me he saw Gavin Ceely go into your shop. When he peeked in, you were liplocked with the guy. Rick didn't like it."

"Is that a question?"

"Let me tell you how this is going to work. You'll tell me what I need to know, or that boy is going to spend a lot more days in the cell. And if I happen to pick up a felon or two to keep him company, that'll be on you. I'm not putting up with your sass." LaCott watched her, one corner of his mouth turning up in a smile.

Lexi crossed her arms, squeezing herself. Hot curses shot rapid-fire through her mind. She squeezed herself tighter. She was here for Rick. This was about Rick—not her. She would smother that ember sparking inside and cooperate for his sake. She gave LaCott a nod, still trying to bore a hole through him with her eyes.

"Now, what was your relationship with Gavin Ceely? Obviously, he was more than a friend."

Lexi decided the best defense was offense. She gave him her eye-roll perfected in her teen years. "Your age is showing. That's not how it works now. For that matter, I think even your generation used to say, 'A kiss is just a kiss.'"

"I'm not that old. That was World War Two—"

"Whatever." Lexi interrupted, noting he seemed touchy about his age for a fifty-something-year-old. "Friends kiss friends now. They've done it in Europe for years. It's a greeting. It's a goodbye. It's no big deal."

"Okay." LaCott rearranged himself in his chair. "Was Gavin Ceely carrying anything with him?"

Lexi let out a huff of air. "He had a briefcase."

LaCott leaned forward. "I oughta arrest you for withholding evidence. What else?"

"He pulled a laptop out of the case."

"And?"

"That's all I've got." Lexi spread out her hands. "He was working on something confidential for NASA. He swore me to secrecy. That's why I didn't say anything. I don't know anything beyond that. Call his partners at Celesto—Joe Leeto and Steve Stone."

"Have they been in contact with you?"

"Nope. I've never met them."

"So you're intimate with the guy, but you haven't met the people he works with?"

She decided to test his age-sensitivity again. "That's the way we do it in the twenty-first century. You don't have to be in the same room to get to know someone anymore. We call it the internet."

LaCott didn't look at her. His lips tightened against his teeth. After several moments he said, "What'd he come in to print?"

"Don't know. Didn't ask." Her answer rolled through her mind. Technically that was true. Gavin was likely printing a part for his project, but she hadn't checked the file for more than viruses, so she couldn't confirm exactly what he was printing. She leaned back in her chair, loosening her grip on herself.

"Do you have it?"

"No."

"We didn't find the laptop, the briefcase, or any 3D-printed objects on or near the body. His car was found at the trailhead to Kissing Rock. Wiped clean. Maybe he went there with somebody after getting it on with you. Maybe you got upset about that."

Lexi squinted, her voice rising. "Why would his body be at the shop, but his car there? That doesn't make sense."

"Because your employee and friend in jail back there got mad, overreacted, and you're trying to help him cover it up and confuse the situation by moving cars around."

Lexi's face went slack-jawed. "You have got to be kidding me. That's the most moronic theory I've ever heard. Gavin will never have justice with you on the case. And while we're discussing your policing methods, I want to thank you for tearing up my shop, finding nothing, and proving I'm not a gunrunner, a terrorist, or mafia grunt. You did me a favor sweeping the cobwebs out of the rafters."

"You seen your mother lately?"

"Okay. That's it." Lexi stood. "You're just trying to push my buttons. I've told you what I know. What's Rick's bail?"

"He can go. I just brought him in for questioning."

"Overnight?" Lexi's voice rose. She gripped the back of the chair, her knuckles whitening. "In a jail cell?"

"He said he wanted to lie down. So the deputy gave him a bed. He could've asked to return upstairs anytime, but he didn't." The sheriff smiled. "Got you to tell the truth, didn't it? You shoulda been honest in the first place."

Lexi ached to throw the chair at his head, but somehow managed to rein in her temper.

"By the way, you can have your shop back. We're finished with it."

"We'll see what an attorney thinks about your interrogation methods." She stalked toward the door.

"I'll probably question that kid again. It seems he's got some anger issues." LaCott paused. "He even uses that snake-hand on you."

Lexi froze, turned with a deadly stare and walked two paces back toward the sheriff. She pushed the folding chair over, clattering it onto the floor. "I don't appreciate being used."

"Pick it up," the sheriff said.

She turned her back to him.

"Pick it up or the kid stays here longer."

Letting out a deep breath, she nabbed the chair and dragged it toward the door.

"And Miss Depriest?" LaCott called before she crossed the threshold. "You're now a suspect, too."

16.

At BrainSmith Printing, Lexi crammed papers into a trash can as she ranted to Mrs. Blackburn. "The Phams are not going to bring charges against the sheriff's department. They don't want to make a fuss."

"You got Rick home—that's the important thing." Mrs. Blackburn picked up bulletin boards and leaned them against the wall.

"But LaCott *used* Rick to get to me." Lexi sat down on the floor and scraped scattered paperclips into a pile.

"He did. And you made it easy, taking the brakes off your feelings and going full throttle with your mouth."

"I underestimated him. I thought he was a pinhead. He's more like a sociopath, sacrificing innocents, wearing their blood as bravado. Probably has an altar to Satan at his house."

"And there she goes." Mrs. Blackburn stuck a sheaf of documents inside a blue folder. "Brain out of gear. Mouth accelerating."

"I think LaCott was watching the jail's surveillance cameras. Rick's never given me a snake-hand before. LaCott saw it." Her eyes went wide. She stood and hurried to the door.

"Now where are you going?"

"I forgot about Davina's eagle."

Mrs. Blackburn dropped the folder, hollering after Lexi, "I'm not doing this alone. I'm not your secretary, you know!"

❧

Lexi found Davina outside her back gate, the scent of ozone and burnt metal hovering in the air.

Davina pulled her welder's mask off. The visor left an indentation across her forehead. "I'm adding sharper spikes to the top. If some *bampot* tries to come over the gate and pilfer my copper and magnets again, this'll leave scars on the idiot."

She slipped off her TIG gloves and turned off the gas. Today she wore her regular uniform: heavy canvas overalls and thick-soled boots. She pushed her sleeves to her elbows as she spoke. "Oh, my girl, I meant to talk to you about the eagle. Sorry, the camera in it hasn't worked for a while, what with folks shooting at him. I meant to get you to fix it, but forgot. My mum always said, trouble travels in threes. I'm bracing for the next one."

"My camera in the crow worked, but the video was wiped when they destroyed my computer," Lexi said. "Do you think the Pizza Shop's owl was recording?"

Davina waved her off. "Go along. I'm done with you 'til you check it out."

At the Pizza Shop, Mr. Pham nodded. "Rick makes sure it works. He sleeps now." The small man wore a white apron and a white cap on his head as he kneaded pizza dough.

"May I look at the recordings?" Lexi asked. "I want to check who was on the street last Wednesday night."

"Yeah, yeah." Mr. Pham pointed a flour-dusted hand toward a closet-sized office.

The camera in the bellies of the metal birds on the roof had been her idea to catch whoever was taking pot shots at the bird sculptures. The recordings had captured surprising antics of public urination, kids with BB guns and slingshots, and how PeeWit's mother had been hit by a car.

On the computer, she easily found the right folder. Inside "Owl recordings," Rick had organized videos by date. Lexi fast-forwarded through the night of the murder. She replayed it several times, chewing on her lip as she watched. Her gut told her she was seeing something, but what was it? She made copies, determined to see if the sheriff's sleuthing skills were any better than hers.

In forty minutes, Lexi walked into his office without knocking. His legs stretched out, his feet resting on an open desk drawer. "Whadda ya want now?" LaCott grunted when he saw her.

Lexi held a purple flash drive between two fingers, waving it like a tiny flag. "It's video of the street the night Gavin was killed. You can see—"

"Where'd you get it?"

"From the camera in front of the Pizza Shop. Fifteen people picked up pizzas that night, but there's one guy—"

"Nobody has permission to put cameras on the street. What's that Pham guy up to?"

"Who needs permission to protect their property? Mr. Pham's store has been vandalized since he bought the shop. Davina's copper has been stolen. And we discovered she has a magnet missing. What've you done to solve those crimes?"

"I can't talk about active cases, but you and your drones and cameras—they didn't prevent anything, did they? You can't spy. Surveillance permission has to be run past me. Maybe even the county commissioners. You don't seem to get that people have privacy rights."

"Not on a public street, they don't." Lexi counted to five to calm down. "Do you want me to show you this or not?"

"Give it to me." He took the drive and inserted it into his computer port. Lexi stood at his side. "What am I lookin' at?" he said. "There's people milling around, waiting for a pizza."

"Mr. Pham said it was an average night. Even you dropped by to get pepperoni with pineapple." Lexi made a face.

"Like I do every Wednesday night, and sometimes on Saturday."

"There you are. There's Ash. There's Bill Brandt. Now look at the guy that walks by and into the shop. He isn't from around here. There was a stranger in town that night. Didn't you notice him? Did you say something to him?"

"No, looks like I was talkin' to Bill Brandt."

"It's a little after eleven o'clock. It's not like the Pizza Shop is a destination eatery. Why would this guy stop there? What's he doing in town? Mr. Pham remembers he ordered a chicken pizza with alfredo sauce. You looked right at him as he walked by. This is the guy you need to find. Circulate pictures of him."

"Give me a break." He pinched the ridge of his nose between his eyes. "I'm not searching for strangers who buy pizza. Does this video show who took Ceely's Subaru?"

"You can see the tail end of the SUV as it backs into the street, but the periphery of the camera wasn't wide enough to catch who got into the vehicle. The time stamp indicates it was one-thirty. Rick was at home in bed at that hour. Mr. Pham will testify to that."

"What about you? What were you doing around then?"

"Home. Waiting for Gavin to arrive."

"And did you go looking for *your friend* when he didn't show?"

"No." The guilt she'd so carefully crammed under a mental manhole cover arose, settling on her like a shroud.

"Well, you shoulda. He was killed between seven and midnight. Maybe if you'd gone to see what was wrong, he'd still be alive."

17.

The last funeral Lexi attended was her father's, which had also been on a Wednesday. Most memories of that day were gray and fogged, but occasionally an image would crystallize, and once again she'd plunge into a taut, anxious feeling. She could sense it now, making her want to run for the exit. Instead, she told herself it was fortunate Gavin's ceremony wasn't at her mother's funeral home. At least she didn't have the added stress of dealing with that woman.

She surveyed the room. There was no coffin, only a memorial table at the front. Gavin's family must've chosen cremation. He would have approved of the environmentally friendly option. She snagged a seat ten pews back; having all those heads in front of her felt like a shield, blunting the main action.

Tribute sprays of purple and white flowers stood on either side of the lectern. Lexi clasped her hands tightly in her lap. During her father's service, had the scent of lilies and roses floated through the chapel like they did now? The same unhummable tunes played on the organ. All around her, people spoke in solemn tones, saying the same thing, saying nothing. She caught snatches from her seat. "He was a fine man." "He'll be missed." "He went too soon."

Many of the young people at this service sported well-dressed, well-styled twentysomething bodies. Quite a few were women. Professionals. Manicured nails. Unfreckled complexions.

The longer Lexi gazed at them, the more her dreams of a life with Gavin twisted into embarrassment. Ugh. She'd surely misread Gavin's helpfulness and kisses. She'd been a fool. Why had she thought he'd be interested in her? She hoped she hadn't made herself too pitiful, too needy in his eyes.

She smoothed her hand over the only dress she owned. The purple A-line, cinched with her father's black tooled western belt, hung loosely on her. She couldn't find her own belt, so she'd rummaged through her dad's closet.

The image of a black dress burning in a barrel popped into her head. She closed her eyes, watching the flames turn the rayon gray, then eat jagged holes through the chest. With a smile, she drew a breath. The scent-memory of smoke almost pushed away today's florals in the air. Her mom had bought that black shift and insisted she wear it for her father's funeral. Burning the dress afterward had been satisfying. She should burn more things.

The sudden chord from the organ startled her. A soloist began singing Eric Clapton's "When September Ends." The ceremony became lighter and livelier as people stood at the lectern and shared stories about Gavin. Slideshows of him from baby to adulthood played. A Gavin-designed drone delivered a bouquet of flowers to the memorial table. Lexi felt as though she had tears inside that she couldn't wipe away. She wished she'd been in his inner circle and known the Gavin who'd discovered a hole in the elbow of his shirt right before a big business meeting, so he painted his elbow with White-Out before his pitch.

When the service finished, she stayed in the pew. Let the others leave. Let the crowds thin. Express condolences and get out of here. She had no desire to exchange small talk with anyone. It was like standing in a vat of worms--everyone was uncomfortable and no one knew where to look.

When the assistant funeral director entered the empty chapel and picked up a spray of flowers, Lexi asked her to point out Gavin's parents and his partners. The grieving parents stood close together at the back of the room. Lexi quietly offered her condolences. The conversation was short, weighting Lexi with more sadness.

Crossing the room, she waited at the fringe of the group surrounding the partners. Shifting from foot to foot, she imagined the relief of being in her truck and driving away, leaving sorrow and small talk and strangers behind. At the first gap in bodies, she held out her hand to the tallest of the duo. "I'm Alexandra Depriest. I'm so sorry about Gavin."

"Joe Leeto." His long, thin fingers took her hand, but his angular face and focus turned elsewhere as if scanning the room for someone else. "You knew Gavin, how?"

"We went to college together. I had to quit to care for my dad, but we kept in touch. He taught me how to make circuit boards. Got me started in 3D printing."

Joe's eyes snapped to her face. "You're Lexi." He grasped her arm, making Lexi's eyes widen with surprise. "Steve," he called to a tall fellow several feet away with a shadow beard. "Steve!" The man broke off his conversation and joined Joe.

"This is Lexi. You know ..." He shot his friend an exasperated look and lowered his voice. "Where Gavin was ... last seen."

Conversation around them stopped as everyone's attention seemed to shift to Lexi. She felt herself shrinking, pulling into her body like a turtle.

"We need to talk." Still holding her arm, Joe led Lexi through the crowd into a back hallway, with Steve close behind. Joe pushed open the first door and peered into a janitor's closet before pulling her onward. "Why haven't you answered our calls?"

"I turned off my phone." She stutter-stepped beside him, and tried to keep up. "I've been too overwhelmed to—"

He opened another door, flicked on the light, and pulled her into a storage room lined with candle stands, music holders, and flower pots. Steve followed, shutting the door behind them.

"Tell us what happened." Joe let go of her arm.

"Haven't you heard from the sheriff?" Lexi took a step back, looking from man to man, her heart beating faster.

"He says it may be some local kid, and that they'll have it wrapped up soon."

She shook her head, her anxiousness pushed away by disgust with LaCott. "That's not what happened." She tried to keep her voice even as she shared what she knew. "The sheriff tore my place up in the search, but I'm not sure if he was looking for clues or because I ticked him off. My computer was magnetized or else I would've had the video of who did this."

"Magnetized?" The men exchanged a look. "We've been told Gavin's laptop and messenger bag are missing. Did you see him use a flash drive?"

"It's sort of a blur." Lexi lied, staring at the floor. "So much has happened."

Steve said, "Each of us is working on part of a highly secret project—"

"I know about the NASA competition," Lexi interrupted. "It was my barn you used to test the drones."

Steve shook his head. "Of course. Sorry. For security, our design is never together in one place. Each of us kept our sections on separate flash drives and kept the drives on our bodies." He held up a small duck in green and yellow colors. Joe held up a University of Washington Husky in a purple shirt.

"The beaver!" Lexi gasped. "I checked it for viruses."

"He let you put it in a computer?" Steve leaned forward, crowding her.

She scowled, using her fingertips to push him away. "My printers. My barn, remember? I didn't download or copy it," she said.

"It's okay. It's okay." Joe put his hand on his partner's chest. "Gavin trusted her." He looked at Lexi. "He liked you. Said you were too brave for your own good."

"He did?" The secondhand praise made her momentarily happy.

"It was more along the lines that you had a temper," Joe said.

Lexi noted that Steve gave him a stare that would kill flies. "That was someone else. *This woman* he liked."

Lexi looked from one face to the other. "I don't know what's worse." She hooked her thumb at Joe. "His rude honesty or your subterfuge. I'm not an idiot. I'm sorry for your loss. I hope you can continue in the competition. My condolences and good luck with your effort." The need to get away from these phonies who only cared about their stupid competition overwhelmed her. She pushed between them and opened the door, but Steve caught the edge of it, holding on firmly.

"Not if any competitors get that flash drive. We need it."

"I haven't seen it since that night." Lexi's voice carried a hard edge. "Nothing of Gavin's was left in the shop except his body."

"You said you had cameras recording at the time?" Joe pressed.

"Yes, but the sheriff took my computer. Not sure what he hoped to find. Someone stole an electro-magnet from the welding shop and bricked my hard drive."

"Get the computer back." Steve looked at his partner. "We have resources. Maybe we can retrieve something off of it."

Joe nodded. "We'll buy you a new computer if you'll give us that one."

"I'll try"—Lexi frowned—"but I've irritated the sheriff so much, he's not likely to do me any favors. I'd like to go now."

"Oh, sure. I apologize." Steve opened the door and stepped out first, looking up and down the hall.

"Again, I'm sorry about the loss of your friend and partner," she paused, "even if you two aren't. It seems you're only missing his technology, which is sad. He was a really fine human being." Lexi hurried along the hallway. The back of her neck chilled, feeling their eyes on her as she walked away.

"Wait!" Joe called, but Lexi picked up her pace. She almost made it to the safety of the vestibule before he caught up to her. "I apologize," he said. "You're right. We haven't made a good impression, but we did care about Gavin and considered him a friend. May I ask one more question to clarify something?"

Lexi glanced at the group of people nearby. Maybe it was because Joe and Steve had shut her in a closet, or perhaps it was their uber-focused attitude, but whatever it was, she wanted away from everyone, including them. "Let's keep walking." She stepped toward the door.

"Please." Joe grabbed her arm but let go when she stared at his hand. "This is about you," he said quietly.

"I'm listening."

"Did you say a magnet was stolen to wipe your hard drive?"

"From the welding shop in Telos. Strong enough to lift six-hundred-fifty pounds."

He looked at the people chatting, drinking coffee, eating cookies. Taking a step closer, he bent, whispering in her ear. "Then this was premeditated. You were being watched. Probably still are."

She stepped back, her mouth gaping as though someone had poured ice water down her back. "Surely not now," she said. "Not since Gavin isn't … around."

He looked at her for several long seconds, and she sensed anger and determination behind his eyes. "We want to know who did this," he said. "We have security information. We've got contacts who can run fingerprints and background checks. If you discover something—no matter how small—it might help us find Gavin's killer and our technology. Will you let us know—day or night?"

She nodded. A dread rolled over her, trebling her heartbeat. This project went far deeper than she'd thought.

With a final whisper of, "Watch your back. I mean it," Joe left, joining a group of young men in gray suits and brown shoes.

She walked to her truck, her long shadow stretching across the parking lot. She felt silly scanning the area. She did it anyway, then peered under the truck and glanced inside before getting in. Had Joe's words been a threat—or a warning?

ॐ

The moon had already set. Only the stars watched as he paused on the gravel drive, looking at the house. She was still up. He imagined her sitting behind the monitor, which blocked his view of her. But she was there. That's where she spent most of her time when she was at home. That or chores or bed. She was a terrible housekeeper. That was okay. He didn't mind a mess. Life was messy.

The glow of the computer screen colored the whole room in a witch's-brew green. He'd wait until the house went black. Then wait a little longer before making his move.

18.

The next morning, Lexi fell onto the floor from her bed. She had to. That was the only way she could force herself to get up. The alarm didn't inspire her. The dusty light coming through the windows didn't motivate her. Not even the birds holding a choir-sing outside her window roused her.

Last night, sleep had come in fits and starts. It had been like scratching the sides of a dark hole, trying to gather enough sleep dust to send her into a dream. When she'd finally settled into a nap, Chicken had awakened her with a dream of his own, growling, pawing the bed, trying to jump off as though wanting to chase cattle. Wide awake, she'd checked the house just in case, but hadn't found anything except a couple of skunks digging in the yard. It had been a short night.

She yawned. This Thursday she had no meetings. No need to look like Office Barbie. A red sweater, jeans, and black-and-white Keds would be fine.

Once in town, she bought coffee and a S'more cinnamon roll from Latte-Da II and headed to her shop. Inside, papers lay several inches deep on her plywood desk, but the floor was clean, mainly because she'd thrown everything from it to the top of her desk.

The paper mound felt like a tsunami ready to bury her. Her business was a sinking ship with no sales coming in. Why should she bother bailing the flotsam and jetsam? Instead of attacking her desk, she organized the spools of filaments, arranging them by type and color in the closet. Each footstep reminded her she treaded where Gavin had lain.

By noon, she'd called LaCott three times to no avail. "I want my computer," she told the deputy, her anger rising with each call. On the last call, she'd added, "LaCott owes me since he shut down my business for five days. I know the hard drive is shot, but maybe I can make a little money recycling the network card and some other parts." She wasn't selling parts, but didn't want to reveal why she really wanted it. Knowing LaCott, he'd keep it if he thought it was important to her.

She shoved papers out of her way and plopped her laptop onto the cubbyhole of space she'd carved in the mound. Unwrapping her peanut butter-and-potato chip sandwich, she tapped computer keys, opening the network to her house.

At home, beneath the dining room table, the iPad mounted to a feeding bin awakened from its sleep-state. "Chicken? Chicken?" she called. The only objects she could see on her monitor were the hardwood floor and table legs. "Where are you, boy?" She whistled several times. Usually, he was waiting in front of the iPad to hear her voice, but today he wasn't there. She checked the time. Early. The feed bin was a few yards from his window lookout, so he must have stiffly moved elsewhere, bored.

She took several bites from her sandwich, intermittently calling to him. Finally, the dog crawled into view. "Oh, Chicken. Are you okay?" She leaned close to the camera on her laptop as though that would help her see better.

He pulled himself into position, paws extended around his bowl, and licked the screen a couple of times. "Are you in pain, buddy?" He stuck his nose in the bowl and sniffed. "Okay, okay. Here it comes." Spreading her fingers wide, she punched three buttons on her keyboard at the same time. The bin opened and dropped a cup of special dog chow into the bowl.

They ate lunch together. Lexi told Chicken about cancelled orders and hanging up on Truvy Orvice, the KDW news anchor. "I'm sick of people bothering me. I don't want to talk about this."

Chicken laid his head on his half-empty bowl and closed his eyes. "You didn't eat much, buddy," she said quietly. She studied him in the monitor. He had more gray in his muzzle than she remembered. One ear had always cocked crookedly, but now it hung flat. He let out a breath that seemed like a sigh to her. "I'm coming home early this afternoon. We'll see the vet again. Get something else to make you feel better, okay?"

He didn't open his eyes at the mention of "vet." Lexi touched the screen, stroking between his ears. He must really be sick. "But don't leave me now," she whispered. "Not now."

At two o'clock, Mrs. Blackburn came through the door leading PeeWit. The older woman had agreed to move back in if Lexi promised to stop throwing chairs at the sheriff. The jabber of the four high school girls of Club Club accompanied her.

Fresh air breezed in with them, carrying the scent of pizza from next door and ruffling papers on the bulletin boards still leaning against the walls.

PeeWit, wearing red fleece pajamas dotted with images of ducks and umbrellas, bounded toward Lexi but stopped five feet away. Stepping from one foot to the other, he stared, then ran back to the safety of the girls.

"He acts scared of you. Probably because you look like a crack addict." Mrs. Blackburn waggled her hands around her head. "When's the last time you took a shower or brushed your hair?"

"I don't know. I don't care." Lexi shoved hair away from her face. "You hang with a lot of crackheads, do you? Just go in there and paint. I've got enough problems without you ragging on me."

Mrs. Blackburn turned and pointed to The Other Room. "Girls." They filed through the door with Mrs. Blackburn at their heels.

For the rest of the afternoon, Lexi worked at her laptop, attempting to slice the files on an eight-inch cowboy statue for

Davina's life-size version. A burst of laughter came from The Other Room. Lexi got up and shut their door with a *bang*.

In a few minutes, Haisley came out and stood behind Lexi, tugging her curly black hair. "Lexi, I'm really sorry the murder took place in your shop."

"Me, too."

"My mother didn't want me to come here today, but I told her it was a safe place to meet after school. Whatever happened was at night. And it wasn't your fault."

"Okay. Thanks." Lexi ignored her, hoping she'd go away. For a few hours, she wanted to focus on something besides her problems. Was that too much to ask?

"Mom's sort of worried about the funny kid next door, but I told her he seems nice."

Lexi's hands froze on her keyboard. She took a breath and let it out slowly. "Rick is innocent. If people would get to know him better, they'd understand that, and maybe like him, too. Now, excuse me, I need to finish this."

"Could I watch over your shoulder?"

Lexi's hand went to her forehead. She closed her eyes and took another deep breath.

"Sorry," Haisley said. "It's just that I'd like to do this, and there's no other opportunity in this town. I'd like to help out."

"I've already told you, I'm not hiring." Lexi gripped the desk as though it would keep her from launching into a fit. "I don't even have enough business for a student apprentice." Her voice sharpened more than she'd intended.

"I'll volunteer."

"I can hardly get myself organized. I don't want to manage another person."

"I'll wipe the dust off. I'm guessing that's where they took fingerprints." Haisley pointed.

Lexi looked at the white-chalked printer. She hadn't used it since—why would she? There were no orders. Worry thundered through her thoughts. Without thinking, her words exploded from her mouth "Please. Go back to your room. Leave me alone."

Hearing herself, she froze. She'd become a she-devil. A dragon. She'd turned into her mother. She needed sleep. She needed work orders to come in. She needed some relief.

Lexi watched Haisley walk away, telling herself when she had spare energy, she'd apologize to the girl. Her focus turned wholly to her project. It was what she liked about programming. Time stopped. Hours passed. It seemed as though she was gone days, visiting another world.

When she finally checked the clock, she mumbled a curse. The vet had offered to work her dog into the last appointment of the day. The office closed in forty minutes. It would take her a half hour to collect Chicken and get there.

Something moved in the periphery of her vision. When she turned and looked, it was gone. Hurrying into the back of the shop, she peered between the row of printers and wall. Red ducky pajamas were ten feet away, its wearer teething a black cable.

"Stop that!" she screamed. PeeWit bolted.

Lexi ran to where the kid had been. The silicon insulation covering the electrical cable had been gouged, but was mostly intact. Lexi wriggled from behind the printer, spotting the goat under her plywood desk, a pink invoice in his mouth.

"Get over here, you!" She ran toward him. He dashed to the other side of the room.

They went back and forth twice, her cussing, PeeWit bouncing, kicking his back legs out as though flying with each jump. "I hate you. You little fuzz rat!" she screamed, filling the rafters with her frustration. Mrs. Blackburn and the girls emptied from the room.

Lexi dropped flat on her back on the concrete floor, her arms at her side, lying like a corpse. The kid took tentative steps toward her.

Haisley hurried forward. "Run, PeeWit, run!"

But it was too late. The temptation to stand on top of something was too strong for the little goat. He jumped on Lexi. She snapped her arms around him with a "Gotcha!" twisting him so his legs slashed the air in front of her, his body writhing as she stood up.

"Who"—Lexi shoved the kid into Haisley's arms—"is supposed to be watching him? He was chewing on a cable. I'm surprised this place isn't in flames right now. Or worse, he'd be electrocuted. His eyes blown out of his head."

"That's enough," Mrs. Blackburn said.

"I'm sorry." Haisley's eyes became shiny as she struggled with the goat.

"And why doesn't he have a diaper on?" Lexi threw her hands in the air. Strands of hair escaped her topknot and dangled in her face. "If that goat is here, then he's supposed to be diapered. But he's not, is he? Now we'll be stepping on balls of goat crap. Way to be responsible."

"Girls." Mrs. Blackburn flourished her hand toward The Other Room, but none of them moved. They seemed frozen, watching Lexi stomp to her white board, still leaning against the wall. She scribbled, "No GOATS!!" and pounded the exclamation points onto the board, making it fall over. Lexi bent and kept writing, adding more exclamations and several underlines.

She straightened, standing as wide-armed and wide-stanced as Bigfoot. "Just think"—she yelled while the teenagers gaped—"if any of you worked here, only bricks and rubble would be left." She threw down the marker, bouncing it off the whiteboard to roll across the concrete as she walked away.

"Lexi! Get back here and apologize," Mrs. Blackburn commanded.

"My dog is sick." She went out the door, slamming it behind her.

19.

Friday morning, Lexi flew the drone and finished chores without incident. She gave Chicken his new meds. He seemed more comfortable, giving her a moment of relief, but the strange sensation of being stuck on railroad tracks, awaiting an approaching train, still dogged her every move. She drove to Telos, gripping the steering wheel, replaying last night's vet visit.

The doc had suggested tranquilizing Lexi would be more calming for Chicken than making *him* take pharmaceuticals. Then the woman had added a weak laugh, as if joking.

Hadn't she heard about the murder? Lexi gave her the sharpest look she could muster, offering her own suggestion. "Why don't you stick your syringe in your own butt?"

The visit had chilled quickly.

She'd lain nose to nose with Chicken through the night, replaying her words, trying to make herself sound better. By daybreak, she admitted she'd acted like a barbarian.

The tiniest situations made anger boil out of her gut and swamp her mouth without warning. Grit scratched every nerve ending. Maybe the vet was right, and she should be medicated.

With effort, she relaxed her grip on the steering wheel and straightened her spine against the truck seat, putting her shoulders back. This was a new day. Chicken wasn't in pain. That would make things better. The sun broke through the clouds, their edges glowing in brilliant whites. Pine trees waved green tips of new growth. She braked to allow a squirrel time to scamper all the way across the road. Life continued and she would too. She'd treat herself to a decent breakfast. A healthier diet should improve her mood. She'd mainly lived on cereal and Hot Pockets for the last week.

As soon as she entered Crusty's, Sull Wixly bellowed across the restaurant, "Hey, Shorty!" He wore his usual uniform of boonie hat, flannel shirt, and camo-green pants, and sat with his regular cronies. She ignored the ol' coot and sat in the corner with her back to him. After ordering, she pulled out her phone and made a list of community presentations to drum up business.

Sales had slowed to a trickle. Only one request for a quote had come in yesterday. Her biggest accounts, the hospitals, had switched to a 3D shop in Boise while her shop had been shuttered by LaCott.

When her eyelids began to feel heavy, she crossed her arms on the tabletop, laid her head on them, and closed her eyes. But instead of relaxing into sleep, Coot's droning voice grated her consciousness. Wearily, she turned to stare at Sull Wixly.

He glanced at her, ending his story with, "Ain't that right, Shorty?"

"You know what a recursive loop is, Coot?"

"Something electronic?"

"It comes from math, but the theory can be applied to anything," Lexi said. "It's when the output is added to the input, thus increasing the output even more."

He pulled a face, goggling his eyes and wagging his head like he'd been smacked with a mallet.

"Here. I'll put it in terms you can understand. When you broadcast your BS stories, the people at the next table have to talk louder to hear themselves. Then the table next to them talks louder, and it spreads through the whole building. Soon, you and your whoppers are getting drowned out, so you amp it up even more, and it starts all over again. Recursive loop. Nobody can hear themselves because *you* can't carry on a quiet conversation."

"Here's your scrambled egg and biscuit." Rosalee, big-boned and horsey-faced, stepped between Sull and Lexi's sight line. "I put some of Osiah's special peach jam on the plate 'cause I know you like it. Now eat up. You're as gaunt as a canner cow."

"Thanks. That's the look I was going for."

"Well, no wonder, what with all the tragedy at your place. They let Rick loose, huh?"

"You *know* he's not guilty." Lexi gave her a pointed look.

"Don't get snipey, hon. I think it's good you're trying to help him out, but when's the last time you had a solid night's sleep? You look droopy and dark-eyed."

"I can't—" Loud laughter rose from the men's table. Then one of them called for coffee. Rosalee rolled her eyes. Lexi waved her away, murmuring, "I'm fine. Never better." Rosalee frowned and left.

Coot's voice continued to carry through the diner. "We were never supposed to go beyond the wire."

Lexi watched a small man at Coot's table stuff his mouth with pancakes, then try to talk. "Yeah, yeah. You told us a hun'erd times. 'Never go beyond the perimeter.' Danger, death and a million Vietcong were hidin' beyond the perimeter."

"This time I *did* go past it. Volunteered to do it." Coot squinted at them. "Somebody had to pick up the wounded and the bodies after a recon. You'd never know where one or two of those little brown men would pop up. They had tunnels all through that hill."

Lexi called across the diner, "Would you mind keeping it down? I'd like my eggs without a side of prejudice and war."

"Sull Wixly is a veteran. You should thank him." Ted Billis made a fist, jerking it in an atta-boy signal.

"Thank you. Now, keep it down, please." She turned back to her plate.

Coot began again, same decibel as before. "It'd been quiet during the night, so we knew those little guys were up to something, digging somewhere. Tunnels yay big." He held his hands ten inches apart. "But they could zip through 'em. So, I said, 'I'm gonna die someday anyway. May as well make it count for something here and now.' I climbed over that perimeter wire.

"Their first shot got my arm. That was all it took. Now we knew where they were. I hunkered down, and we sprayed and cratered that hill till it didn't exist no more."

Lexi dropped her fork onto the table with a clatter, her face becoming sharp angles and shadows. She pushed her chair back and strode to his table and spoke with a deadly evenness. "I could not help overhearing because you're broadcasting like a loudspeaker, so I'm letting you know ... they are not little guys or whatever derogatory name you want to call them. They have given names and a culture like you do. A family of Vietnamese live in this town. The war's over. Someone may look and sound different, but lots of things are different—and the world is going to keep changing."

She drew in a breath. "You think about this ... your ancestors were once foreigners and new here too. They probably threw a fit about traction engines, saying the exhaust and noise scared the horses. Now, even *you* own a tractor, proving your ancestors wrong. Obviously, all change isn't bad. But you still think it's okay to make fun of or shoot anything you're afraid of."

"No, I don't think that at all," Sull said. "We're just old men tellin' old stories."

Lexi's fingers clenched at her side. She knew what to do. She'd been taught by the best bullies in the high-school lunchroom. One of the jerks would turn a drink upside down on Rick's plate—or hers. Hamburger, fries, or pizza floated in a pool of cola. Ice had mounded on top of the food with a few pieces skittering onto the table. Each time the jerk-trio succeeded in the prank, they thought it got funnier, cheering, giving high-fives, and gladly accepting detention for their victories.

"This is your reminder not to tell bigoted stories anymore." Leaning over the table, Lexi grabbed Coot's coffee mug. She shoved it forward, trying to turn it upside down onto his waffles, but the cup caught and whacked the edge of Coot's plate. Hot liquid arced into the air, hitting the old man's face and chest. The mug jumped from her fingers, somersaulting across the table, joining the plate sliding onto the old guy's lap.

"Mother, Mary, and Joseph!" Coot yelped as he stood. The plate and mug fell, hitting the floor. White ceramic pieces bounced across the tiles. Globs of egg and syrup stuck to Coot's pants. Coffee dripped from the edge of the table, pooling around his boots.

Lexi gasped, her hand frozen in midair. Such a deceptively easy stunt required skill—skill she obviously lacked.

Rosalee rushed from her work station. The other men at the table stood, lifting their plates as though the spreading coffee would melt their dishes. Three women at a nearby table scooted their chairs back as coffee trailed across the floor.

"There was no need to do that!" Rosalee growled, glaring at Lexi and tossing out dishtowels. "Sure, he's loud and irritating, but you know better."

"I'm sorry. I really didn't mean for—"

"Move outta the way." Rosalee huffed.

Lexi hurried to the register, pulled a credit card from her wallet, and waited. When Rosalee had the table wiped, she threw the wad of towels at the mess on the floor and took long-legged strides to the till. She punched the register's keys like an angry, one-fingered piano player.

"I didn't mean to make extra work. I'll pay for everything, including the old coot's meal. I didn't expect him to stand and the dishes to break. I thought—"

"You *don't* think!" Rosalee gave her a doomsday stare. "We all know you're stressed-out trying to help Rick, keep up a ranch, and run your business, but you need to go home, lock the door, and rest up until you stop acting like a bull fighting bumblebees. That'll be forty-eight dollars. And we don't take credit cards."

"Okay." Lexi stared, wide-eyed. The undertones of her voice cracked as she whispered, "That's a little stiff, isn't it?"

"A plate. A mug. Your breakfast. And you're buying Sull Wixly two breakfasts, the one you ruined and another one."

Lexi nodded; her eyes closed as she took a breath. Finally, she whispered, "I know I don't have it all together. I'm sorry." She glanced sheepishly around the diner. Customers stared back. She knew each face, but couldn't gin up enough bravado to ask for money to finance her idiocy. Coot was the only one not looking at her. He grumbled, rubbing egg deeper into his pants as he attempted to clean them. Lexi leaned over the mints and fishbowl of business cards on the countertop, saying quietly, "I could help clean up … maybe wash dishes?"

The waitress gave a snort. "You've got fifteen minutes to bring me the money. You hear me?" With a quick nod, Lexi headed for the door.

The loud growl of her stomach turned off her brain and goaded her into her next stunt. In a sideways dash, she grabbed her plate of eggs and biscuit from the table and ran through the door. Rosalee's shouts followed her.

20.

Caws, tweets, and whistles sounded as she dashed from Crusty's. Rounding the corner of the building, she jogged onto Main street. The squawks rose to a jungle crescendo. Holding the plate to her face, she pushed the eggs into her mouth with her fingers, hurrying toward her shop.

Five people stood in the street, staring at hundreds of birds lined wing to wing along the roofline. Scratching, pecking, and screeching, even more birds bobbed over the walkway, on the table, and across the bench in front of the Pizza Shop. Pigeons and crows acted as gang leaders, strutting and jabbing at a thick layer of maize. They flapped their wings when they got too close to each other. The ducks, wrens, and chickadees darted along the edges, stealing seeds.

Above the sidewalk scene, Mr. Pham stood on the flat roof, swinging a broom. Two crows took turns dive-bombing him. He cursed "*Chét tiêt*," damning them. Between the moments of their assault, he hurriedly brushed maize into a dustpan and threw it to the sidewalk below. On the ground, birds fluttered away each time he pelted them with seed, but quickly hopped back into the feast.

"Good grief. What's this?" Lexi, her stomach still growling, stopped next to Bill Brandt, eating and staring at the bird circus.

The forty-something-year-old president of Rotary wore khakis and a black polo embroidered with the name of his insurance company. He transferred his briefcase to his left hand so he could pat Lexi on the back. "Morning. Eating on the run?" He watched her scrape her biscuit across a blob of jelly and take a bite.

"Rick must've gone a little crazy with the food," he said, glancing from her Keds to her face. "Guess he went nuts after being cooped up in jail. Pham's been heaving seeds off the roof for the last five minutes." His eyes followed her swabbing the last of her biscuit in the jelly and putting it to her lips. "I was wondering … maybe sometime … you'd like to go for coffee …or lunch? I'm a good listener. I know you've had more than your share of hard luck lately. Maybe you'd like a shoulder to lean on?"

Lexi barely heard Bill. Absent-mindedly, she licked her fingertips, focusing on the one thing she could handle right now. "Rick would never overfeed." Creases lined her forehead as she shook her head. "He's too worried about rats." She pushed the plate into Bill's hands. "Give this to Rosalee. Something's terribly wrong here." She ran to the Pizza Shop. Birds rose in fluttering clouds as she dashed through them. Yanking on the door, she found it locked. She pulled her keys from her pocket.

It was Rick who had discovered that one key opened all the front doors in the old brewery for every shop. They could've changed them, but found it handy. Rick used his key to do night work at Lexi's shop. Lexi used her key to get rebar or steel posts from Davina's. The Scottish woman used her key to visit Mr. Pham's shop in the mornings, where he left a plate of fresh-made doughnuts on the counter for her or Lexi.

Kicking, she flushed birds away from the door. Quickly, she entered, locking it behind her. Dashing down the hall, she knocked keys off a peg and the phone off its base without pausing to pick them up. Turning, she took narrow steps, two at a time, up to Rick's secret Eden.

He had made a niche on the roof, surrounding his lounge chair with potted cedars and snowberry bushes to hide it from view. It was one of the few outside places he felt safe. Now the plants had been pushed over, soil fanned across the black rooftop. Roots stuck out like skeletal fingers, drying in the air. A thirty-pound burlap bag lay discarded in a corner. Round pellets of orange maize lay scattered everywhere.

Lexi retrieved the sack and held it open on the surface. "Sweep it into the bag!" she shouted over the bird calls.

"Too loud for Rick!" Mr. Pham yelled. "He agreed to go home."

"Too loud for anybody!" Lexi nodded as seeds rolled and bounced in front of his broom.

The grain disappeared into gullets or the burlap sack. Groups of birds began flying away. After a while, the squawks toned down to the decibel of a chicken coop. By the time Lexi and Mr. Pham moved from the roof to the front of the shop, a third of the bag was full of seed, and the street was full of spectators. Mr. Pham phoned Rick.

Lexi looked up at the building. White-and-gray crap covered the metal owl. It oozed across the pizza sign and ran in globby streaks down the brick walls.

Davina arrived, a scowl on her face as she carried a stiff-bristled broom. Grumbling indecipherable Scottish, she began sweeping seed from the cracks in the sidewalk and street. "Move!" she growled at Sull Wixly and his cronies who, like everyone else in town, had heard the noise.

Mr. Pham bowed to the crowd. "Everything is okay. No birds in shop. Pizza still good. We are open soon. Everyone come back."

In a few minutes, Rick arrived. Stone-faced, he connected a hose to the spigot, and began hosing down the sidewalk, just as he did every morning after the ducks had visited. Davina pushed the broom in front of his spray, scouring away dollops of crap.

"Okay, folks." Lexi clapped above her head. "Thanks for all your help. And if you didn't help, then you have to ask yourself, 'What kind of a selfish son-of-a-monkey am I? Why wouldn't I help a neighbor?' She stared at Sull Wixly, his crotch and shirt stained with syrup. "This is what happens when you run your mouth about people."

"Twern't me. I was being attacked by a wild woman while this was goin' on."

"Then why don't you help by buying a pizza before you go?"

"I don't eat pizza." He added something Lexi couldn't hear. His buddies broke out in laughter. He grinned at her. "That second round of pancakes looked good"—he winked—"but I was full. Sorry you gotta pay for something I didn't eat. You want a loan? I don't charge much interest." He turned, mumbling something to his friends.

Lexi grabbed the hose from Rick, aiming a jet of water at Sull. The stream popped him in the ear, knocking his hat off. Sull turned from the spray, his hands on his head as he tried to move away. The men around him scattered.

Davina made jabbing attempts to grab the nozzle, but Lexi twisted, pushing her back, holding the sprayer beyond her reach. Lexi followed Coot down the street, keeping the blast aimed at his head. Finally, Davina put an armlock around her and wrenched the hose away.

Sull Wixly stood alone, a few strands of hair pasted to his balding head, his flannel shirt clinging to his rounded shoulders, water dripping from his fingertips. He coughed several times, flinging water off his hands. His face wrinkled with confusion. "*What* have I ever done to you?"

Her words came out in a hot-tempered hiss. "That was for my dad."

"Your dad and me got along fine."

"Liar! I was sitting there that day." Her voice strained as though it were burning her throat. "I heard every word you tried to break him with."

Sull winced, his mouth tightening as he looked down.

A blast of water hit Lexi in the face. "Cool your head, girl!" Davina shouted. "You're losing yourself!"

꙳

Lexi stayed at the Pizza Shop and talked with Rick—how it felt like high school again, except this time, she was the one who couldn't control her anger. Together, they watched the morning's street video from the owl sculpture. She needed to keep busy, to burn off anxiety crawling in her like ants marching through her veins. She wanted to forget the spectacle she'd made of herself, hosing down an old man, even if he deserved it. She needed to get out of town—maybe move to another continent.

Kewake, Oregon, nine miles away, was all the travel she could afford at the moment. As she drove, sunshine broke through wracks of gray clouds, spotlighting fields turning green again. Along the highway, birds sat in groups on the electric lines. She wondered if they'd been at the banquet in Telos. She honked at them. They didn't fly away.

On the north side of town, she parked at a blue ranch house in need of paint. No vehicle in the driveway, but she figured he probably kept his Dodge truck in the back. A small drift of leaves lay against the front door. The moldering welcome mat was frayed and chewed on one corner, evidence a dog had once lived there, but it must've been long ago. Using the side of her fist, she pounded the door.

After several door-beatings, LaCott swung it open, appearing in old jeans, a belly-stretched black t-shirt, and stocking feet. "This better be important," he growled.

Lexi held up a red flash drive. "Here's video footage of the juvies who vandalized Pham's Pizza Shop. The Phams are being persecuted since you falsely suspect Rick of murder."

"Yeah, I heard about it—even though it's my day off. I suppose this video came from that illegal surveillance camera you put in those oddball bird sculptures on the street. I told you to take them down. You tell Pham if he wants to file a complaint, he can go to the station."

"Like that worked so well when I lodged a complaint about shooting my drone. Let's just say this is your chance to show the state attorney general you actually understand justice and are doing your job."

"Are you threatening me? Haven't you learned anything?"

"Apparently not. I'm on a roll today, insulting people and surpassing my previous benchmark for being hellish and acting brainless. So you want this or not?"

He snatched the drive from her hand. "Who was it?"

"The Bilyeau twins."

"Figures. Little pinheads. They probably stole the seed too." He pinched his nostrils and gave a snort. "All right. I'll call Darrel, which is what you shoulda done." He started to close the door.

"Wait!" Lexi pushed against it. "I came to you because I really need my computer. I've called your office five times. I can't do business without it."

"Then you got a problem. I sent that hunka junk to the state's technical forensics. Don't know when you'll see it again, but I'm pretty sure you can kiss it goodbye."

"Who's in charge of that department? I'll talk to them."

"Good luck working your way through bureaucracy." He gave her a look as though she'd ask for the sun to rise at midnight.

"Did Gavin's autopsy reveal anything?" she asked.

"No. And Miss Depriest"—he let several beats pass—"don't ever come to my house again. You understand?"

"Oh, sure. You can count on it." Lexi turned and walked away.

⁂

When she finally opened the door to BrainSmith Printing, it was late afternoon. The drama, energy, and resolution that had bullied her through the morning had frizzled, leaving her in a deep funk. She'd been dive-bombed, crapped on, sprayed, air-dried, crazed, and threatened by the sheriff. Now she was starving. There was no cereal or snacks at the shop. Cursed rats.

She looked for her chair and found it in the middle of the room. Standing on the seat was a tiny 3D figurine.

The two-inch Daughter of Khaine was part of the Warhammer collection Mrs. Blackburn was painting. The vicious warrior was frozen mid-leap, mouth wide, screaming. Her red hair streamed behind her. One hand clenched a bloody saber, the other held a banner of tribal symbols above her head. Across the base of the statuette the old woman had painted "Lexi."

Beneath the toy figure lay a note in Mrs. Blackburn's precise handwriting.

My house. Tomorrow. 9:00. Dress for church.
No show. No rent.

"Ugggh!" Lexi let her head fall back and her gaze focus on the ceiling. "I do not have the energy for this!"

She rolled her chair to her desk and turned on her laptop. Plopping into the seat, she set the small statue on the desk, studying its saber. All the other statuettes she'd printed for Mrs. Blackburn had swords in both hands, ready for action, but this one was burdened with fighting *and* carrying the banner. "Mrs. Blackburn got that right," Lexi mumbled to herself. "Even my figurine has to multi-task."

21.

Lexi had three surprises when she went to church Sunday morning.

They began when she picked up Mrs. Blackburn. She was astonished when the older woman loaded PeeWit into the cab of the truck. He wore his Sunday best, a black and white sweater with a rolled collar. He looked like a pastor and was dressed more stylishly than Lexi in her baggy purple dress she'd worn to the funeral.

"Sunday school," Mrs. Blackburn said before Lexi could ask. "People have yoga with goats, this is like God with goats, and it tires both PeeWit and the little ones for the rest of the day."

Mrs. Blackburn looked Lexi up and down, but didn't comment on the tooled belt slouching around her hips or the dog hairs. Another surprise.

In Kewake, Davina waved as their truck pulled into the graveled parking lot of the Lutheran church. Lexi got out, eyeing the Scotswoman's red silk blouse, beige slacks, and tartan shawl around her shoulders. "For a welder, you clean up real good. Why're you here? I thought you were a Methodist."

"I heard God sometimes drops by here on Sundays. Thought I'd see if he had anything different to say to this bunch." Davina pushed the truck door closed behind Lexi.

Maybe it was the haunted-house creak of the door, or perhaps it was how nice the women were being, but Lexi adopted the same head-tilt Chicken had when he was working on a problem. Something was off here. Church was a twice-a-year-affair for her: Christmas and Easter. However, she would endure an extra hour of righteous living if it ensured Mrs. Blackburn continued her rent.

The other women walked away, chattering about egg salad. PeeWit bounced behind them as far as his leash allowed until Liz Gray's children spotted him and began a game of pet-him-up.

Lexi looked around the parking lot. This felt like a killdeer's broken-wing act, the bird fluttering along the ground, luring others from its nest. In this case, she felt she was being lured from her truck.

Davina glanced back and waved. "Come along."

Lexi sniffed the air like her paint did when something was different. Silly, of course. Horses had a more acute sense of smell than humans. Molly could nose out medicine even when hidden inside a molasses ball. The morning carried only a hopeful scent: a fresh breeze, damp air, and soft earth being broken up by daffodils pushing through it. Still … something was definitely off.

On the drive over, she'd expected Mrs. Blackburn to rip her about hosing down Coot. Nothing happened among the Telos residents or the surrounding area without the old bat knowing about it, yet she'd rattled on about using a slow cooker to bake a pecan pie. It had taken four hours to cook it. Lexi snuck side glances as the old gal critiqued the crust. "… a little soft, but overall, it was blue-ribbon delicious." The whole conversation was weird.

Now Davina was holding the narthex door open, the bass notes of the organ floating outside. Mrs. Blackburn had gone in. Lexi slowly walked forward like a fawn taking its first steps. When she finally crossed the threshold, Davina let the door hush shut behind her. Lexi glanced back, feeling like a hippy at an opera, unsure whether to move forward or rush back to the comfort of her truck. Gathering her resolve, she closely followed Davina, stepping on her heel as they entered a row of pews. Thankfully, it was near the back.

Mrs. Blackburn sat, hymnal open, lips moving to a song, but Lexi didn't hear any words. She took a seat, sandwiched between the two women.

The usual standing up and sitting down of the liturgy ticked by. She began to relax with the familiarity of the routine. Children's sermon. Singing. A homily. More singing about a deer running, "parched and weary from the chase." She could relate to that desperate feeling of being "hurt and hurried, thirsting for grace." It seemed trouble stalked her. The question was how to be free of it. When would people stop judging her? Lexi's eyes widened. Grabbing the top of the pew, her words burst out before she could throttle them. "This is an intervention, isn't it?"

"Shush." Davina patted her arm. Everyone kept singing, but Lexi twisted, looking right and left.

"Stop it," hissed Mrs. Blackburn.

"Where's my mother? Balcony?" Lexi checked behind her. She saw Bill Brandt, two rows back and mouthed, "Save me."

He cocked his head, his lips forming a silent, "What?"

Mrs. Blackburn shoved an elbow into her ribs. "Catharine isn't here. Now stop acting like a two-year-old who can't sit through church."

Lexi daggered a glance at her and refused to sing any more songs.

At the last "amen," Davina murmured, "Let's get out of here before people start asking you questions."

"Fine by me." Lexi popped out of the pew.

Davina took her by the arm and herded her down the side aisle, through the sacristy, down the back stairs, into the Lottie Lubach Reading room, and closed the door. "We'll wait for Shirley."

Shortly, Mrs. Blackburn arrived with a tray of sandwiches and a pitcher of lemonade. "What do you say to lunch? Davina was kind enough to bring food. And you look like you haven't eaten in a long while."

Lexi gave her a wary look. "She brought food before we arrived? So … why don't we take it back to your house?" Mrs. Blackburn ignored her, continuing to lay the table with lacy green placemats, white plates, and a vase of mums in a gumball array of colors.

Eyeing the stack of egg salad sandwiches, Lexi weighed it against her hunger. Slowly, she sat down, calculating there was only one sandwich per person. That wasn't enough for the Give-Lexi-Leftovers Campaign. "Where's PeeWit? And you haven't said why we can't go to your house."

"He went home with the Grays. And we're here because *this* is the intervention. I don't want you throwing chairs in my house."

"I knew it." Lexi thumped the table with her fist. "A church? Really? This is despicable, suckering me to church for a surprise blitz. Besides, I wouldn't break your furniture."

"You have no idea what you're going to do next, do you?" Mrs. Blackburn slapped a sandwich onto Davina's plate, her voice getting louder. "What was going through your head, having a hissy fit in the street yesterday? Calling everyone selfish sons of monkeys!"

"It was kind of a cathartic release. Letting go—"

"Shut up. Stop making excuses for bad behavior." Mrs. Blackburn crossed her arms.

Davina fiddled with her necklace. "This is not how we agreed we'd do this, Shirley."

"And where's my mother?" Lexi asked. "Are you the warm-up act?"

"She's not coming," both women said at the same time, then glanced at each other.

"Typical." Lexi nodded.

"All right. That's it. I've had enough of your prissy attitude." Mrs. Blackburn splatted a sandwich onto Lexi's plate. Lexi leaned back, her eyebrows rising toward her hairline. Several hunks of egg had spattered out. A blob stuck to the side of her lemonade glass, beginning a slow slide downward.

"Do you know who sponsored those orders you received for different high-school mascots?" Mrs. Blackburn slung a sandwich onto her own plate. "Your mother."

"No. That was from the schools' booster clubs."

"And Stewart Funeral Home is their biggest booster. Why do you think you have accounts from hospitals?"

"Gavin Ceely." Lexi squirmed, not liking where this conversation was headed.

"He may have seconded your mother's recommendation, but it was Catharine Stewart who did the groundwork and set you up."

"I don't believe you." A sick feeling swirled in Lexi's gut.

"I don't care if you do." Mrs. Blackburn dropped the tray onto the table and began pacing. "You're too busy being angry and feeling sorry for yourself to notice anything. The only time you see your mother is when you've pulled such idiotic monkeyshines, she has to step in and threaten you back in line. You're like the complainers who never go to the dentist, then when a tooth makes them cross-eyed with pain, they go in. But they whine that the dentist always hurts them—that's why they never go."

"Shirley, sit down." Davina pulled at the silver chain around her neck as though she were winding a cuckoo clock. "We had a plan."

Lexi's focus turned toward the Scotswoman. "What are you doing here, Davina? It used to be Mother and Shirley who set these ambushes."

"I'm backup. Shirley's on her own. Your mum doesn't know about your recent antics."

"Oh … she knows." Lexi rolled her eyes. "She's a witch with a crystal ball. It's just that she doesn't care."

Mrs. Blackburn leaned over the table, her face inches from Lexi's, but Davina stuck her hand between them, staving off the next outburst and waving Mrs. Blackburn back. In a voice so quiet, Lexi had to lean forward to hear her, Davina asked, "Remember today's gospel? Jesus sent disciples out two by two?"

Lexi picked up her sandwich, chomped a bite, and chewed. "I didn't really listen."

"We hoped the lesson might wiggle through some crack in your hard head," Davina said. "He sent them in teams. Any major accomplishment in this world means you need others to help you. And you need to be the kind of team member others can count on."

"I've always been on my own. What I heard in the gospel is that when people won't listen, you should forget them. So, like the disciples, I'm shaking the dust of this backwards little town off my feet."

"Ha! You were listening." Mrs. Blackburn smacked the table. Davina threw her a tired look, but the older woman went on. "Why should anyone listen to you? You're about as professional as the next food fight you'll surely start."

"What do you expect?" Lexi yelled. "As you say, I was raised by a horse and a father who didn't know what to do with me, so I have a few anger issues."

"I'm kicking that crutch out from under you right now. You were the one telling your mother to stay away from you. It's not up to me to explain why she left. But I'm informing you, she was always there in the shadows. That horse you love so dearly ... your dad couldn't afford that paint, but you fell in love. So ... it appeared in the barn. Your mom bought Molly. For you."

Mrs. Blackburn let that sink in for a few seconds, then added, "Your dad fed it and took care of the vet and farrier bills. That was their agreement."

"No ..." Lexi frowned, searching Mrs. Blackburn's face.

"Who do you think paid for college—the few years you got to go?" Mrs. Blackburn tapped her foot on the floor.

Lexi hesitated, her mind racing for proof of what she knew. What she believed. "Dad …"

Mrs. Blackburn shook her head. "You wouldn't have gone if you'd known it was your mother giving you the opportunity. She wanted you to have choices."

Lexi lay her sandwich on her plate, wiped her fingers on the napkin, her hands becoming still in her lap. When she'd needed new reins or a printer, her dad had assured her he'd find a way. And somehow … he did. "Dad wasn't the kind of man to take credit for what he didn't do."

"Did he take the credit?" Mrs. Blackburn gave her a pointed look. "Or did you assume, throwing your arms around his neck, thanking him? And he couldn't say a word. That was what he and your mom had agreed."

"No. Lying would've eaten him up inside." Lexi's mind raced.

"Maybe it did. But he loved Catharine as much, if not more, than you. He wanted her to be happy," Mrs. Blackburn said. "I admit, she's not a warm, outgoing person, but she tried to be in your life. You didn't want her, so she lived on the edges, working behind the scenes. And your father accepted whatever she wanted."

Lexi replayed the times she'd asked for something and had gotten it. She poked the soft white bread of the sandwich, staring at the indentations left by her fingernail. "Dad never said a bad word about her. Just changed the subject. He was a weak-willed man. I didn't want her because she abandoned him—and me."

"I'm here to tell you she didn't abandon you, Lexi. She was at your events. You just didn't see her. She made sure you had people in your life to watch over you. Why do you think *we* put up with you?"

Lexi's focus snapped toward Mrs. Blackburn. The truth of the old woman's words showed in her unwavering gaze and set jaw. Lexi swallowed, summoning words, thin and stretched. "Why … on earth would you do that for her?"

"We have our reasons. Believe it or not, she's a mighty friend. Haven't you figured out it would be easier for me to work at home?" said Mrs. Blackburn. "Catharine begged me to stay close by. And I wouldn't be here if I didn't want to."

Lexi looked at Davina. "Are you part of her spy ring, too?"

"Nobody's spying on you," the Scotswoman said. "You're twisting this to suit your wrong-headed ideas. I'll tell you this for nothin'—Catharine took care of us when we needed her. We'll gladly repay her the favor. There's no question you're a chancer, but you're mostly good fun. Headstrong, but a proud challenge. Lately, however, you've been a little gobshite."

"Okay. I admit I've been"—Lexi's mouth pinched in on itself—"touchy. It feels like the world has caved in on top of me."

"Touchy? You've been a seething pit of anger," said Mrs. Blackburn, "and it's festering, oozing over bystanders. Have you paid Crusty's for the dishes you broke?"

"Oh." Lexi's hand went to her mouth.

"See what we mean?" Davina said. "You want this community to support you, but—"

"I know!" Lexi held up her hands, closing her eyes. "I know, all right?" Her throat narrowed, making it hard to swallow. She blinked, focusing on the floor. "Something's wrong with me. I can't stop … I wake up angry. I go to bed angry. I don't know what's going …" Her voice trailed away.

No one spoke.

She hoped one of the women would continue scolding her; she deserved it. Maybe she'd feel better after a good chewing out.

But the women continued to sit. The only sounds came from upstairs, footsteps fading, doors closing as people abandoned the church, hurrying home to their Sunday lives.

The silence went on. The air felt heavy. The sharp, bitter words she'd yelled earlier filled her ears. Her idiotic, mean-spirited stunts blanketed her thoughts. It was hard to breathe, impossible to look at Davina or Mrs. Blackburn's faces.

She swallowed and blinked back the wetness in her eyes. "I know I've been a colossal jerk. I hate myself for it. It's like being eaten from inside." She palmed her chest. "Taking it out on others gives me a little relief. Then—I realize what I've done and feel worse, even angrier at myself.

"When I think about Mom leaving, Dad's death, Gavin's murder, Rick's problems, the hassle with the sheriff, my struggling business, selling dad's life's work—the ranch. Everything I touch—I mess up. And I mess up everybody who's around me."

Davina and Mrs. Blackburn looked at each other. Mrs. Blackburn let out a sigh. "Oh, Lexi, you probably caused the Vietnam War, too, even though you weren't born yet."

Lexi's voice rose, her forehead furrowing. "What?"

Davina gave Mrs. Blackburn a sharp frown, touching Lexi's arm. "What Shirley is saying—though she's using a sledge hammer to voice it—is that you're not responsible for everyone and everything—only you. You can't control others. The choices they make are theirs, just like you demand to make your own decisions. Do you really think you could've changed your mom and dad's marriage or kept Gavin from being killed or solved all of Rick's challenges? That's quite a load to tote around."

Lexi ran both hands over her face. "No. I just want to be an adult on my own terms and be successful at it. But I can't even eat at the diner without causing chaos. I don't know how to stop being me."

"Oh, I hope you never do." Davina leaned close, tapping Lexi's arm. "You're strong. You're smart. You don't let others dictate who you really are. We Scots love a rebel, as proven by our years of uprisings. You don't have to become somebody else, just try to understand all the parts that are you. Nobody's perfect. A wise lass is one who's simply learned how to work with what's inside her."

Lexi nodded, sniffled, and wiped her nose with the back of her wrist. "So ... what now?"

"Well"—Mrs. Blackburn took a deep breath, handing her a tissue—"we'd like to propose a plan."

Lexi wiped her nose, then covered her mouth, her fingertips pressing against her lips as she focused on the women.

"We can start by putting a little more space in your schedule," Davina said. "Otty Fuller can be at the shop in the morning. He retired from the lumber mill's front office last month. He's making his wife crazy. He'll come in several days a week to file, do maintenance, whatever, just to get out of the house. Free—until you get on your feet."

"He'll drive me—"

"Shush. We'll take comments at the end." Davina pointed for Mrs. Blackburn to take over.

"You owe all the girls of Club Club an apology, especially Haisley Starkey. She's like you. Clever, intelligent, hungry to learn about computers, and you stomped all over her dreams."

"I feel awful about that. But I had very little sleep and—"

"This isn't a poor-me session. This is about those girls." Mrs. Blackburn's leaned closer. "You can't publicly shame young people. They don't know who they are yet. Those young women looked up to you—a smart business woman. Well, they used to, until you had a meltdown about PeeWit's poo and hosed down a war veteran in the street. So, you *will* apologize to each girl and make the shop a welcoming place they can come after school. Heaven knows there's nothing to do in this town except get into trouble. I think you'll agree you're proof of that."

Lexi chewed her lip. For a moment she wanted to respond to that insult, but when her years of stunts and stupidity flashed through her mind, she had to concede the old gal was right. With a long breath, she gave a single nod.

"And you'll hire help with the ranch. It's obvious you're being pulled from both ends and unraveling in the middle," Davina said.

Lexi's shoulders drooped. "How am I going to afford that?"

"You're going to ask for help," Mrs. Blackburn said. "Your mother, townsfolk, the bank, I don't care, but you *have* to ask for help. And you can start by talking to a counselor about whatever's bothering you. I have some names I can recommend."

Lexi's face twisted. She'd rather sort through a pile of manure for coins.

The two women looked at each other. "I told you she'd balk at the counselor," Mrs. Blackburn said. "Her grade cards were always marked, 'Needs to learn teamwork.'"

"Okay! Okay!" Lexi ran her hands through her hair. "Obviously what I'm doing isn't working. I'll try it—at least for a while." Even after being raked over the coals, she felt a strange sort of relief as though small lights marked a path through her darkness.

"Good. And we'll be supporting you every step of the way." Mrs. Blackburn nodded.

"Is this why you hauled me to church this morning? A sermon about teamwork? If so, I'm glad I only have to deal with you two as a team."

"In your case," Mrs. Blackburn said, finally picking up her sandwich. "It'll take a village."

22.

Otty Fuller met Lexi at the shop at nine the next morning. He wore tan slacks, a striped green polo shirt, and a big grin as he rubbed his hands together. "I've always wanted to learn how this 3D stuff works."

"Let's start by clearing up this mess." Lexi pointed to the papers mounded on her desk. Together, they set up a new color-coded filing system and began sorting. When Mrs. Blackburn came in at one o'clock, she commented the place looked much better. Lexi updated her on their progress.

"Excuse me, Lexi," Otty interrupted their discussion. "Could you move something off your desk so I can get at the invoices? Shirley warned me not to handle any 3D objects until you gave me the okay. She said you're really picky about that."

"Well, that's putting it nicely." Lexi cast a look at Mrs. Blackburn, suspecting the old gal had probably warned him using stronger words, like 'unnaturally manic,' when someone messed about with her 3D items. She followed him and he stopped by her plywood desk, pointing at the 3D skull lying on its side in the middle of the tabletop.

"Oh, that. Yeah, I think the roundness of the head tempts people to pick it—" Her hand froze, hovering above the object. "Mrs. Blackburn!"

"What now?" The older woman said, as she slipped off her jacket.

"Do you remember who was holding this skull the last time you saw it?"

"I do."

"And how was she holding it?"

Mrs. Blackburn closed her eyes. "As I remember, she held it by the jaw."

Anticipation pinged Lexi's spine. "So, there may be fingerprints on the top of the skull. People tend to palm the top of it to pick it up. They have a hard time keeping their hands off of it. Whoever was here the night Gavin used the machines may have touched it."

"That's a rather slim conjecture," she said.

"You want me to call the sheriff?" Otty asked.

"No." Lexi quickly shook her head. "Rather than waste his time with false leads, would you find a clean sack to put it in? Gavin, the man who was killed here, was part of a team of security experts. They have connections and offered to look at any clue I found. They want answers even more than I do. I'd rather start with them. And Otty"—she gave him a warrior-woman stare—"do not mention this to anyone. We work with several confidential projects. What we do here, stays here. Don't even mention this to Janice."

"Who's Janice?"

"Your wife." Lexi cocked her head. Maybe having Otty help wasn't such a great idea after all.

"Her name's Jackie."

"Oh, sorry." Lexi fidgeted. "I'm not good with names."

Mrs. Blackburn gave Lexi the look teachers use on their densest students.

"But don't worry—I won't tell anyone about the work here." Otty rubbed his palms together as he headed toward the storage room. "I knew this was more than just a plastic factory."

⁂

That afternoon, Lexi placed a box of Reese's Peanut Butter Cup cupcakes on the table of The Other Room. A cooler of soft drinks and vitamin water sat on the floor.

Two o'clock came and went.

Lexi leaned into The Other Room. "Was there something after school today? Why haven't any of the girls dropped by?"

Mrs. Blackburn held a brush, her eyes covered by jeweler's loupes as she stroked red paint on a two-inch long 1953 Buick Skylark. "Why would they? They're not welcome."

"I brought treats. I thought you talked to them." Her excitement about the moment evaporated. What had she messed up now? She'd never invited the girls here in the first place—rarely saw them outside of the shop. When would she talk to them? Mrs. Blackburn was the "organizer." It was another social tripwire in an ever-changing world. That's why she preferred coding; she could count on it. An equation yielded an expected action. "What now?" she asked.

Mrs. Blackburn looked over the tops of her loupes. "Here's a little lesson you might find helpful. When I was young, I was taught I had to be sweet and nice so everyone would like me. I don't subscribe to that notion anymore. It teaches girls that who they are is based on the opinion of others. So, as a mature woman, I've come to realize I don't have to like everyone, and everyone doesn't have to like me."

"Sounds right to me." Lexi shrugged, still confused.

The older woman took off her loupes, framing Lexi in serious stare. "But I still believe it's important to be kind and know how to work with others. Having good social skills is imperative if you want cooperation. So, I'm telling you, when it comes to apologies, face to face is usually the best way." The thin lines around her face deepened. "Do you understand?"

"Why didn't you just say, 'Ask the girls yourself'?" Lexi huffed. "You could've skipped all that stuff I tuned out."

"I know you have gaps in your social graces"—Mrs. Blackburn took a breath—"but Davina has pointed out that I may have contributed to some of your missteps. Maybe she's right. The exchanges between you and me are often … brusque. I'm now endeavoring to model better communication."

"O—kay. What am I supposed to graciously say to that?"

"Whatever you wish."

"Thanks." With a single nod, Lexi walked away, adding over her shoulder, "But I prefer you let 'er rip, tater chip."

⁂

At six p.m., Lexi turned off the overhead LEDs in the shop and switched on her desk lamp. It made a small bubble of light in the cavernous darkness. She packed up her tote bag, feeling tired but satisfied. BrainSmith Printing finally looked like a functioning shop again. She'd asked Otty to leave at one o'clock, but he was so excited, he'd stayed until four, putting papers in drawers and whiteboards on the walls.

BrainSmith's new computer would arrive tomorrow. Gavin's partners at Celesto had said they'd attempted to retrieve her bricked hard drive from the state investigators, but the forensics department couldn't find it within the backlog of cases.

With a yawn, she toggled her desk lamp from white to an amber light for night and turned to leave.

"Lexi?" A voice came from the blackness of the back doorway.

She gripped a pair of scissors, her pulse jumping under her skin.

"Are you going to fire me?"

She dropped the scissors. "No, Rick. Come into the light."

He looked worse than when he'd spent the night in jail, with greasy hair, wrinkled clothes, and dark circles lining his eyes. "Dad said I need to tell you." He looked down, thumbing his rubber band on one hand, carrying a sack with the other. "I think it's my fault your friend died."

"No, Rick. You had nothing to do with it." Lexi closed her eyes, massaging the back of her neck.

"I lost my keys."

His statement brought her focus back to him. "The keys to our shops?"

147

He nodded. "The night your friend died, I found my keys in the alley. They were by the dumpster when I took out the trash. I don't know how they got out of my pocket. Dad said I had to tell you. And I'm sorry for spying. I didn't like him kissing you, but I didn't hurt him. Someone else got inside, and it's my fault."

She frowned, shaking her head. "But you're always so careful … even with things that don't matter like pencils and sticky notes. You have a place for everything, and you don't do anything until you've put something in its place. Have you ever lost your keys before?"

"Once. When I was little. Now, I hook them to my belt loop and cram them down in my pocket when I go out."

"And when you're not using them, don't you keep them on a peg by the stairs in the Pizza Shop? I knocked them down the day of the bird invasion."

He nodded again.

"Could someone have taken them while you were on a delivery and your dad was dealing with customers or the ovens? Is that possible?" she said.

The rubber band made *thwooping* noises as he rapidly snapped it between his fingers. After several moments, he looked at her and nodded.

"Then, when whoever took your keys was finished with them, they could've tossed them in the alley," Lexi said.

His eyes darted back and forth, as though reading his own thoughts. "I could look on the surveillance video. The sheriff ordered Dad to take the camera down." His voice dropped to a whisper. "But I haven't yet. The Bilyeau boys may come back."

"We've looked at the video, but it never hurts to look again."

"Here's teriyaki chicken wings to say I'm sorry." He held out a takeout bag. "They're new. Dad's adding them to the menu."

"I'm eating alone. Chicken's been fed for the evening. Do you have time to drag up a chair? It's been too long since we shared a lunch. And now nobody's around to throw milk cartons at us."

"It's ten minutes past six. That would make this dinner, not lunch."

His literal interpretation brought a smile to her lips. "You're right as always, Rick." With her foot, Lexi pushed her roller chair toward him. "Sit down. I need to talk to you about a crazy idea I have."

23.

He liked Monday nights at the bar. Like most red-blooded men, he sat in front of the TV, eyes glued to the football game. It's what real men do. The cheerleaders bounced across the screen, defying gravity. How could they keep themselves tucked into those deep-cut tops as they wiggled and jigged on the sidelines? Those shirts had to be glued on.

It made him think of Lexi Depriest.

Not that she dressed like that. And she wasn't big-chested. Smart women usually weren't—for some reason. She dressed like a ranch woman should. She'd be perfect as soon as she learned to tone down her sass. He'd enjoy breaking her from throwing fits. Fortunately, she had acres and assets to offset her mouthiness.

At midnight, when the bar closed, thoughts of women doing splits made him drive north of town. He parked east of the Depriest ranch. He put on his sneakers and walked across the pasture.

There was a bite in the air. Chilly for early April. A thousand stars dotted the sky. No moon. Perfect.

He avoided the barn—the horse still nickered at him. Instead, he cut through the calf lot, making one hooky old mama-cow snort and lower her head.

The windows of the house were dark. He stood in front of the door, arms wide, welcoming himself.

He wiped his feet with the towel as he'd done before, then in inchworm increments, eased the side door open. Each footstep was a minefield. She left shoes and boots everywhere in the mudroom.

The place looked a little tidier tonight. She'd collected the cereal bowls and greasy plastic clamshells from takeout food. Hopefully, she was over that drone-flying boy trying to edge in on a great deal. The guy had fought like a girl. Good riddance, sucker.

He eased himself into a chair at the dining room table. From there, he could see through her bedroom door. How long ago had she gone to bed? Was she lying there, wondering if she'd heard a noise, straining to hear him breathe like he was straining to hear her? The thought excited him.

He needed to slow down. He'd entered the house too quickly, anxious to see her. He'd wait. Let the air settle. Let his heart slow a bit. His next move must be done carefully.

She had changed the brightness of the bedside clock, maybe to help her sleep better. The numbers now dimly shone in charcoal gray. She certainly tossed and turned. He squinted, focusing on the mound of covers, trying to tell if they rose, then fell in time with her breathing. He willed her to turn on her back.

When she didn't, he passed the time, snooping through the tote she'd left on the table. He lifted a couple of envelopes. An object dropped out, clattering to the hardwood floor.

He froze, holding his breath, his eyes focused on the mound on the bed. He waited.

The dog must be medicated or the mutt would be making those stutter-growls like a heater cutting in and out. On an earlier visit, he'd found the pills a vet had prescribed. Good thing they were working.

He bent and picked up a tiny toy. Holding it close to his face, he examined it by the starlight coming through the windows. A woman with ample cleavage in a low-cut vest held a flag and a sword. "Lexi" was painted across the base. Tucking it in his shirt pocket, he patted it against his chest. She was too messy to miss it—or she'd blame the dog. The mutt was handy. She probably blamed it for lots of stuff. He would, too, when he moved in with her.

The covers rustled from her room. Silently, he counted to 200, then moved, peeking one eye past the doorframe. At last, she was on her back, laid out before him, waiting. He gripped the fingers of his hand and rubbed them, making sure they were warm. He'd practiced while watching football games, trailing his fingertips across his own palm, so lightly it made his gut swirl and groin tighten.

He smiled. Tonight, he'd touch her—his cheerleader—and if she happened to see him in town, she wouldn't even know. It was the secret he would have with the cheerleader part of her body.

Focusing on the sound of her breathing, he watched the shadows on her face as he took slow steps into the room. His foot stepped on something soft. A high-pitched shriek cut the air.

He jumped back. Why was the dog on the floor? It never slept there.

Then it lunged.

He ran. Teeth snapped. Toe nails clawed across the hardwood floor.

"Chicken!" he heard her yell. He passed the table, swinging his arm, knocking a chair to the floor.

Cursing, he hit the screen door and threw it closed. The dog slammed into it with a sharp yelp. Its whimpers rose into the night behind him.

That was a shame. The old mutt was just doing his job.

In one bound, he hopped the fence and ran across the barn lot. There'd be footprints. He'd have to burn these shoes. Jumping another fence, he raced through the pasture, but not toward his vehicle. Mama didn't raise no dummy. He'd do what he did best. Shift the blame. Behind him, a light came on. A quick backward glance revealed she'd turned on the vapor light mounted on the telephone pole. The windows across the front lit up. Good. In that bubble of light, she couldn't see him fading into the darkness.

He'd hear about this—the whole county would.

24.

Sull Wixly sat on his horse staring at the tracers. Trailing green lights screamed overhead. Explosions churned the earth, each eruption coming nearer and nearer. He and his horse remained at their post. A mountain of dirt rose in front of them, tall and dark as a shroud. Clods hurled toward him, thudding his chest. The palm tree overhead cracked. Fingers of fronds fell on top of him, trapping him like a net.

He bolted awake, a sheen of sweat slicking his chest. It had been years … but every so often, nightmares from the Vietnam War niggled their way into his sleep. Probably because he'd been thinking about his neighbor's eye-in-the-sky drone. It would've helped back then with surveillance, probably saved a few more men.

He rubbed his bad arm as he got out of bed. It ached when he was cold, and he was cold most of the time now. He'd started wearing flannel pajama bottoms and a t-shirt to bed. When had he become an old man? Sliding into beat-up slippers, he pulled on a jacket and stepped through the back door.

The sky was as it should be. Black. Silent. Full of stars. Safe. Nothing here to maim or blow the bottom half of your best friend away.

He didn't drive people off the road anymore, yell, or slam his fists on the table like he had when he'd first come back. It hadn't seemed fair he'd fought and lost so much, only to return to the land of the free and still feel miserable.

Now they had names for it. Treated vets for it. Back then, his wife and daughter shouldered his moods, dark looks, and outbursts. If only he could do that part over.

No longer did he have to guess about the invisible chain squeezing his chest. He'd mined his soul until he'd found the fear inside. Anger crept right behind it. The neighbor-girl didn't see any of that. He could guess what made her angry, but she was walking in the dark, swinging blindly at her demons.

A branch snapped to the east, the sound carrying up the hillside through the trees. He walked across the dirt yard, squinting into the dark.

As he rounded the corner of the house, blue and red lights pulsed at ground level, flashing across the pasture a half-mile to the north.

His arms hung at his sides. *What has she done now?*

❧

As soon as the sky turned a cement color, Sull saddled Marvin. He rode for a while, breathing cool air, watching the stars fade and the sticky fingers of the night slide to the west.

Miles away, the Blue Mountains tumbled in a dark line against a salmon sky. Rays of light bladed the horizon. It would be a bright spring day, but still wouldn't melt the frost hiding in the shade.

He sat on his quarter horse, watching the girl. She walked across her pasture, head down, staring at the ground, the reins looped between her and her paint as they worked their way toward the gate.

"Lotta fuss over at your place last night, Shorty," he called out. "You okay?"

She'd squatted down, studying the dirt. "You come through this gate last night?"

He nudged his horse forward across the dewy grass. "Shorty, to my knowledge, that gate hasn't been cracked open in years. What's goin' on?"

She had her ball cap off now, running a hand over her head, still focused on the ground. "I honestly don't know what's happening." Her voice sounded like she was at the bottom of a pit, exhausted from trying to climb out.

"Somebody was in my bedroom last night," she said. "Stepped on the dog. Chicken slammed into the screen door, chasing them. The vet came out at two this morning to give him a shot for the pain."

"Good grief! That poor hound. I saw the sheriff's lights. He doesn't go anywhere at night without his flashers. He likes the citizenry to see he's working."

"LaCott came in like he'd been chewing bumble bees. Right off, he warned me not to let my 'bulldog mouth overload my hummingbird butt.' Accused me of being a drama queen, dragging him out because the wind was banging my screen door."

Sull listened to her story, unease growing in his belly.

"The vet told him his scenario wasn't consistent with the dog's injuries. Then the poor deputy said he'd found sneaker tracks in the barn lot. LaCott got even madder, being shown up like that. He probably has that deputy picking up roadside trash the rest of the week. He ordered him to check all my shoes for mud because the prints were probably mine. What a moron."

"In a county that has nothing but DUIs and the occasional speeder, it doesn't take Einstein to enforce the law." He paused. "Is the dog okay?"

"He's gonna be," she said with more certainty than her face showed. "Vet said if he gets well enough, she can do surgery to relieve the pressure on his spine and joints." She swallowed, her eyes shiny as she stood up. "This isn't the first time Chicken has woken me up. For several weeks now, on some nights he's growled and tried to get off the bed. I thought it was the medicine giving him bad dreams. He fell asleep on the floor last night. I didn't want to move him and wake him. Then someone stepped on him." She glanced around as though eyes were watching from behind the cows or trees or clouds.

He knew that face—when home didn't feel safe anymore. "You find somethin' out here?"

"I think it's another sneaker print."

"Mind if I look? I used to do some tracking during … well, never mind. You throw stuff if I talk about the war." He dismounted, opened the gate, and led his horse to the print, clearly outlined in a dirt patch. "I'd say it's a size eleven, headed toward my place. Are you thinkin' it's me? I wear a size eleven boot."

"No. You're full of long-tailed stories, but I doubt you'd sneak around my place, looking for adventure. I believe you'd show up, banging and blustering at the door. Besides, you can't move fast like this creep, and I doubt you even own a pair of sneakers."

"Nope, I don't, but you're welcome to look if it'll make you feel better. C'mon. Pass through. Let's see where your varmint went."

They walked, leading their horses, both studying the ground. "I suppose I owe you an apology," Lexi said. "I didn't believe you when you said you didn't shoot my drone." She sighed. "I'm sorry. I guess somebody else is hanging around."

"S'allright." Shame pricked him. When he was with the guys at the diner, he hadn't missed opportunities to poke fun at her. But darn it, she shouldn't be so touchy. Although … it probably wasn't easy for her, bein' without her dad, runnin' a ranch. And now some lowlife was pestering her.

New green sprouts muffled the crunch of dried winter grass under their feet. Lexi cleared her throat. "And I'm sorry about making you wear your breakfast, then hosing you down. I acted kinda crazy."

"Like frog-in-a-sock crazy."

"I finally went to pay the diner yesterday. Rosalee said you'd already picked up the tab. I'll pay you back. I need to make things right."

"That won't mend a thing, Shorty. The only fix is to talk about it."

"I'm seeing a counselor."

"That's good, but you might as well say to my face how you think I broke your dad." He didn't look at her.

"You know what you did."

"You tell me how you see it."

"Dad swallowed his pride." Her voice was thin. "He came to you, asked for your help."

Sull paused, inspecting the ground, then pointed to the east. They walked in that direction. Keeping his eyes on the ground made it easier to talk. She wasn't looking at him either. "This isn't an excuse, just an explanation. I came back from 'Nam like I'd eaten thorns. Maybe you know that anger? I'd boil over, then be okay for a while. Then in 2002, my girl died in a car crash, and nothing made sense again. I'd left a lot of unspoken apologies between her and me.

"That was when your dad asked for a loan. I blew up—all the anger exploded—he didn't deserve that. He just stood there and took it. I went to him later and apologized. You know what he said to me? That he didn't even remember what I said."

"You called him a failure. 'A pissant who was barely fit to herd cattle. A worm-rider who'd scraped up enough to buy a few acres.' You wouldn't trust him with a wild goat, much less any money to buy several head and improve his herd."

Sull stopped, his head down, tonguing a tooth. He huffed through his nose. If she recalled every word, then she had a terrible hurt inside. "That's the problem with being horn-tossing mad. All I remember is the venom I was getting rid of. And I didn't think about you, sitting in the corner, hearing your father being cut down. I'm sorry you've been carryin' that all these years. He never told you I apologized?"

Her stare scalded his face. "Would it matter? After you put it out there, you can't take it back. It lives in here." She tapped her chest.

"No. You're right." He shook his head. "I was like a cut bull, but he and I worked it out long ago. I don't think I broke your dad. I think I broke the way *you* think of him. My words might have eaten at him, but they didn't stop him. He pulled his ranch together, made a go of it, and proved me wrong. To my shame, he never said an unkind word to me. We even worked together on roundups."

"He let people run over him all the time. He was a nice man with a spine that bent with the weight of bullies."

Sull gave her the look men reserved for the holes in their lives they can't fix. "If I made you think that about your dad, I'm sorry because your dad was the finest example of a human I ever met. If I could burn what I said outta your head, I would. I'm shamed I ever spoke. You can cuss me, drop bird crap on me, spray me down, and buzz drones over my house. I deserve it. But I won't allow you or anyone else to disrespect Darron Depriest."

"He was never the same after that."

"He was better. Your dad taught many a person to rise above their demons, including me."

"Is that supposed to make me like you?"

"Not a lick."

They walked on in silence. The sun burned away the mist in the valleys. The tops of pines glistened in the sunlight. He leaned over a clump of bunchgrass, inspecting broken stems, then waved them forward. Lexi stayed where she was, her eyes on the thin wisps of cirrus clouds above. "Weather's coming. You or I can't stop it."

He paused, looked up, adjusting the brim of his boonie hat to see better.

Her voice was barely louder than a sigh. "I've tried stopping the future. I yelled at Dad, trying to keep him from being a pushover. I tried to stop Dad's cancer. I tried to stop Mom from leaving. I acted as good as I could, then really bad just to get their attention. It didn't matter. Maybe what you said to me at the diner was right. 'The future doesn't always work out like we think it will.'"

"Sometimes." He nodded. "But it's easier not going it alone. That's why they send a squad of soldiers on a mission instead of an army of one. Less chance of being left stranded."

He moved on. She followed in silence. They passed behind his house. Sull stared down the hillside into the brush and trees.

"The tracks disappear into this jungle. I heard something down there last night. You got your eye-in-the-sky?" He circled his finger in the air.

"A drone?"

Sull nodded. She pulled it from the leather scabbard laced to the saddle, opened the struts, and handed it to him. Activating the app on her phone, she said, "Toss it in the air. Up, not in front of Marvin. He isn't used to it."

Sull did as he was told. The drone hovered for a few seconds, Marvin's ears flicking at the sound of the soft whirr. Several Angus looked up as she flew it above them.

"What're we looking for?" Lexi angled the phone screen so he could watch.

"How close can your eye get to the creek?"

She zipped it over the thin, snaking line of water in the brush below. The camera peered through black tree branches, a few of them tipped by green leaves. "I don't see tracks," she said, "but he must've crossed the creek and climbed the fence onto the road."

After several zig-zag flights over the area, she flew the drone back. Holding out her hand, staring at the controls, she let it free fall from eight feet above her, dropping into her upturned palm. A self-satisfied smile spread across her mouth.

"Fancy flying," Sull said.

She ignored him, folding up the unit. "The sheriff said he'd be out to talk to you today. He refused to bother last night. Wanted to get home. He'll probably accuse you. He seems to point a finger at the nearest person."

"LaCott and I butted heads when I was a county commissioner. He doesn't wanna see me. He'll send a flunky. Why didn't you use your eye last night to follow your intruder?"

She stared at him, her face losing its smile and becoming blank like an eggshell. "I didn't think of it." Her eyes widened as she shook her head. "Am I stupid, or what? With Chicken howling and the shock of it all, I just didn't ... but it wouldn't have done any good. I couldn't have seen him in the dark. I'd need to use a drone with an infrared camera."

"You think he'll come back?"

"I never thought he'd come in the first place. I don't know why he's here."

Sull forked a leg over his saddle. "The place is changing. Hun'erd-fifty years ago, people were killing each other for bits of gold. Now we're after each other over what? Plastic? I got somethin' I want you to see."

"I should get going."

"This'll only take a minute, and it's on the way." He rode off, but in a few moments, he heard the hoofbeats of the paint behind him, then it moved beside him.

"My daughter was thirty-nine when she died," he said as they rode. "I tumbled down another hole I thought I'd never get out of. I guess I'd never really climbed outta the first hole after the war. Sometimes I'd visit her grave. I'd talk to the dirt, tell her things I should've said to her face. One day I found something there."

Lexi rode without looking at him.

"It about broke me in half when I saw flowers planted on her grave." He glanced at her.

Lexi stared at the horizon. "Dad told me to stay off your place, but I'd sneak over and explore. I thought I was getting something over on you. That little headstone named Mary looked so lonely. I'd sit with Mary, tell her my problems. When I found flowers growing in a crack up on the hill, I brought them to her stone—to make her spot prettier. They were the

161

coolest flowers I'd ever seen, like rockets, the petals fanning behind them like blue flames."

"They're called shooting stars. When folks rolled through here on the Oregon Trail, those flowers covered most of this land. But then farmers brought in sheep. That's change for you. A hun'red-fifty years later, there's hardly any shooting stars left."

"That's a real pity. They were cool." Lexi dragged her fingers through the paint's mane, combing it as she rode. Sull allowed himself to smile; sometimes Mary had done the same thing with her horse.

The sun had topped the horizon, chasing shadows from the pasture. Crows pecked the ground and fluttered to the sky as they approached.

"Mary's got company now," Sull said. "Maggie, my wife, is with her. But you should see this."

He got off his horse, glancing behind him to check if she dismounted. She had, and he held drooping branches up for her as they ducked beneath them, their footsteps crunching frost-covered leaves from last fall. He chided himself for letting the alcove go wild. Two headstones stood in the center of a ten-foot clearing. Tiny nose cones bobbed on tall stems, standing as thick as bristles on a brush. In a day or two, they would open, and the area would be covered by bright blue shooting stars.

"Oh … they've spread." Lexi kneeled, taking one of the stems between her fingers, its tiny petals starting to unfurl. "This brings back memories," she whispered. "Some of them painful."

He didn't answer. The morning breeze rolled down from the mountains and soughed through the top of the pines. It was as much as he could take. He walked back to his horse and mounted.

Soon, Lexi appeared and climbed on her paint, murmuring, "Thanks for showing me that."

He rode toward the gate, practicing his words in his mind. Finally, he cleared his throat. "You're always telling me about old ideas changin', so I looked somethin' up the other day."

"In an encyclopedia, I bet." She nudged her horse to keep up.

"What's wrong with that?" He reined Marvin to slow him down.

"Nothing. Go on."

"It said the Pony Express, which was a big deal for its time, only lasted eighteen months."

"Can't say I knew that—or particularly cared."

"The point is do you think your eyes-in-the-sky and 3D print-stuff will stay around?" He stopped when he reached the gate and opened it.

"I don't know. I doubt it." She rode through to her side. "Everything gives way to faster, more efficient, less costly methods. The Pony Express was replaced by stagecoaches; the stage was replaced by trains and telegraphs. A few trains are left, but the telegraph was replaced by phones, then the internet. It all keeps changing."

"Growing beef has hung around for two hundred years." He swept his hand toward the dawn. "And this view has eased many a soul since humans first walked here. Sometimes I tell myself the sun will still rise, the land will still be here, but there'll be some other insignificant bent-back fool workin' this dirt, tryin' to get by. But until then, I'm here for the peace I get from it. That's why most of us are here. I believe that's why your dad was here."

The silhouettes of two meadowlarks flew across the morning sky.

"That's sort of profound. Is it supposed to make me like you?"

"No. Just pointing out some things change, some things don't. If you get tired of your other interests, you've got this place under you. I know Bill Brandt wants it." He pushed the gate shut. "I'm only sayin' I watched you grow up here, ranging over these acres. There's a lot of your heart planted all around this land."

She slid the latch shut from her side with a *clank*. "If it's okay with you, I'm going to put a camera and alarm on this gate. I'll make it ring in both your house and mine if it's opened."

"Do whatever you need to feel safe." He gave her a nod. "Just remember, you can come through here whenever you want. We may not be good friends, but we're neighbors."

25.

Wednesday morning, Lexi put on her business suit and drove to Telos where Otty and Rick were waiting at the shop. They spent an hour fleshing out the ideas she and Rick had come up with.

They'd have computer-assisted design classes and recruit attendees by having a 3D Fair next week. People could choose from several simple projects, watch an object print, and then take it home. When she left at nine to drive to Kewake, Otty was making phone calls and Rick was excitedly creating an organization chart of who would do what.

She drove under a gray sky. Not a leaf turned or weed bobbed. The air felt dead. She considered it might be an omen but chose to ignore it, rehearsing her spiel instead.

Bill Brandt stood when she entered the cafe. He wore a basil-colored shirt with gray tie and slacks. "I'm so glad you called." His voice resonated in bass tones. He opened his arms. "Where's my hug?"

"I'm … I'm not much of a hugger." Lexi sidestepped him.

"No worries, but you dropped your smile. Should we look for it?" He gave her a half-grin, pulling out a vinyl-padded chair to the right of his own. "I ordered you a coffee." He waved to a waiter. "Let's get the rest of your breakfast, then we can talk."

After she'd ordered, she filled Bill in on what had happened in the past week. At first she was hesitant to dump the details of her life, but he was a an excellent listener, focusing on every word. She found herself telling him more than she'd intended, even after the waiter had delivered their breakfasts.

No wonder he excelled at selling insurance. He made a person feel as though they were the only one who mattered at the moment. She could learn important business lessons from him if she paid attention.

"You've been through so much." He chopped his eggs, mixing the runny yolks with the cooked whites. "Let me buy your property and help get that burden off your mind. You know I'll give you a premium price."

His words chilled her for a moment. She shook her head. "I'm not quite ready yet."

"Then let me help you with it. It's always handy to have a man around. I know you've got a lot going on right now. I don't mind helping."

She gave him a half-smile and forced herself to eat small bites of French toast instead of stuffing her mouth as she usually did when she was in a hurry. After chewing and swallowing, she ventured, "Actually, I asked to meet today because I need your help with a fund-raising project."

"Okay. Interesting. I'm all ears." He gave her a confident look as though reading a significance that only he could understand in her proposal.

"Well…" Her spiel evaporated, replaced with an anxiousness about something she couldn't read in his expression and tone.

He was a good-looking man. His blond hair made him appear younger than the fifteen-year gap between them. But he seemed friendlier than usual, his attitude more familiar. She shook off her thoughts, focusing on her plate. "I'd like to start a computer assisted drawing class. A CAD program. It would be an after-school activity, but it'll be housed in the old theatre in Telos. I need at least five computers, and I need someone like you who can sell organizations on the idea, so they'll donate funds."

"You flatter me."

"No. I need you. Mrs. Blackburn told me to ask people for help. I'm asking you."

It was hard to say those words. When her father had made himself vulnerable, he'd been shredded. Easier to go it alone than risk being drawn and quartered. She tried to smile, thinking it probably looked like a wince.

"At a science fair in Washington DC," she continued, "three teenagers, using CAD software and a 3D printer, designed and built a prosthetic leg that allowed amputees to hike and even use skateboards. A seventeen-year-old in California printed a 3D spirometer. You blow in it and her design can diagnose obstructive lung problems like asthma, emphysema, or chronic bronchitis. It's surprisingly accurate. But the best thing is it only costs around thirty-five dollars to make, so patients can carry it and monitor their respiratory conditions."

She drew a breath. "What I'm saying is if we give local kids knowledge, access, and tools, they'll change the world. And we'll *all* be better for it—even if technology scares us."

He wiped his lips with a napkin, then he cupped his hand over her wrist. "I'm glad you're inviting me to join you on this. Quite honestly, I've been worried about you. I've admired you for quite some time. You have a mind of your own, and you're not afraid to shake things up. A program for the youth—great idea."

She leaned back, sliding her hand from under his fingers as she reached for her coffee. He was involved in every organization for a hundred miles. She should be flattered he even noticed her, but adrenaline flooded her legs. For some reason, she wanted to run like a deer.

"It's not exactly a radical idea," she said. "I begged for a program like this when I was in high school. The girls who come to my shop after school told me there still aren't enough computers or teachers for such a program."

His face became solemn as though she'd asked him to solve world population control. "I'm not clear. The school needs more technology, but you don't want to donate the computers to the district. You want to keep them in Telos?"

"We need activities in our tiny town for the kids to do after school. They'll learn a vocational skill. I've lined up people who can monitor the program for a couple hours Monday through Friday. Mrs. Blackburn, Otty Fuller, Rick Pham, me."

"Forgive me for saying this, he paused a moment. "But aren't a few of Rick's pages stuck together? I mean, would he be able to oversee kids?" He lifted his palms. "I'm simply telling you what others would be thinking. This will be a harder sell with him on the team."

"I see." She placed her hands on either side of her plate, staring at the crispy over-fried edges of French toast sopped with maple syrup. She took a couple of slow breaths, speaking slowly. "Or maybe people will discover how knowledgeable Rick is about computers."

She breathed in and out, then picked up her fork and slowly carved off several bites. "There are plenty of adults who have no idea why their computers are acting up, or how to make their TVs connect to their networks, or even how to put contact information into their smartphones. There's room in our town for adult education too. And once they discover Rick can help them, they'll get over their prejudices."

"It won't be easy, but that's what I admire about you." He touched her wrist again, his smile changing into a flat line of concern. "But you want to use my contacts for something the school could be doing?"

"It's for the *community*. Others can join us, but it's for the people who live in Telos—all of us. I've made a list. You can pick out those organizations you want to ask to support the project, and I'll take the rest. What do you think? Are you on board?" His fingers felt hot on her skin but she was afraid to move her hand away while asking for a favor.

He leaned closer. "I have a lot of experience in what it takes to sell people. It'll go better if we make the presentations together. A team approach. We need to strategize. A positive side effect is it'll help your business as well. You could use that right now, couldn't you?"

"Oh, I don't want to take up too much of your time." She moved her hand, waving away his suggestion, still feeling the heat of where he'd touched her. "I figure divide and conquer is the most expedient route. Both of us will have quotas. Kind of like when everyone in Rotary has to sell ten tickets to the Christmas dinner."

"Don't you want to work with me?" He arched an eyebrow, adding a wounded look. "It's for a good cause."

She blinked at him. "Sure, but my life is crazy right now. I'm afraid I'd hold you up. And strategizing isn't my thing. Rick and Otty are already working on curriculum and a project name. I'm—"

"Okay. Stop." He clasped her arm. "Here's the deal. You have to eat. We'll meet during meals. Starting tonight. If it's not worth spending the hours planning it, then it's not worth doing. That's the condition I'm putting on it."

She sat back and stared at her plate. "I'm feeling … I don't know …"

But she did know. She needed fresh air. Open space. To ride bareback, hunched-over, a two-handed death-grip on Molly's mane, galloping hard in the opposite direction of Bill Brandt as though dodging the wind.

She folded her napkin. "You'll have to excuse me."

"You've hardly eaten. You're way too thin already. Have a couple more bites. Did you hear the elevator in the Smythe Building in La Grande got stuck with a couple of kids in it?"

She stood and signaled the waiter. "I'm so sorry. If we're meeting tonight, I have a hundred things to do. Stay and finish your breakfast. I've got this. And thanks for talking to me. I'll text you when and where to meet tonight."

"Make it seven. At Tony's in Kewake," he said.

"Uh, okay. I appreciate your help." As the waiter approached, she snatched the check from his fingers and hurried to the cashier. After paying, she glanced back. Bill still watched her. She couldn't tell if his smile matched his eyes, but something seemed off. He gave a single wave.

She stepped outside the cafe and took a deep breath. Man, she hated working with people.

26.

On the way back to Telos, the clouds spit, then turned to rain. She dashed inside Latte Da II and picked up cupcakes wrapped in marzipan to make them look like mugs of hot chocolate. Marshmallows decorated the tops. Seven individual aqua boxes tied with glittering ribbons filled her bag. They'd been expensive but an appropriate offering for mouthwhipping high school girls out of her shop.

Hurrying back to her truck, she tripped on a heaved-up corner of sidewalk. Boxes tumbled from the bag, bouncing through puddles. The air fogged in front of her lips as she cursed, bending to pick up boxes, cold raindrops spattering her back. Two cupcakes had crumbled; the others were whopper-jawed in appearance. Most had lost their marshmallows, which rattled around inside the boxes.

Grumbling, she drove to her shop, water dripping from her hair, running down her neck and into her bra. There wasn't time to go home and change. The day had more meetings she didn't want. She'd go by each girl's house, apologize, invite her back—and offer a cupcake. But first, she needed Mrs. Blackburn's brain because she didn't know all the girls' names or addresses.

As she waited for the older woman to arrive at work, she sat in her truck, eating a mutilated cupcake, scraping icing from inside the box with her finger. She thought of Rick. He was fortunate in some ways. Often, he was blissfully unaware he'd misread someone or missed a social cue.

Unfortunately, she *knew* she had big voids in her social upbringing. Bill triggered her alarms, but whether it was because he was too friendly or because she was too clammed-up remained a mystery. She needed to talk to someone, and it would be five days before her appointment with a counselor. She ate another maimed cupcake instead.

Her rearview mirror framed Ash sitting across the street beneath the covered walkway of George's hardware/feed store. She got out and crossed the road, adding more rain to her clothes. As she went inside to get a bracket for the gate alarm, she handed him a misshapen cupcake. "I dropped the box, but it's still tasty." It was a clumsy gift, but it would keep her from eating another one. And he looked hungry. He probably rarely got treats.

When she came back out, the box was against Ash's face as he licked the marzipan from the corners. She ignored him; she'd seen it all in high school. Gathering her nerve to get soaked again, she stared into the clouds muttering, "Just stop raining, would you?"

"Doesn't look like you've got much pull with the weather." Ash glanced at the sky.

"I've got a fence to fix. Cattle to sort. Vaccinations to give."

"I could do it for you," he said.

She gave him a sideways I-don't-think-so glance.

"Tell you what …" He closed the box. "If the fence doesn't hold for ten years, I'll come back and fix it."

She frowned. "Who knows where you or I will be by then?"

He wiped the heel of his hand across his chin. "I'll be here. And so will you. This is our county. Lookit, I understand there's barbwire between us 'cause you testified against me for Rick. That's water long gone. People change. Or do you not believe in second chances?"

"Heaven knows people have given me another try, though I don't know why."

"How 'bout this. You don't have to tell Rick—or nobody—I'm doin' work for you. That way, they can't get in a twist about it. I know a few things about crapstorms, and you seem to be in a doozy. I'll help you out. I admire you."

"You're the second man who's told me that today."

"Maybe it's 'cause you look like a drenched cat."

"You're really bad at job interviews, you know that, right?" She watched raindrops plunk circles on a puddle. "But I've been told I need to hire help. So, what's your phone number?"

"Don't have a phone. How's about I go out to your place, fix your fence, and see what else needs doin'?"

Puffing her cheeks full of air, she blew out slowly, watching water drip off the eaves. Neither of them spoke. Finally she said, "All right. Sure." She walked down the steps into the downpour

"Stay dry," he called.

She turned, squinting up at him, drops spattering her face. "At this point, what's it matter?" She turned and walked to her shop.

"Exactly." He tossed the cupcake box next to him on the walkway.

Through the afternoon, she visited each high school girl and a few of their parents, apologizing for her moods and the state of her cupcakes. "And I need your help planning a 3D Fair next week. Please?"

By the time she'd gotten to the fourth girl's house, she'd run out of cupcakes, and the fair had expanded into an educational event where youth could learn to knit or paint too. "And even weld?" Cecily Bennings asked.

"I'll talk to Mrs. Duff to see if she's interested in doing a presentation."

"You mean Davina?" the pony-tailed girl asked.

Lexi nodded, realizing that nowadays only the formidable Shirley Blackburn was called "Mrs." The teens used everyone's first name, even the mothers of their friends.

She'd grown up knowing she was not trendy and had been raised with old-fashioned ways, but she was only ten years older than these girls.

For a fleeting moment, she understood why Sull Wixly felt out of place.

27.

"After the day I've had, I need a drink." Lexi draped her jacket on nearby chair. "Whatta ya have?"

Davina stirred the coals in her firebox at the welding shop. "Fizzy juice." She pulled two cans of 7-Up from the mini-fridge. Lexi made a face, but took one, then described her meeting with Bill Brandt. "Am I being weird?"

"No," Davina said. "Do you know why this shop is called Paul's?"

Lexi shrugged. "You were too cheap to paint over the name outside?"

"Aye, that's part of it, but Paul was my husband, you know."

Lexi nodded, trying to remember the last time she'd heard Davina talk about her marriage—hardly ever.

"What you may not know is that he was a charming but worthless cur. That's not who he'd always been, but life has a way of wearing a man down. A woman, too, but women are made of different metal.

"The first time he gave me a hidin', I took it. I'm a tough woman. A welder. But I got him back, burning him with a metal plate. That taught him to behave for a while, but the more he caroused and drank, the more I had to pick up the slack in our shop. I was fed up to my back teeth. Then he began *fobbin'* me off. It got where I couldn't work with him around.

"Fobbing?"

"Tricks, lies, excuses. Fires broke out under my feet. Manganese fumes rose behind me. He'd sling hot slag across my arm. Always said they were accidents. I figured it was the alcohol, but I'm telling you, Lexi, when you hear drums in your ears, sounding an alarm, you'd best heed it. Don't go second guessin' yourself."

"I'm sorry. I didn't know about Paul."

"I wasn't in your life back then. I hardly had a life. And then he electrocuted himself—not payin' attention to what he was doing. He'd become sloppy. Drunk and dangerous with his tools. By that time, most folks were used to coming to me, so I stayed on with the business. I keep his name out front to remind me to trust the voice in my head when somethin' doesn't feel right. That's th' lesson you need to learn here."

"I don't think Bill Brandt would hurt me. He seems upstanding. Maybe he wants some kind of emotional connection—but maybe not. We all know I can't read signals."

"He divorced a few months ago. More than once I've found that recently separated folks are shaky, clinging to the nearest support post. Cut him wide berth for a while. Do your guts say they want to meet him tonight?"

"No. Not really."

"Well, there you go. Trust your guts." She took a sip of her soda.

Lexi's phone thumped out a six-note musical drumbeat. She answered, "BrainSmith Printing."

A voice came through in a whisper. "Open the gate."

"Do you mean Davina's back gate?" Lexi said, but the phone was already black. "C'mon." Lexi stood. "Rick sounds like a Sith Lord from *Star Wars*. How did he know where I was?"

"You've been walking 'round in the rain all day like a sea duck. People notice that sorta thing." Davina dug in her pocket and handed her a loop of keys. "*Skedaddle aff*. I'm not getting wet."

Lexi left and returned in a few minutes, shaking water away like a dog. Rick followed in a gray rain jacket with only a small circle of his face peeping from the hood over his head.

He peeled off his jacket, revealing a large flat parcel in a black garbage bag belted around his waist.

"I hope that's a pizza," Lexi said. "I'm starved."

"This was in my closet. At my house. Dad said to show you." He upended the garbage bag. A Cole Hahn messenger bag slid out.

"That's Gavin's." Lexi felt as though an ice spike had been jammed into her stomach.

Rick tugged the hair on the back of his head. "Not mine. It wasn't in my closet this morning. Showed up this afternoon."

"Crivens! It needs to disappear again." The Scotswoman looked sick.

"Did you touch it, Rick?" Lexi asked.

"The handles. Nothing's in it."

"Do you have any bleach, Davina?"

"I've Drano and other chemicals."

"Get me the Drano."

Davina left and returned with the bottle and rags. "It's a shame to ruin such a tidy-rich bag."

"I'm guessing that's why someone kept it," Lexi said. "They wanted it, then decided to use it to frame Rick."

"But why now? What's happened?" Davina said.

"Am I going back to jail?" Rick began to rock back and forth, tugging his hair.

"We've got to be rid of this," Davina said. "Call your mother, Lexi."

"What is it with you and my mother? I've got an even better idea," Lexi said. "Instead of destroying it, we'll give it to Gavin's partners at Celesto. They know experts who may be able to find fingerprints on this bag. They've already taken prints off the skull. This is evidence the killer took. Maybe he slipped up and left a trace of himself."

"Are you havin' me on, girl? Rick touched it. Slop it good with Drano and be rid o' th' thing," Davina said.

Lexi ignored her, stepping from the room and pushing Celesto's phone number on her phone.

When she returned, Rick was swirling metal parts between his fingers, burning off anxiety with a fidget spinner he'd made from magnets and ball-bearing cylinders Davina had just given him.

The Scotswoman paced the room. "Whoe'er planted that bag will be tellin' the authorities where to find it. LaCott is probably scratchin' through Rick's house at this minute."

Lexi grabbed her friend's shoulders, forcing her to stand still. "Then it's a good thing the bag is leaving town. I'm giving it to Celesto."

"Think, girl! You'll be the first person LaCott will look for if he doesn't find it. Everybody knows Rick will come to you. You won't make it to La Grande."

"Then it's fortunate the drop off is at Tony's in Kewake at seven, and we're lucky an upstanding man in the community is taking me there. I also called Bill Brandt and told him my carburetor was on the fritz. He's picking me up in fifteen minutes. Now, we've got to find some way to disguise that messenger bag. What do you have to hide it in?"

Davina closed her eyes, her body seeming to deflate. "That plan is even worse. You need a long spoon ta sup wi' th' devil."

Lexi rolled her eyes. "Half the time, I have no idea what you're saying."

"You can't be alone in a car with a man on the rebound. You need your own vehicle so you can escape when you want. We don't know ... he might be the fella creepin' 'round your house. Here's a *tidy* idea. Let's douse the leather with phosphoric acid. Or I can burn the sides with a torch. I'll sneak into the hills and bury it. Just don't be goin' with Bill."

"All of those things, if discovered, can be traced back to you or Rick or me. Stop worrying. Bill's not a psychopath—he sells insurance. I've called Joe Leeto and told him to meet me at the restaurant. It's taken care of."

"Why do you sandpaper every soul's patience?" Davina threw up her hands. "The more I talk against it, the more donkey you'll become, won't you? You'll fob me off and do this anyway, won't ya?"

Lexi nodded.

Davina shoved a finger in front of Lexi's face. "You text what's happening ever' ten minutes, you understand?"

Lexi folded Davina's finger down, grasping her hand. "Let me make my own mistakes, will you?"

"You don't hafta make every one o' them." The Scotswoman squeezed her eyes tight, shaking her head. "Shirley's going to kill me."

"I do need a favor," Lexi said.

"Anything." Davina nodded.

"Could you go to my place, check on the dog, feed the horse, muck out her stall, and make sure somebody hasn't stolen my cattle or burned down the house? Maybe Sull Wixly would help if you asked him nicely."

The worry on Davina's face faded into annoyance. "Aye, right, yer ladyship."

"And I know you've got beer in that fridge. Give it to me. I'm not going to this meeting sober."

※

As soon as Bill's silver Camry drove up the alley, Lexi slipped through Davina's back gate. By the time he got out of the car, Lexi had already slung her large flowery bag onto the passenger seat and was hopping in.

Bill took his seat again behind the steering wheel. Lexi gave him a bright, "Hi!" adding a toothy smile. "Davina and I were working on my carburetor, that's why I had you come 'round back. Good to see you. How ya been?"

Uggh. She reprimanded herself. Too loud. Too fast. Too much information. Take a breath.

He eyed the large pink bag dotted in white flowers with green piping. "You want me to put that in the back? Give you more foot room?"

"No. It's fine. Really."

Only moments ago, she'd argued with Davina, "How am I supposed to explain this ridiculous duffle?"

Davina had yanked her yoga mat and workout clothes out of it and stuffed Gavin's messenger bag inside. "It's all I've got." She zipped it and pushed it against Lexi's chest. "Tell him it's notebooks and such. Boring stuff." She wagged a finger. "You text me, you hear?"

As the Camry pulled onto the highway, Lexi arranged her feet tightly together, giving herself more room and patting the bag. "It's woman-stuff. You know what I mean." She gave a single nod, as though he were an expert on what women carried inside their purses and hoped it was such a frightening subject, he wouldn't pursue it.

"Oh, I know, all right. My ex kept a big hair-dryer in her bag. Can you imagine? I don't know why she couldn't go natural like you do."

Lexi's breath caught. Was that a compliment or a criticism about her bedraggled appearance? She decided to be neutral, flatlining her lips with a one-shouldered shrug. "Who knows?" She glanced behind them.

"How are you really doing?" Bill's voice was heavy with concern. "I worry about you. I know you keep your feelings close to the vest, but you've been through several deaths. Did you know there's a grief support group in Kewake?"

"There is?" Lexi tried to sound interested as she looked in the side view mirror to see if a patrol car followed them.

"When I was in high school, the librarian's husband died," Bill continued. "The strength Mrs. Crowell showed during her loss inspired me. She started the grief group.

"For a long time, she was the only member. It made me sad, so I went to the meetings and sat with her so she wouldn't be alone. I remember we would sit on that couch in the Home Ec room, just sit in silence, eating cookies."

The lulling hum of the wheels on the asphalt filled the car. Lexi searched for appropriate words. She tried to imagine two people sharing a lonely silence because they didn't know what to say. Or maybe there had been too much to say and no clue where to start.

She glanced behind them again, then dug deep in her memory, searching for the only conversation starter her mother had taught her. "If you don't mind, I feel more like listening than talking tonight. Tell me what it's like to, uh, do insurance stuff?"

"Oh!" Bill's face registered surprise. "I never get to talk about myself. This is a treat. In my line of work, it's always about the customer. I wish my ex could've been a listener like you. Well, you'll get a kick out of this …. I recently processed a unique claim. Did you know falling coconuts kill a hundred-fifty people a year?"

28.

Early the next morning, Lexi installed the solar alarm for the good neighbor gate. It took ten minutes to install and thirty minutes to prove to Coot the tiny box she put in his house would *ding* if someone passed through the gate.

"What if they crawl over the top?" he said.

"Don't tell anybody at Crusty's, and they won't know to climb over it." She managed not to roll her eyes at his question.

"Buncha hoopla if you ask me."

"I thought you'd approve of arming your perimeter."

"Right over the top." His hand sailed through the air as he shook his head. "And where's the electric line?"

"It's wireless. Runs off this little solar panel." She tapped the square of plastic.

"If you say so."

"I suppose you'd prefer I tie tin cans to the gate?" He didn't say no immediately, and appeared to be considering it. She shook her head. "Never mind. I've got to pick up Mrs. Blackburn."

By mid-morning, she sat in Mrs. Blackburn's kitchen. "I've become like that tattooed spy-girl," she said, watching the older woman slip PeeWit's front legs into a pajama coat.

"You have tattoos now?" Mrs. Blackburn fiddled with the snaps beneath the kid's belly. She huffed an exasperated breath and pulled the pajamas off. "Watch him." She pointed at the goat as she went into another room. "He needs the next size."

"Don't make him wear those. They're embarrassing," Lexi called after her. "All the other kids make fun of him." She

182

grabbed PeeWit's ears, bonking their foreheads together. He returned the bonk.

Mrs. Blackburn came back and put red ladybug pajamas on the goat. "Where are your tattoos?"

"I don't have any," Lexi lied, not about to share that bit of personal news. "I was referring to a spy in the movies who does secret missions on her own."

"Does she dress like a CrossFit instructor, because you obviously aren't styled to do business today." Mrs. Blackburn gave Lexi's purple tunic, black leggings, and athletic shoes a scan. "Let's go." She picked up the diaper bag and her purse.

"We have to talk here. Otty's at the shop, remember? There's no privacy anymore. That's on you."

Mrs. Blackburn sat, her face as stiff as her straight-back Victorian chairs. "You can trust Otty. But all right, we'll talk here. Just don't throw anything. Now why all this drama? If you'd done something appalling, I would've heard about it by now."

"I used Bill Brandt. I've become one of *those* people. I *hate* those people. I'm using him to help fund my cause. I used him to take me to the drop-off in Kewake. The whole drive there, I asked questions and kept him talking like I was interested in him, while actually I was watching for flashing lights behind us. I think I sweated right through the seat."

"And nobody stopped you," Mrs. Blackburn said in a tired, know-it-all way.

"That simply extended the torture. We were seated at the restaurant and having drinks when my phone buzzed. I didn't look at it. I told him I had to go the restroom, grabbed the flowery yoga bag—with Gavin's briefcase inside—and hurried to the lobby. And what did I see? *Davina* standing there."

Lexi's body slumped as she closed her eyes. "Now what was I supposed to do? Dash to the lobby every time my phone buzzed? What spy has a problem like this? So, I gave Davina the bag and made her huddle outside, under the portico, and wait in the rain for Joe Leeto from Celesto."

"So the drop took place. What's your problem?"

"Because fifteen minutes later, Davina came to our table. She still had that big, stupid flowery bag with her. My eyes about fell out of my head. She said she'd found it in the restroom. Then she sat down like she owned the place, jabbering that she was so thrilled to be part of the fund-raising team—which she is not. She announced, 'Let's get started,' and gulped my wine." Lexi groaned at the image playing in her mind.

"Go on." Mrs. Blackburn circled her hand in a wrap-it-up gesture.

"At first, Bill looked like he'd been dropped into a bad dream. Then Davina began asking him questions. So now he had two women hanging on his words as he talked about his marriage, his divorce, his kids, his love of jet skis. I swear, Davina's accent got worse the longer we were there. Who knew what she was saying, but that didn't stop Bill from talking about himself. I know more about him than I do myself. Each time he looked away, I pointed to the bag, but Davina was busy mouthing something to me.

"I finally gave her the stink eye and said, 'Why don't you just text me?' And I'll be darned if she didn't pull out her phone and try to type. Of course, she'd drunk most of our third bottle of wine by then, including my glass each time Bill refilled it."

Mrs. Blackburn fiddled with PeeWit's leash. "Davina was worried you might overdo your drinking. You seemed off your game last night."

"You were in on this?"

"You take a village."

"Thanks for the vote of confidence. I spent most of the evening wondering if the drop was successful. Then I had to drive Davina home because she'd drunk too much."

"All part of the plan. Since his divorce, Bill Brandt has been acting strange, and he's been asking questions about you and your ranch. It seems a bit suspicious."

Lexi studied the floor for a moment, then shook her head. "I don't think he's a murderer. Besides, what would he gain from killing Gavin?"

"Maybe ruining your business, making you so stressed you'll sell. Who knows? But there's no reason to take chances until he's ruled out."

"I think he's very lonely and broken-hearted."

"That's another reason we didn't want you two vulnerable people drinking, and then driving—or however the night would've ended. This way you didn't say too much. There was no accidental romance. No traffic mishaps. No problems."

"You meddling old women!" Lexi's posture straightened as though bracing for another insult.

"But you're relieved you didn't have to meet with him on your own, right? Never mind. You'd never admit it. Did you get his fingerprints?"

"Why would I do that?"

"That's what Davina was trying to tell you. When she gave Joe Leeto the bag, he told her they'd found a set of prints they couldn't identify on that skull. They're not Gavin's, yours, your mom's, Rick's, or mine. Someone else was in your shop, handling that skull and he, or she, might've killed Gavin. We're trying to get as many fingerprints as possible to eliminate suspects and know who we can trust. We wanted to confirm or eliminate Bill."

"I checked Davina's text when I got in her car, but it was gobbledygook like a butt-text."

"So, both your mission and our mission were accomplished—except for fingerprints. What's your problem?"

"I feel sorry for Bill. And now he thinks he has two women who are fascinated with his every word."

"You were just being polite."

"A special guy was once really sweet to me. I thought it meant ... well, I don't think he was as interested in me as I was in him."

"Who?"

Lexi looked down. "Gavin."

"You don't know that. You didn't get a chance to fully explore that relationship," Mrs. Blackburn said.

"Maybe so." Lexi hugged herself. "I felt like a fool at the funeral when I saw all the other smart-looking women in his life. It hurt. I don't want to do that to anyone. I used Bill, turning him into a mule, helping get my contraband across the county. It's not right."

"Oh, stop it. We agreed we're going to do what's necessary to keep sending Celesto fingerprints until they find a match. And when did your moral compass kick in? Now you become righteous? You've pulled so many worse stunts. What about removing screws from most of the doors and machines at the high school?"

"Nobody got hurt. They were non-essential screws. Everything stayed intact—just jiggly. And there shouldn't have been so much free time in the schedule for me to dismantle things." Lexi refused to feel bad about that escapade. "Besides, I left the bucket of screws for the principal when I graduated."

Mrs. Blackburn hefted the diaper bag onto her shoulder and headed for the door. "I wouldn't worry about Bill Brandt. He's a salesman. He made *sure* you felt sorry for him—which is precisely why we sent reinforcements. This isn't exactly our first rodeo."

"You know, social gaming was easier when the horse was mentoring me."

"It's time we were at the shop." Mrs. Blackburn tugged PeeWit's leash and went out the door. "Lock it behind you. And take Davina coffee this morning. You owe her."

29.

"Otty, you don't have to stay for this meeting." Lexi tugged at her leggings, pulling them from where they'd bagged around her ankles. "You've done enough. You even brought in new orders from the mill and Ag-Services."

"It works out good for them and you." He looked at the three women at the table, pausing at the sight of Davina using both hands to prop up her head.

"You okay, Davina?" he asked.

"*Peely wally*," she mumbled, her eyes closed.

"I think that means she's feeling a bit washed out." Lexi waved. "Thanks for all you've done. See you later, Otty."

But the man didn't move. "I don't have anything else on a Thursday afternoon. I can help here. And don't worry about paying me." He took off his glasses. "These frames would've cost a couple hundred dollars. You didn't have to print driving or sunglass frames, too, but I appreciate it." He opened a folder. "Now for the 3D Fair, Rick and I figured we can print keychains with a person's initials on them. They'll cost two cents each. We're expecting a hundred people, so that's—"

"Otty." Lexi held up her hand. "That's wonderful, and I'm thankful you've put this shop in order and given me cost expenditures, but that's not the purpose of this meeting."

His forehead wrinkled. The corners of his mouth drooped as he closed the folder.

This care about other people tired her out. Lexi sighed. "If you want to stay, I could use your brain and organizational skills. Mrs. Blackburn and Davina"—Lexi gave a head wag toward the women—"say you're reliable."

"I'd like to think so."

"What I'm telling you is strictly confidential." She waited for him to nod before continuing. "Yesterday, the police searched the Phams' house, looking for evidence."

"I saw the cruisers there last night." Otty nodded. "The deputy told me they received an anonymous tip, but didn't find anything. It's a shame how somebody's harassing that young man."

Mrs. Blackburn gave Lexi the look teachers use when they read an essay full of fluff. "Just get to the point and tell him. You can trust him."

"Someone planted Gavin Ceely's briefcase in Rick's closet to implicate him. We unplanted it. Don't ask me specifics. It's too long of a story. The question is why now? We know"—she held up a finger—"Gavin was working on a secret project that NASA might use." A second finger rose. "His laptop and briefcase were taken—as well as his life."

Lexi swallowed and focused. "Number three—after the murder, Rick was kept at the jail overnight and interrogated because he was the last person to see Gavin alive." Her fourth finger rose, then all fingers folded into a fist. "I'm pretty sure LaCott threatened Rick to make me cooperate. I wasn't forthcoming with information until that happened."

She glanced at Otty to see if she needed to repeat anything. He gave her a micro-nod.

"Now we're aware an unknown person was in here that night and picked up the skull," she continued. "According to the Pizza Shop video, there was a stranger in town, but none of us have seen him since. Could be a coincidence, but that's doubtful. Then just when the case stalled, suddenly Rick is framed with the missing briefcase. Why?"

"And someone broke into your house, Lexi," Mrs. Blackburn added.

"I don't think it's related. If they were going to plant the briefcase at my house, why would they sneak in at night? Why not during the day when I'm not there?" She grimaced at the thought of the intruder.

"Because of the dog," Mrs. Blackburn said.

"Oh, that reminds me …" Otty raised his pencil. "I've been using the iPad-dispenser like you showed me. Sometimes it takes a while for Chicken to get to his food. I leave the camera on while I work. I didn't see him today, but I wasn't in front of the camera all the time. You can review it if you want."

"Okay. I'll try to get him to eat tonight. Thanks, Otty. Now, I'd appreciate your opinion. Who do *you* think murdered Gavin Ceely?"

Otty ran his hand over his balding head. "Well …" He readjusted his glasses. "Since you asked, I'd say *you* were the one who had the best means, motive, and opportunity."

"Me?" Lexi's eyes widened. "LaCott once told me I was a suspect, but he didn't do anything about it. He didn't have any proof. What's my motive?"

"There are all sorts of rumors around town. Let's see … you're into espionage or money-laundering. You were jilted. The leading gossip is Ceely groped you, and you had one of your fits and did him in. I tell people it's hogwash. But if I were trying to frame somebody, it'd be you, not Rick."

A muffled noise came from the end of the table where Davina had her head cradled on her arms. She lifted her face slightly, her red-rimmed eyes, pale skin, and uncombed hair so unlike her usual appearance. "Maybe the ranch break-in was to plant evidence. The only time it could be planted was at night when her foreman wasn't around."

"What foreman?" Lexi frowned.

"Ash. He was there when I fed the horse last night. Told me he was foreman. Wouldn't muck the stall for me though."

"He was there to fix the fence." Lexi's tone prickled with thorns.

Mrs. Blackburn looked at Lexi as though she'd removed her head and juggled it. "Tell me you didn't employ him."

"You *said* hire help. So I did. He was probably hanging around the place, waiting to get paid. I think he's living hand to mouth."

"He had a cot in your barn. Back by the tack room." Davina made a sneery face.

"Noooo." Lexi closed her eyes, her head cocking sideways as her shoulders slumped. "I didn't see it there. Ugggh."

"Congratulations," Mrs. Blackburn said. "George has been trying to get Ash away from the front of his feedstore for months. You just solved his problem."

"I don't think Ash should be your foreman," Otty said. "He seems the type that would claim to be your common-law husband after a few years and have legal right to the whole ranch."

"He's not my foreman!" Lexi groaned. "This keeps getting better and better." She rubbed her temples, her eyes closed.

"Ignoring the problems with your hired help, I see two possibilities," Otty adjusted his glasses. "Someone is breaking in your house to either plant something or to take something. What do you have that somebody wants?"

Lexi stopped rubbing her face. "N-nothing."

"I like working here. It's a lot more exciting than the mill," Otty said. "But if you want to keep doing whatever it is you're doing, you'll have to learn to lie better'n that."

"It's a 3D printing shop. That's all I do. The goat-sitting, investigating, evidence-hiding activities are just hobbies. When I went to Gavin's funeral, his partners told me they couldn't proceed without his section of the technology. It's on a flash drive, but I don't have that drive. The last time I saw it, it was in Gavin's hand. Then *poof,* with the murder, it was gone like his laptop and briefcase." She slumped back in her chair, feeling drained.

"Maybe somebody *thinks* you have it," Otty said. "Why haven't they framed you? If you were in jail, you couldn't stop them from tearing your house apart looking for that drive."

"Catharine Stewart," Mrs. Blackburn said.

"Oh," said Otty. "Yeah."

Lexi's hands flew into the air. "What does my mother have to do with this? Why did Davina insist I call my mother last night like I'm a four-year-old?"

Mrs. Blackburn shot a disgusted look at the Scotswoman who kept her head on the table but waved at the mention of her name. Mrs. Blackburn continued, "LaCott knows he'd better have reliable witnesses, several pieces of evidence, and an airtight case before he messes with Catharine Stewart's daughter. They've had a few run-ins before."

"Ooh, yeah." Otty nodded. "Your mom does all our family burials. She's the person to call. People know she's not gonna swindle them or inflate the charges. But she'll give you the short shrift if you try to mess her around."

Lexi put her head on the table, joining Davina. "No wonder I'm scarred for life."

The Scotswoman kept her head buried in the crook of one arm, while lifting a plastic bag from the floor. She slid it onto the table. "I stole Bill Brandt's wine glass from the restaurant. You're welcome."

⁊₹

At three o'clock, five girls from Club Club and Rick came through the door. Four of the girls joined Mrs. Blackburn in The Other Room. "Haisley," Lexi said, "you'll be working with Rick."

The girl's face shone as bright as sunlight on snow as she nodded to him. "I'm not trying to take your job."

"I know. You couldn't do my job," Rick said.

"Okaaaay, I guess my last little pep talk instilled more confidence than I thought." Lexi pointed to two chairs in front of her computer. "Rick, she's only trying to tell you she doesn't want to make you feel anxious. Sit down, please."

"She should say that."

"Haisley, if you agree, you'll be Rick's student. He knows the basics of the CAD program, but he needs practice teaching it to others. Would you be his practice student? As you already know he's very literal. I'm hoping together, you can work out the best way he can teach."

"Shouldn't you do that?" the girl asked Lexi.

"She says she has too many irons in the fire," Rick said. "There's not a blacksmith around here. The closest is the welding shop. She could say she has too many MIG welders arcing, but Lexi doesn't weld. Mostly we are trying to keep her calm so she doesn't start yelling and throwing things again. That sometimes happens to me."

"Me too," said Haisley.

Lexi left them and appeared at The Other Room door. Keily tried a partially knitted sweater on PeeWit while the other girls painted figurines.

"I'm going across the street to pay Ash for the fence repair." Lexi tapped an envelope against the doorframe.

"Did he finish the job?" Mrs. Blackburn stared over the top of her jeweler's loupes.

"From what I could tell from the drone video, yes. I'm going to clear the debt and be done with the whole thing."

Lexi grumbled to herself when she didn't find Ash in front of George's hardware/feedstore. She had a sinking feeling he might be at her house, lounging on his cot. When she asked inside, George told her, "He's not here and don't leave anything for Ash with me. I don't wanna be responsible for it. Nate Spils took him off my porch this morning. They're building a shed. Might be late when he drops him off. Ash parks by the bar so he doesn't have far to stumble to get to his truck. I'd say just leave your envelope in the cab. I doubt anybody will bother it. He doesn't have nothin' worth stealin'."

Lexi located the green Ford F-150 at the far end of the Lost Nickel's lot. When she opened the door, the stench of sweat, old french fries, pizza crust, and mold hit her in the face, making her step back. He must've been living in the truck for a while.

Afraid to leave the envelope on the dash, she put it on the driver's seat and picked up a wadded shirt to lay on top of it. She shook it out so it would look strange lying flat on the seat. Surely he'd notice it and then find the envelope.

Something fell from Ash's shirt pocket, hit her knee, and bounced onto the gravel. The figurine of the screaming warrior with LEXI painted across the base lay next to her foot. Her breath felt like ice in her chest, constricting and burning in a thousand cold needlepoints.

Gravel crunched under tires as a truck pulled into the lot. Hunching over, she took sly peeks until she was sure the newcomer wasn't Ash. Then she tossed the shirt onto the pile in the passenger's floorboard. She arranged a different shirt on top of the envelope instead. Using the hem of her tunic top, she picked up the figurine, rolling it in the fabric, keeping her hand tucked around it and her fingerprints off of it. Swearing, she promised herself she'd never buy another piece of clothing that didn't have pockets. She waited until the truck's passengers went inside, then jogged toward her shop.

The Lost Nickel was a little over a block from BrainSmith Printing. She had twenty yards to go when red and blue lights flashed behind her. A siren made a *bip-bip* sound. She kept running.

The cruiser pulled even with her. LaCott could have chatted with her from his open window, but instead he held a mic to his mouth, amplifying his words. "You wanna pull over, Miss Depriest?"

"Am I speeding?" she yelled.

"I thought turtles were slow, then I saw you. I only have a couple of questions."

Lexi slowed, noting several people stood on the sidewalk, watching the exchange. She stepped off the curb to approach the cruiser and put one hand on the window strut so LaCott would have to look up at her.

"Why ya running?" he asked.

"Exercise. Oxidizes the brain. Makes a person smarter. You should try it."

"Where were you last night?"

"Not far from your house, actually, but I told Bill Brandt we should stop by and see you."

He studied her a moment. "You got anything to report?"

"I do." She took her hand off the car and bent over to meet his gaze eye to eye. "The night of Gavin's murder, there was a skull on my desk. It has an extra set of fingerprints on it, so there was a stranger—"

"How do you know it has fingerprints?"

"I took it to a private agency."

"What's the matter with you? It's like you're purposely fouling things up. Like you don't want anybody to get caught. You've made that skull inadmissible as evidence. There's a chain of custody that has to be followed. How do I know it was even there? You could've taken it to a kids' soccer game and passed it around."

"But I didn't. Others will testify it was in the shop the night of the murder. I'm just keeping you in the loop." She squeezed the figurine in her tunic tighter. "So now there's a set of unknown prints that can be compared to other fingerprints. If you won't find who killed Gavin, then I will, because it wasn't Rick."

His face hardened and jaw tightened. "Nothing you've got can be used in court. I won't look incompetent because of some bumbling girl. Butt out or I'll turn up the heat under you, your friends, and your mother."

Taking a deep breath, she walked away, calling, "Good thing your opinion doesn't matter to me as much as you think it does. Go ahead. Go after Mother."

Back at her shop, she told Davina and Mrs. Blackburn, about LaCott as well as what she found in Ash's truck.

"I wouldn't worry about him. His bark is worse than his bite," Davina said. She handed Lexi a plastic bag and watched her drop the figurine inside. "So how did Ash get that?"

"It was in my house. I brought it home to put by my desk. When I couldn't find it, I figured it would turn up the next year I cleaned house."

"Maybe Ash used the bathroom and took it when he was working for you."

"Since the break-in, I've locked the doors. He had to steal this before last Wednesday, and that means he's been in the house uninvited."

"So maybe he's been in your shop uninvited, too?"

Lexi's eyebrows rose, her face full of questions.

"We could ask him," Davina said. "But I'm not drinking with him to find out."

30.

Ash pounded a nail into the corrugated roof of an open-front shed at Lexi's place. His phone vibrated, breaking his concentration. He hopped off the ladder and looked across the field dotted with pines. Lexi was still digging weeds in front of her house. He stepped inside the shed and pulled out his phone. "Yeah?"

"Do you have it?"

"Nah. But I'm closer."

"How close?"

He shielded himself behind the gray-planked wall, watching Lexi with one eye. "I'm sleeping in her barn. The dog'll get used to me. Then I'll be able to go through the house with a fine-tooth comb."

"We don't have time for that. If you'd gotten that flash drive in the first place, we'd be done."

"Not my fault the geek put up a fight, knockin' stuff around. I didn't expect him to die, but crap happens." He silently cursed. Nobody appreciated the time and effort he'd put into this job. "I was doin' good to magnetize the computer, grab what I saw, and get out of there pronto. I've told you, I didn't see any flash drive."

"He must've dropped or hidden it. Find it. Whatever it takes. We're on a deadline."

Ash moved to the back of the shed, his voice rising. "You keep saying that, but I'm tired of you pushin' me. I'm the one who'll have to pick up the pieces after this is over. She may not even have the drive. Or she may be burying it in the flower bed right now. I can't tell 'cause I'm talking to you. Let me do this my way."

"What was the idea of trying to plant evidence?"

Ash blew out a breath. Having to explain himself was really annoying. "To put the blame on Rick Pham. She's his buddy. If she did have the drive, maybe she'd say so to save him."

"Do you have anything else you haven't turned over?"

"No, you've got the laptop and piece of plastic he printed."

"Don't do any more thinking on your own. You've screwed this up beyond repair."

"Don't be calling me. I told her I don't have a phone. I'll let you know when there's something to tell. I've got this handled. I'm taking her out tonight. Got new clothes and everything."

"You were told not to start spending money."

"It's just a shirt and some new boots."

"You are what is commonly known as a total screw up. You've got two days—then you're out of time."

"If you mess with her or hurt her—I'll come find you, Bullet."

The caller hung up. Ash's fist opened and closed, his jaw tightening. He stared at the dirt, hard packed from cattle standing in the shed during the winter. A bug zig-zagged between smashed patties of manure. He stomped the bug.

Shoving the phone in his pocket, he walked outside. Lexi still rested on her knees, pawing through dirt, but now someone had joined her. A saddled horse stood in front of the flower bed, the reins leading to a man in a camo jacket and a boonie hat.

"Crap."

31.

Lexi jammed a shovel among the brittle weeds in the front flowerbed and pried up a mound of dirt. Red worms wriggled and twisted between the clods. She watched their segmented bodies squeeze back toward broken holes. It used to be her job to drop them in a can. Every year her dad had turned the flowerbed, then they went fishing.

She looked at the sky. The sun had the same early evening light she remembered glinting off the pond. Their red-and-white bobbers would dance between the wind-ripples. When a bobber disappeared, she'd shout. Her dad always let her be the one to reel it in. "Keep the tip up!" he'd coach—over and over. "Rod up."

"I am!" she'd yell back. She lost a few, but he never seemed to mind.

An electronic *ding* sounded. Lexi dropped the shovel and looked down the driveway. When she didn't see anything, she went in the house and began mining the trash for a tin can. She hadn't cooked in a long time, so her efforts yielded a plastic yogurt tub. When she came back outside, Coot and his quarter horse, Marvin, stood by the flowerbed.

"Hey neighbor," he said. "I used the gate."

"I heard it ding." She hooked her thumb toward the open window behind her. "I checked the driveway, but didn't see anyone, so figured it had to be you coming through the other gate." She squatted down and threw a handful of dirt in the tub, then tweezed a worm between her fingers, watching it writhe and kink up. "I'm collecting."

"This is fortuitous." He unwrapped the end of a gunny sack from the horn of the saddle and handed it to her.

She peeked in, then smiled. "Shooting stars."

"You want a hand with that?"

"Actually"—her mouth pinched as she looked toward the shed in the field—"I'm out here keeping an eye on Ash. I fired him yesterday and paid him off, but he showed up anyway. Put a cot and his clothes in the barn. Says he has to fix that flapping piece of tin on the shed roof."

"I don't think so. If you told that wasted bag of excuses to leave, he needs to be moving." Sull started to lead Marvin toward the field.

"Stop. I don't need saving. I can take care of myself. And if I'm honest … I'm glad that sheet of tin won't be banging whenever the wind changes. It's just that …"

Coot stood, giving her an impatient stare as he slapped the end of the reins against his thigh.

"It seems selfish not to let him sleep in the barn, but he gives me the creeps. I'm pretty sure he's been in my house—while I was asleep." She gave a shiver-shake.

"Reason enough to kick his backside here to Idaho. Whatta ya gonna do about it?"

"Pay for today's work and ask him to leave."

"You want backup?"

Lexi shook her head and went inside to get money, but when she came back out, Ash stood in the driveway talking to Coot. The older man listened, his arms crossed over his chest and his stare the same expression cops used on shoplifters. As she approached, Ash pointed around the place, noting work that needed to be done.

Lexi interrupted, putting cash in Ash's hand. "This is for today. I appreciate your help, but I can manage from here."

"This is too much." He stared at the bills. "I'll finish what needs to be done. I told ya you'd get your money's worth outta me."

"No. We're done. But I want to know, Ash, have you been inside my house?"

"Why would I? There's plenty of trees I can go behind if I need a bathroom. I'd knock on your door if I needed to see you. As a matter of fact, I planned on doing that tonight and taking you to dinner. If you won't take your money back, I'll just spend it on you." He stuffed the bills in his hip pocket. "Might have to borrow your bathroom to clean up."

"Thanks, but that's not going to happen," she said. "I need you to leave."

He squinted as though she were speaking a foreign language. "You can't. I got a new shirt and boots so I wouldn't embarrass you. This place is too big for you. You need me."

Lexi heard the desperation in his voice. He truly seemed concerned, but why would he think she couldn't hire someone else to help her out? She studied his crazed face, deciding it was time to end any misaligned hopes he harbored. "The truth is, Ash, I don't feel safe with you around. I want you to go."

"That's wrong," he declared. "Gimme a chance. You'll feel comfortable after we get to know each other better."

Coot stepped closer. "She's the boss. Pack it outta here, bud." He nodded toward the green F-150.

Ash raised a hand. "Okay, I'll get my stuff for now, but—"

"Nope." Coot moved his horse, blocking the path to the barn. "No excuses. No dilly-dallying. In the truck and outta here. Now."

"Or what? Fight me with your gimped arm?" Ash's fists balled.

Lexi tensed, her mind racing. This was like high school, trying to figure out how to stop Ash from picking on someone.

"I'm just her backup." Coot nodded toward Lexi. "But while you're trying to get a lick in on me, Marvin'll be stomping you into a greasy spot. You wanna have a go at it?"

"Just leave, Ash," Lexi said. "Working here didn't pan out."

He took slow steps backward toward his truck, pointing at her, looking as though his brains had been stirred with a drill. "I want my stuff. Bring it to me at George's."

"Yeah, I'll get right on that." Coot followed him, leading Marvin.

Ash jerked open the truck door and climbed onto the running board, yelling, "I defended you, Lexi. Without me, you're gonna get hurt. You need me whether you know it or not."

"Okay." Coot dropped the reins and strode toward the truck. Ash jumped inside, slamming the door. He cranked the engine and ground gears. Coot reached the truck, grabbed the handle, and yanked the door open.

Ash stepped on the gas. Gravel sprayed behind the tires. The old Ford shot forward, ripping the door from Coot's grasp. As it neared the barn, the truck made a sharp U-turn, missing the building, the back tires slewing across gravel tracks. The engine roared as Ash leaned out, trying to grab the flapping door of the moving vehicle while aiming it at Coot.

Marvin, in the middle of the driveway, went white-eyed. He crow-hopped a foot into the air, then side-stepped through the flowerbed, his reins catching on weeds. By the time he'd cut around the corner of the house, his legs had stretched into a gallop.

Coot ran for the field fence next to the drive. The wires bent as he climbed it. He held onto the top as he dropped to the other side, the upper strand of wire ripping his flannel shirt.

Ash roared past, cussing, still grabbing for the door.

"Coot!" Lexi ran through the dust fogging the driveway, afraid his fall broke an arm or his hip.

The seventy-year-old man leaned against the fence, staring up at the sky. "And that's how we did it in 'Nam."

"Are you okay? Your arm's bleeding."

"Go find Marvin. He may be in the next county by now."

⅊

Marvin had been cornered by the fence in back. By the time Lexi caught him and lead him to the front, Coot sat on the front step. She gave him the reins and went in the house. In a moment she returned with a first aid kit, a couple of hard ciders, and an apple.

He looked at the label on the can. "You got anything stronger?"

"Give it a try. It's what young people drink. Let me bandage that." She rolled up his sleeve and pressed a towel against the jagged tear in his arm.

"Hard cider's been around since Egyptians stuffed snakes in baskets. Now it's what young people drink. *Pfffft.*" He shook his head. "You got a gun?"

She daubed the uneven edges of his skin with antiseptic. "I've got a dog." She turned to see Chicken watching them from the window. "A friend in college had a creepy guy follow her home several times. Then she noticed him hanging around outside her apartment. She bought a twenty-two pistol. About a week later, he kicked in her door at two in the morning. She shot him. He took the gun away and shot her. She lived. Lost her spleen, but she's not the same person. You know what the trauma of being shot is like." She pressed a couple of butterfly bandages against the wound and rolled down his sleeve.

Coot rubbed his arm. "She shoulda had a bigger gun."

"Then she'd be dead. She was only trying to scare him. Wing him. She's tough, but not a killer. Neither am I. What I learned was don't point a gun unless you plan on really using it." She closed the first-aid kit.

They drank their ciders in companionable silence, sitting on the steps.

Marvin finished his apple and lipped the new sprouts pushing up next to the house. Lexi's paint hung her head over the fence, snuffling at the interloper.

"I don't trust that guy to keep away. You wanna stay with me? I got extra rooms." The old man watched Molly, who'd started pacing the barn-lot fence, nickering at them.

"I've got a Louisville slugger and my cattle prod is charged. He can't get closer than thirty-six inches without getting bashed or 10,000 volts."

"That'll only make him jump. It won't stop him."

Her gaze remained faraway, looking at nothing. After a while, she got up, jammed the shovel into the flowerbed, and turned more dirt.

Coot massaged the top of his shoulder where he'd landed going over the fence. "You know, some woman on the Oregon Trail probably had the same quandary. Independent. Wanted to be left alone, but some stupid honyocker wouldn't let her. Strange how the world changes, but it really doesn't."

Lexi paused, the shovel stuck in the ground, her foot resting on top, her back to him. To the northwest, the sun had dropped below the Blue Mountains, turning the sky golden. Black silhouettes of birds flew over the peaks, heading somewhere safe for the night. A single tear escaped. She smudged it from her cheek with a quick swipe.

"Would you"—she cleared her throat—"wanna go fishing sometime?"

"Sure. How about"—he pushed to his feet with a groan—"letting me spell you on that shovel?" Not looking at him, she put it in his hands.

He turned the soil, groaning several times as he worked. She pushed damp, tangled roots of shooting stars into the ground. Slowly, they worked until the breeze turned cool and above them, a star winked in the gray-pink sky.

32.

Thursday night, before bed, Lexi checked the front door. Locked. Moving to the side door, she frowned at the old knob. The spindle was as loose as a bone in a paper tube. With enough twisting and pushing, it would pop open. She wedged a chair under it, feeling a bit safer.

It didn't help much. She startled awake all night, listening to the house creak and settle. Chicken slept on the floor beside her bed, the medicine helping him rest and eat better.

When the sky finally turned a dim gray, she pushed herself out of bed and fed him breakfast, which he wolfed down. The vet had said removing the bone spurs should improve his movement but he'd need to gain a few pounds before surgery.

She pulled the chair from under the knob and stepped outside. The sky was fading from gray to pink as a full moon disappeared in the west. The air had forgotten the dregs of winter and was laced with the scent of growing grasses. Lexi inhaled as she walked to the barn, cattle prod in hand. No one was in the stalls except the paint, who raised her head, puffing two fluttering breaths through her nostrils when she entered.

After feeding Molly, Lexi checked where Ash had nested. A folding cot sat by the tack room door. A shiny, uncreased pair of black boots stood next to it while a brown gunfighter's shirt hung from a nail. Its yokes and cuffs glittered with the scroll of gold embroidery. Amber snaps, grouped in threes, lined the front plaque, and the price tag dangling from the collar read $90.

Maybe he could take it back to the store. She felt bad for him to have gone to all that trouble, but not bad enough to actually go out with him. She'd asked Coot to take the clothes to Ash. He'd snorted. "Yeah right. I'd burn the stuff." She backed away from the cot. There were too many other jobs to do today than deal with this problem.

She dressed in jeans and a red quarter-zip sweater, then drove to the shop. A line of cyclists in Spandex and yellow helmets pedaled in front of her for several miles. One fellow waved heartily as she passed them. It looked like Bill Brandt. She sighed. She'd have to deal with him too—some other day.

Otty greeted her at the shop door with an Almond Joy muffin from Latte Da II. He'd arrived early to work on tomorrow's 3D Fair, which included knitting, painting, a presentation on how to sell on Etsy, and the opportunity to weld a simple yard ornament. The girls of Club Club had put up signs advertising the event. By the afternoon, BrainSmith Printing was filled with young people and adult volunteers, including Bill Brandt, setting up booths.

In all the busyness, her worries slipped away, even with Bill's frequent winks and grins, and Otty's report that Chicken hadn't shown up at the iPad for food again.

"Maybe he doesn't recognize my voice?" Otty said as he hung the last of the red and gray balloons. "The iPad is recording in case you want to check it."

Lexi shrugged. "He ate a good breakfast. He's probably not hungry."

At five o'clock, spirits rode high. The place looked ready, and Lexi shooed everyone home. "We'll be swamped tomorrow. Get some rest, and please be ready to start at eight. I'm bringing coffee, juice, and donut holes for everyone." The group applauded. Voices faded as they went to their vehicles.

Lexi stopped next door for the *Canh chua*, a special Vietnamese sweet and sour soup Mr. Pham had made just for her. While waiting for the order, a text came in from Joe Leeto of Celesto.

Fingerprint on statue matches fingerprint on skull. Do you know who it is?

Her stomach tightened, squeezing into her chest. She texted back: *Ash Felway*

Joe replied: *Will see if I can get access to his records. Does he have what we're looking for?*

There was only one way to find out. She closed her eyes. It had been such a good day until now. She'd go home, get his belongings, and use that as an excuse to confront him. She texted back.

Will check it out.

Lexi stared out the Pizza Shop window at the empty chair in front of George's hardware/feedstore.

"Your food."

She turned to see Rick slide a plastic tub across the counter. "And the new menu item—chicken wings." He held up two cartons. "Dad says the one with a smiley face is for your dog."

Lexi returned her gaze to the empty spot where Ash usually sat. Rick came from behind the counter. "Are you okay?"

"Sorry." She pulled away from her thoughts. "It's just that I have to talk to someone I don't want to see."

"That's my world. Every day," Rick said.

They stood, silently watching through the window as though waiting for something to change. After several moments, Mr. Pham called out, "Rick-delivery!"

They looked at each other, then wordlessly Rick returned to the kitchen and Lexi left.

At home, she entered through the side door, stepping over boots and balancing cartons on top of each other. She glanced at Chicken, sleeping in front of the window. Best to let him rest. Returning outside, she hurried through chores, but an hour and a half passed before she could return to her cold soup.

"Chicken. You hungry yet?" she hollered, pulling off her boots as she came inside. "Mr. Pham made you wings—without the spice. And he removed the bones."

Silence answered her. Not even a tail thump.

"Chicken?"

He lay with his head on his paws. Unmoving. She squatted and stroked between his ears. His eyes didn't open. His tail didn't wag. His fur was cold. Putting a palm on his ribs, she shook him. His whole carcass rocked.

She fell back on her bottom, her hand over her mouth, muffling a strangled cry. Tears filled her eyes. In front of her, blackness filled the window, her constricted image reflected on each pane.

After a while, she pushed to her feet. In the kitchen, she stared at a dingy piece of paper taped beneath the wall phone. Biting her bottom lip, she dialed the first number.

At nine o'clock at night, she expected to get a recording, but someone answered. Lexi's voice cracked. "Mother? I need help."

Less than an hour later, the *ding* of the gate sounded from Lexi's computer. Soon, Catharine Stewart's Cadillac XT4 pulled to the side door.

Lexi, sitting beside Chicken's body, heard her come inside. When she looked up, her mother stood across from her, a maroon velvet blanket draped over her arm.

"May I cover him?"

Lexi nodded. "He's cold."

"I won't cover his head." Catharine arranged the blanket, tucking it around his paws. She sat on the floor next to Lexi. "Tell me what happened."

Lexi spoke, remembering images as they'd unfolded minute by minute.

After a while, Catharine encouraged her to the table, then heated the Canh chua soup. "I'm sure you're not hungry, but you'll need to eat at least a quarter cup to do what needs to be done."

Lexi didn't answer, toying with the spoon but not eating.

Catharine fixed a small bowl for herself. "Do you remember the time Chicken unwrapped all the Christmas presents under the tree?"

Her mother's question broke her silence, and memories about Chicken spilled out. Somewhere in the middle of Lexi's fifth dog story and second bowl of soup, she realized how good her mother was at her job. And she hadn't mentioned the piles of laundry, the countertops covered in projects, or the emptiness of the fridge.

"Otty Fuller told me you were the best person in the county to call whenever there's a death," Lexi said. "I didn't know what to do. You took care of everything with dad, so …"

"We'll do this together."

Lexi nodded. "Thanks. I didn't want to dig that hole in the boneyard by myself."

"The boneyard." Catharine wore a sad smile as she shook her head. "I'd almost forgotten. Many a cow and coyote were hauled there. Wouldn't it be better if Chicken was cremated? He'd have a lovely walnut container. You could always keep him with you."

Lexi glanced at the dog's corpse. Sometime during their running conversation, her mother had covered him completely and lit a candle. "Maybe I could print a 3D statue of him, put his ashes inside, and keep him on the desk." Lexi twisted the heels of her hands into her eyes like a child rubbing away the image of him lying so still.

"That's a good idea." Catharine picked up their bowls and ran hot water in the sink, adding soap. "Are you still going to do your big event tomorrow? It sounds wonderful. I've seen the posters all the way to La Grande."

Lexi's head jerked up. "I completely forgot. Yeah, I guess we'll go ahead."

Her mother stood at the sink with her back to the room. She shifted from one foot to the other, first soaping, then rinsing. It all seemed so familiar. And Lexi was eleven years old again, doing homework at the kitchen table. Her mother was cleaning up. Always cleaning up. "Why did you leave?"

Catharine's movements stopped. Her head dropped to her chest. After a moment, she shook the water from her fingers and sat at the table, drying her hands on a dirty dish towel. "Do you remember anything before this ranch? The pigs trying to eat you? Playing with roaches?"

"I remember you screaming at a pack of mean cow dogs."

"When you were born, we didn't have two beans to rub together. We went from cow camp to camp, your dad picking up work where he could get it. In one shack we moved into, the previous guy had kept goats in the house. Crap and pee and chewed walls everywhere. We peeled up the carpet, but the stink had soaked into the floorboards. You were only a year old. It took five buckets of paint before I could set you down in that place." Lines of misery tracked across her face.

"It took nine more years of living in hollowed-out shacks before we finally scraped together enough to buy this ranch. We could've borrowed the money from my dad, but Darron wouldn't abide it. By then, I knew this was not the life for me. And your father knew the undertaking business was not for him."

"He needed you. He wasn't a strong man." Lexi's voice rose.

Catharine wore a brittle smile as she shook her head. "Your father's resolve was like iron. Once he got his teeth into an idea, he didn't let go. The difference was, he wasn't loud or showy about it like most men."

"I hated you for leaving."

"I know you did."

"And you left anyway. You could've worked at the ranch and the funeral home."

"So could your father, but he wouldn't have enjoyed it. I wasn't happy. And I couldn't make your dad happy. You loved it here, though. We agreed this was where you should grow up. You were always exploring. When you told him you wanted to go to college to be an electrical engineer, he accused me of luring you away, but by that time he understood ranching wasn't for everyone. We wanted you to have a choice like both he and I had."

"I'm thinking of selling the place. Getting out of here. Just saying that aloud would've killed Dad."

Catharine slowly smoothed her hand across the table, pushing crumbs into a pile. "I understand. But now is not the time to sell. You're not sure what you want. You're still grieving."

"I've been grieving something all my life." Lexi turned a stony face toward her mother. "And I'll do what I want with this property."

"You probably haven't noticed—because the estate is paying the taxes—but I'm on the deed with you. We're partners. And now isn't the time to make quick decisions you may regret the rest of your life."

"Like you did? You don't deserve to be on the deed."

"Maybe not. I have many regrets."

"Your minions told me that it was you who paid for college, not Dad."

"They're friends, not doormats. And they've done me a great favor in watching you since you and I don't"—she looked down—"speak to each other much."

"Why do they do it?"

"Friendship. And your charm, of course." Her mother gave her a sideways glance, encouraging her to smile. "That's enough about the past. We've got to look to the future. Why don't you stay with me tonight?"

Lexi shook her head. "It'll be a busy day tomorrow. Morning chores will be easier if I'm here."

"All right." Catharine got up and headed for the living room. "Come and rest." She moved a pillow to the end of the couch. "We'll talk while I take care of Chicken." She paused, staring at the pillow. She picked it up again, scratching at a smudge on it. She sniffed her fingernail. "What's this blue smear?"

Lexi flopped down, glancing at the pillow her mother held in front of her nose. "Looks like that sticky blue medicine Chicken was taking."

"Did he crawl on the couch?"

"Stop fussing. I know the mess here is probably driving you crazy. Chicken couldn't climb up here. He hurt too much. I carried him to the bathroom and changed the pads under him. That's the stink you smell in this room, but aren't mentioning."

Catharine went to the dog, flipped back the cover, and tweezed open his eyes. Using both hands, she prized open his jaw, then looked back at the pillow. Pulling up a corner of the pad beneath him, she ran her hand over the floor.

"Just leave it alone," Lexi said.

Catharine returned, tapping Lexi's legs, making her scoot them over so she could sit down. "The man who was murdered in your shop ... how's that investigation going?"

"LaCott's a moron, but Gavin's partners have been running fingerprints to help me prove Rick didn't do it. And maybe find who did. Ash Felway was in this house and my shop. I think it was him."

Catharine gently put her hand on Lexi's shoulder. "Please listen to me. You can't stay here tonight. Chicken was smothered."

33.

"Chicken was old. He was weak." Lexi paced as she ranted. "The vet said the meds may affect his heart. He could've died from the meds. Why are you telling me he was murdered?"

Her mother sat on the arm of the couch, her hands crossed in her lap, her voice low and soft. "I have experience with this sort of thing."

Lexi felt like she was sliding down a steep cliff, clutching for handholds and coming up empty. "What? You're a dog detective now?"

"I've seen many accidental deaths. And this was no accident."

Lexi whirled to face her mother. "Is that why Mrs. Blackburn called you to the shop when Gavin died?" She shook her head. "But that was obvious. Anyone could see he was strangled."

"I was there to make it easier on you. Let's just say I know how to finesse a death scene to make it less stressful for my clients. If you'd have let me help you, LaCott wouldn't have torn up your shop."

"What do you mean by finesse? Is that why LaCott threatened me, saying if I didn't stop investigating, he'd come after you?"

Catharine let out a long sigh. "All you need to know is sometimes people die suddenly and leave their family in a terrible situation. A man may jump off a roof, invalidating his life insurance policy. The man's problems are over. But what about the gambling debts he ran up and left for his widow? Perhaps a knocked-over ladder and an alibi that the widow was gone when it happened would be all it takes to remedy one of the problems he left her."

"Didn't Shirley Blackburn's husband fall off the roof?" At the sound of her own words, Lexi felt the blood draining from her face. Her eyes widened as her brain connected old dots. "Davina's husband electrocuted himself, didn't he?"

"Yes, that was very sad." Catharine's expression became as solemn as her voice.

"You're a fixer."

Catharine shook her head. "I have certain knowledge that can sometimes help friends."

"And you use this knowledge?"

"Occasionally. When it's absolutely necessary."

"No wonder Dad didn't want me to stay with you."

"He knew nothing about it."

Lexi turned and gazed out the window into the blackness. "And now you think Chicken was murdered?"

"I'm ninety-nine-point-nine percent sure of it."

"I know how to check." Lexi hurried to her desk and woke up the computer. "See that iPad attached to the leg of the dining room table? I use—used it—to see and talk to Chicken during the day. Otty Fuller set it to record because Chicken didn't eat lunch earlier."

Her hands trembled as she fast-forwarded through the video, stopping at a blur on the edge of the recording. Playing it in slow motion, the video showed only a bent, brown-shirted elbow sticking into the screen. The sounds of whimpers and toenails scratching the floor grew loud, then faded and stopped. "No," she whispered. Pushing from the desk, she hurried to Chicken's body.

"Don't!" Catharine called out, but Lexi was already tugging Chicken's pad sideways. Curved scratches marred the hardwood floor.

Her fingers traced the grooves. "He fought hard." Tears ran down her face. She swallowed. "This was my fault. I fired Ash yesterday. Sull Wixly helped me run him off. He came back and did this."

"Could be, but you don't know that with certainty. I think it's best you stay elsewhere tonight."

"This isn't right." Lexi brushed her palm over her cheeks, smudging tears off her face. "I think Ash killed Gavin. He tried to frame Rick. Now this." Her jaw clenched as she stood. She turned and walked into her dad's bedroom.

"Why would Ash do that?" Catharine called after her. "Come back here. What are you doing?"

A moment later Lexi reappeared in the doorway, her face twisted as though swallowing tacks. "Someone has been in Dad's room. It's a mess. Boxes in his closet jumbled together. The drawers of his bureau hanging open. I was going to get his deer rifle, that Marlin he loved. It's missing."

⁂

Fifteen minutes later, they'd examined every room.

"How can you be sure what's missing among all the clutter?" Catharine batted at a cobweb. The longer they'd looked, the more drawers and desktops they found disturbed. "What were they searching for?"

"I think it's a flash drive." Lexi rested her cheek on the floor as she looked beneath the couch. "It was something Gavin had with him the night he was killed. It's been missing since then."

"I see." Catharine bit her lip. "I'll help you clean up later. For now, we'll go to my place. I'll send someone for Chicken."

"I'm not leaving and that's that. Ash could come back to hurt Molly. I'm going to check on her again."

"What if he's out there?"

Lexi went to the computer and keyed in several commands. "I'm turning on cameras in the barn. Don't ask why they're there. It was part of Gavin's experiment. I don't see anybody lurking around, do you?" Catharine shook her head, staring at the squares on the screen. "You guard the house and watch me. Which do you want? The ball bat or the cattle prod?"

"The hot stick." A grimace crossed Catharine's lips. "I used to be good with it. Take your phone with you. From now on, always keep your phone on your body."

Gripping the wooden bat, Lexi peeked outside before pushing through the screen door. The full moon cast shadows behind buildings and trees. She hurried to the barn, surprised she'd never noticed how loud her footsteps were on the gravel.

Molly greeted her with a nicker. Lexi checked the paint, running her hands over her back and down her legs. She looked in all the stalls, then unlocked the tack room and checked inside. All was clear. Ash's clothing and bedroll remained where they'd been this morning.

When she returned to the house, she found her mother sitting on the couch, sorting through her purse.

"You made me remember something," Catharine said. "The day of Gavin's murder, I arrived before you. I took pictures— and I picked up a few things. Habit." She shrugged. "Could it be they were looking ... for this?"

She held up a small plastic beaver in an OSU shirt.

34.

At seven-thirty Saturday morning, Lexi arrived at BrainSmith Printing. Haisley Starkey waved as Lexi parked. The moment Lexi opened her truck door, the high school girl started talking.

"I brought rubber bands and extra batteries for Rick's headphones. We've worked out a code so I know when he's tired. It's 'bear-hauler', you know, like hauling a teddy bear to bed for a nap."

Lexi nodded and stifled a yawn as she unlocked the printshop door.

Haisley still chatted, raising and lowering herself on her tiptoes. "How can you be tired? This is so exciting. And you said you were bringing donuts."

"Long night. Donuts will be a little late because—" She didn't want to go into Chicken's death. "It was a long night."

Before long, the shop filled with music and young people. An hour later, when Catharine came through the door with boxes of donut holes, cartons of coffee, and jugs of juice, even Lexi cheered.

Catharine wore the same clothes she'd had on the night before, yet Lexi thought her mom looked better than she did. Catharine caught Lexi's eye and nodded toward The Other Room.

When they'd both stepped inside, her mom closed the door. "It's done. Joe Leeto met me at the coffee shop in La Grande. The way he was checking around him, you'd think we were in a spy movie. He didn't even look at the flash drive, just palmed

216

it, sticking it in his pocket. I hope we gave it to the right person and not someone who's selling out his company."

"I hadn't considered that." She pushed the thought aside. Right now, catching Gavin's killer was her main focus.

"You haven't met enough jerks yet. It doesn't matter. The experience is in the rear view mirror. He said to give you his business card and let you know the FBI might be calling since this is a potential government project."

"Then it's not too late for the NASA competition?"

"They have twenty-four hours to turn in a prototype. Read the card."

For your CAD program. Good For 2 Computers-your choice of hard drive and software. Our thanks. Celesto.

Lexi shook her head. "Their project only cost a wonderful man, a good dog, and nearly my business."

"You're your father's daughter." Catharine straightened Lexi's collar. "You've adapted to every crapstorm that's come at you. You're a survivor—whether you realize it or not. You've been gifted with people to help you—whether you realize it or not. And you're helping these kids and businesses—whether you realize it or not. So, worry about the rest of it tomorrow. Each day has enough trouble on its own."

"Mrs. Blackburn says that, too."

"Matthew six, verse thirty-four." Catharine smiled.

"Good grief, how long have all of you been secretly seeding me with righteous advice?"

"Ha!" Catharine coughed out a laugh. "I'm going home. My presence here would wag too many tongues. I'll call tonight. It's important you act normal as the noose tightens around Ash's neck. In your case, that means be your usual hot-headed self."

"Everybody keeps giving me conflicting advice. Thanks." Lexi made a twisted face. "Coot said he'd keep an eye on the ranch while I'm here. Do you think I should take Ash his clothes?"

"For crying out loud, no! He's already been through your place. You don't have to worry about him now. Nobody's seen him around." She opened the door a few inches. "You should only snap at half of the people you'd like to chew out today. Remember, they're irritating only because you're tired."

"Says the ice queen." Lexi looked at her, adding a cocked eyebrow and a mirthless smile. "I'm my mother's daughter."

"Touché!" Catharine barked another laugh and threaded through the crowd and out the door.

※

By three that afternoon, they had printed more than two hundred personalized key chains. Bill Brandt had talked two people into donating new computers to the CAD program. Main Street had no parking spots left. People milled between the shops, buying pizza, eating Crusty's blackberry pie, touring Davina's welded sculptures, and catching up on gossip in front of George's hardware/feedstore.

Rick and Lexi had invoked "bearhauler" twice and retreated to Rick's rooftop Eden to eat rice noodles and nap without the mindless crowd noise.

Around four o'clock, Cal LaCott wandered into the shop. He wore a blue plaid polo shirt with jeans and watched as the printers slid back and forth, extruding plastic.

"You want a key fob with your initials on it?" Lexi halted beside him.

"Nice turnout. This is a good thing you're doing, keeping kids busy. On behalf of law enforcement, thank you," he said.

She leaned back. "Who are you? What have you done with our sheriff?"

He gave her smug grin. "It's been over a week, and I haven't answered an emergency call concerning you or something you've done. What gives?"

"As a matter of fact, I almost called you last night, but figured listening to you would be more painful than what I was going through." Her words slowed, anger underlining each one. "Someone killed my dog yesterday."

"No way. Is that the hound that used to hang over your dad's tailgate, letting his tongue flap like an oil pump? I thought he died years ago. Somebody shoot him?"

"No, they broke in and smothered him."

He gave her the squint eye. "You haven't lost your taste for drama. Why would someone smother a dog when a bullet is faster and easier—not that I'm recommending either."

Lexi pulled out her phone. "This video is from his feeding station at my house. The time stamp shows eleven-thirty yesterday morning, and that brown-shirt-elbow sticking into the screen is someone struggling to hold the pillow over him."

LaCott stared at the video, his forehead bunching up. He scratched behind his ear as he shook his head. "Maybe this is what you say it is, maybe not. Who knows? But look around, Miss Depriest. There's two guys in this room wearing brown shirts. One of them was your date the other night—Bill Brandt. I bet there's four guys out on the street, right now, wearing that color. And if this is what you say it is, how do you know this elbow was smothering your dog? It could've been a woman. Maybe she was petting it."

"What's the matter with you?" Lexi's voice rose. "Did you not listen to the audio or see the scratch marks on the floor that I recorded?"

"Our animals are like family members, and I'm truly sorry you've lost a long-time companion, but most of all, I thank you for not calling me in the middle of the night, like you usually do. I have a hard time buying your story because you're what we call an attention-seeker. Always making a big splash. Why would anybody hurt an old dog?"

"So they could search my house."

"Last time I checked, the queen still kept her jewels in the tower. Are you missing something?"

"My dad's Marlin 336." Her words finally got his undivided attention.

"When did you last see it?"

"I don't know." She should have checked for the gun sooner.

"So he coulda sold it or given it away before he died, or maybe it was taken during your last dramatic break-in, along with your diamond tiara."

"Stop trying to be funny. I want it on record it was stolen. If it's used in a crime, I don't want to be accused of it."

He rubbed his forehead, a red flush creeping up his neck, fanning into a bloom on his cheeks. "Cheez! I'm off work today. I get a few days a month off from this thankless job only to hear your whining. I knew I shouldn't have come in here. You need to march yourself to the office and fill out a form if you want to report something."

"And you need to arrest Ash Felway."

"Why's that?" he snapped.

"Ash swears he's never been in my shop or home, but he touched a plastic skull in my shop and stole a small figurine from my house. Both have his fingerprints. I think someone paid him to kill Gavin and steal what he was working on. Sull Wixly ran Ash off my ranch yesterday, but Ash left behind an expensive shirt—brown, by the way, and boots barely out of the box—so he's receiving money from somewhere. He told me I'd get hurt unless he stayed around. You need to look into his finances, because if you can't do your job, then I know people who can find things out."

LaCott leaned close, his voice rasping as though he'd swallowed a chain saw. "I've had it with your play-detective attempts. If what you say is even half-true, you've fouled up any chances of making it stick. I'll pick up Ash tomorrow, and we'll have a come-to-Jesus chat. Until then, keep your mouth shut. You've messed up so much evidence I could have you mucking out stalls at the Women's Correctional Center. You understand?"

"Aren't you supposed to 'serve the people?' Isn't that what it says on your cruiser?"

"Not today." His eyes narrowed as though centering on a target. "Right now, I'm driving my Dodge Ram. It doesn't say nothin' on the side of it. Good night, Miss Depriest."

⁂

That evening when Catharine called, Lexi reported the 3D Fair had received commitments for five computers and enrolled twenty students in various classes. She also described her conversation with LaCott.

"That was stupid," Catharine said.

"Why? Ash tried to frame Rick. Maybe he stole the gun to frame me. Now it's on record."

"You know who else wears dark brown shirts?" her mother snapped.

"No."

"They're part of the sheriff's uniform."

35.

Bullet had been looking forward to a quiet evening instead, he'd been interrupted by the gangly young man now lounging on his couch, sucking down another glass of his bourbon.

"She shouldn'ta kicked me out." Ash let his head drop onto the backrest. Sunday Night football played across the TV screen.

"What'd you expect? She's outta your league," Bullet muttered. "You had two chances to impress her: slim and none—and slim left town."

"You don't know squat. She needs me. It takes time for a shoe to form to a foot." Ash poured himself another drink, slopping the amber liquid over the side of the glass.

"I'm guessing that's about as likely as an icicle in a forest fire." Bullet toed Ash's leg. "Pay attention to what you're doin'."

"She woulda warmed up to bein' Mrs. Ash Felway."

"Forget her. She would've made you miserable. She's a spiked-tongued witch."

"She's not." Ash's face grew blotchy and hot. "When she slept, her hair fell across one eye. She looked like somethin' from heaven."

"So do baby ducks and kittens. But watching somebody sleep is creepy."

"You wouldn't understand. Your ol' lady got as far away from you as she could." Ash's mouth puckered as though tasting pecan hulls. "It wouldn't be like that for me and Lexi."

"Okay, believe what you want, Romeo." Crease lines deepened across Bullet's forehead as he watched Ash drain his drink. From the TV, the crowd roared. Seattle made a touchdown.

Ash poured another bourbon and swung his cracked, bent-toe boots onto the coffee table letting them rest on a scrunched-up doily.

Bullet frowned. The bric-a-brac was left by one of the ex-wives. It shouldn't matter that it was getting wadded and mashed, but … if he complained, Ash would only say something else stupid. "Listen up. This is the plan. We're gonna retrieve your gear, then you're gonna get out of this state."

"Why?"

"The deadline is tomorrow. Vendix will make the final payment then. It'll be a little less than you thought because you never found Celesto's new design, but you delayed their project till the deadline was up. That's what counts."

Ash's feet hit the floor. "I shouldn't be docked for somethin' nobody could find. I need the full amount."

"Consider it a penalty for botching the job in the first place."

"Not my fault. The jerk shouldn'ta fought so hard. I thought he'd just passed out. Not died on me." Ash downed his drink.

"You left fingerprints at the scene."

"I wore gloves."

"All the time?"

Ash looked at the TV. "For the important stuff, yeah. You ever worn those? My fingers were sweatin' so much, it was runnin' down my wrists. Had to get 'em off."

"And then you got caught trying to search Lexi Depriest's house."

"Nobody caught me." Ash's voice rose. "Th' dog chased me."

"They're on to you. And your attempt to plant that messenger bag at Phams' house—what was that about? You weren't supposed to have the bag. It shoulda been given to

Vendix along with the laptop and plastic piece Ceely was printing."

"Shut up. I waz fixin' things, helpin' point a finger at th' weirdo guy."

"So where did the messenger bag end up? It wasn't found in the search. You probably put it in the wrong house." He silently cursed hiring the fool. It should've been easy to control such a stooge. Instead, it was like poking holes in granite.

"I din't! I'm no idiot." Ash's jaw tightened.

"And what'd you do with the electro-magnet?"

"Iz in my pickup."

"That's really smart, isn't it?"

"You're th' stupid one. Why'd ya tell me to slap it on her computer if the computer had the information we wanted?"

Bullet looked away, disgust in his voice. "I've told you already."

"Then 'splain it again. I wanna know why I'm not gettin' paid fer info I was tol' to destroy. I'm gettin' screwed here. I *won't* be quiet 'bout it." He pounded the coffee table.

"Calm down!" Bullet took a breath and spoke slowly. "I told you to steal a big magnet, so we'd have it when we needed it."

"Did that." Ash made a checkmark in the air.

"And while you were sitting around, looking innocent, I was watching the Celesto group. When all three partners went to the Depriest barn, we figured they had to be getting close, finishing their project." He took another calming breath, telling himself when this job was done, he'd never have to talk to this birdbrain again. "When Ceely split from the group and went to the 3D print shop, it was the perfect opportunity to retrieve his data. Vendix had already reported there were cameras all over that shop. The magnet was the fastest way to get rid of videos of the robbery"—Bullet shot Ash a hateful look—"which you turned into a strangling."

He detested mistakes. That's how trouble started. He straightened the doily on the coffee table. "The information we needed was supposed to be on the guy's laptop—except it wasn't. Then we found out he carried it on a flash drive, which you still haven't found. You aren't being cheated. You'll get part of your money, and it's a good amount. Now, get rid of that magnet."

"I like it."

"You aren't keeping it. You've bungled this job in so many ways you shouldn't be paid at all. The advance cash I gave you was for food, not fancy clothes. That was about as smart as a head crash."

"Shuddup!" Ash hurled his drink against the wall. The jangle of broken glass rang through the room. "Ya think you're so smart. You're right alla time, aren't ya? Thaz 'cause ya hide and don't get yer hands dirty. You jus' remember I can ruin your whole game … like … that." Ash snapped his fingers.

Bullet looked at the spatter on his wall and the broken shards on the floor. His lips flatlined. He breathed slowly. When he spoke again, his voice was calm, but his eyes burned. "You won't say anything because it'll hurt you." He got up and retrieved another glass from the kitchen. "Let's clear our heads and not let a woman mess up our plans. Right? That's what women always do—hold us back. And then when we've got money, they think we're gods. We can do no wrong. You and I can still save this thing. We'll soon have enough to keep us comfortable."

Ash didn't speak.

"Here's what we're gonna do." Bullet stood in front of him. "I'll drop you off at your truck, then we'll get your clothes from the barn so there's no DNA samples lying around. You'll point your truck north and drive till you hit the Canadian border. I'll send you your money."

"What if I don't wanna?" Ash sneered.

"I'm trying to help you here. You're about one cigarette-butt away from being identified. But if you wanna hang around and get railroaded through the system, it's up to you. You're hours from being a rich man if you leave now."

Ash chewed his bottom lip. "Okay, but I'm comin' back when things cool off."

"Sure. Of course. But in a couple of days you'll be a man of means in a new place. Why would you come back to a town that treated you like dog scabies? Besides, you're not leaving anything behind, so there's nothing to come back for. We're gonna quietly get that new shirt and boots tonight, so you can start fresh north of the border, right?"

"Oh, yeah. You bet I'm takin' those boots with me."

"Good. We can still make this turn out fine." He set an empty glass in front of Ash. "I'm changing my shoes. Have a drink till it's time to go. Keep it off the walls."

36.

*D*ing.

    Lexi's phone chimed, the sound penetrating the thin haze of her sleep. She rolled over. Cracking open an eye, she checked the bedside clock. Two in the morning.

Her phone suddenly brightened with a darkened photo.

She sat up, fully alert. The gate alarm. A groan escaped when she looked at the picture. She'd only thought of day visitors when she'd hooked up the camera. At night there wasn't enough light to capture who passed through. Fortunately, she'd made preparations since the last visitor.

Phone in hand, she raced to the mudroom and grabbed one of Gavin's customized drones. Kicking the chair from under the knob, she stepped out the side door.

The air felt damp and heavy. The wind blew in gusts. Above her, curds of low black clouds flashed with internal lightning. Muffled thunder rolled in the distance. A few raindrops dotted the concrete steps, the cold nipping her bare toes.

She set the drone on the steps and opened an application on her phone, turning it into the controller. In a few seconds, the black machine hovered in front of her. At ten pounds, it could barely be heard. She'd modified it to carry a small infrared camera and run without lights. If it went down, she wouldn't be able to spot it. She glanced at the sky, hoping it wouldn't rain and short out the electronics. Covered with goosebumps, she huddled against the house, tapped the phone, and flew the UAV thirty feet over the driveway.

Her screen showed two infrared figures walking up her driveway. One weaved and jabbered, the other signaled with hands for silence. Their faces weren't clear. She buzzed to the road to see their vehicles. Ash's F-150 sat with one wheel lodged in the ditch. LaCott's Dodge Ram angled across her driveway entrance.

The men appeared to be talking as they walked, but the drone wasn't equipped to pick up audio. Lexi scanned the surrounding area. The infrared showed only cows. She brought the drone back and landed it on the porch roof. Hurrying inside, her dirty feet slipped on the linoleum as she ran for the ball bat. She felt like a cartoon character, skidding through the room, bouncing off the doorframe. Where had her mother put the cattle prod? When she reached her bedroom, she dropped to the floor, afraid they'd see her through the windows.

Ash staggered in front of the house, his voice carrying in the damp air. The wind skittered leaves across the gravel drive. "She's 'sleep. You can tell cuz the computer's off. When it's on, it turns the room blue-green with light, and looks like she's wearin' a li'l halo when she sits there."

LaCott mumbled something Lexi didn't catch.

"Th' houndz not at th' window," Ash said, his voice louder. "She sleeps with him. Thaz weird. Don' ya think? She needs a man in her bed—me."

LaCott hissed. "Shut up."

"Shhh. That dog haz ears like tha' big honkin' magnet. Pickz up ever'thin'."

"Not anymore he don't."

When their voices began to fade, Lexi peeked above the windowsill. Ash stumbled toward the outbuildings, LaCott followed. She hunched over in case they looked back, and trotted to her computer.

❧

Outside the barn, Ash stumbled to a halt. "Wait! I gotta ..." he fumbled with his pants, putting one hand against the barn, steadying his swirling world as he relieved himself. "I don' think I can drive to Canada tonight."

"Looks doubtful."

"When's zat Vendix guy meetin' uz at the Pizz' Place with our money?"

"He's not. Too risky," LaCott muttered. "Pham got us on video last time but didn't know what he had. Vendix will pay me tomorrow, then I'll pay you. You'll have to camp at my place till you sober up. But as soon as you get your money, you're headed north. Got it?"

"Thaz nice a'you, Bullet."

᷉

A series of keystrokes woke up the computer and turned on the barn cameras. Lexi squinted at the computer screen, looking for the men. The yellow bulb shining next to the tack room was the only light. Finally, Ash appeared, cast in sepia tones and deep shadows. He picked up one of his new boots and cradled it, his mouth moving, one hand upraised like a Shakespearean actor giving a soliloquy.

The other cameras showed Molly wasn't in her stall. Lexi sat back, relieved. She'd left the barn door open so the paint could go into the field if she needed to escape an intruder. Either Molly had heard them and left, or most likely she was at the pasture shed, bossing the cows around.

Her fingers drummed the desktop. So this was LaCott's cowardly solution to the allegations she'd made. He'd found a drunken Ash and herded him here to pick up his clothes. Most likely, the sheriff would knock on her door and force her to hear Ash's apology for taking squatters' rights in her barn. Of course, Ash would deny he'd hurt Chicken. She didn't have proof he'd actually done the deed, either. LaCott would enjoy all this, especially waking her up in the middle of the night like she'd done to him.

To the south, a flash of lightning streaked to the earth. One Mississippi, two Mississippi—she continued to count, a leftover childhood habit. Twenty-five seconds later, thunder rolled over the house, the storm five miles away.

Now Ash sat on the cot, putting on his new boots. Lexi rolled her eyes. Couldn't they finish and leave? She should hike out there and jab Ash with the hot shot until he admitted to the killings. Now, if she could only find it.

LaCott didn't appear in any of the camera frames, but he had to be nearby because Ash's mouth still moved.

Ash stood, stomping into the heels of his new boots. He walked in a little circle, testing them with a smile on his face. Unbuttoning the top three buttons, he pulled his old plaid shirt over his head. His skinny upper torso looked concave as though he had lost the trapezius muscles to hold his shoulders back. He took his new brown shirt off the hanger, its gold embroidered shoulders glinting as he slipped it over one arm, his mouth still moving.

LaCott stepped behind him. In one fluid swing, he slammed Ash's head with a shovel as though he were hitting a homerun to win the World Series.

Lexi froze.

Ash lurched sideways, his eyes rolling up, showing their whites. Then he dropped in a slow-leaning fall, slamming onto the floor like a fallen pillar. Lexi's breath caught in her chest.

Without a moment's hesitation, LaCott grabbed Ash's ankles and dragged him across the concrete floor, glancing overhead at the beams and platform above. He dropped the body, then tossed Ash's bedroll beside it. LaCott disappeared off camera for a few moments, then returned, lugging a bale of hay. Dumping it beside Ash, he cut the twine, tore off several flakes and scattered it around Ash.

Lexi barely breathed, stuck with horror-paralysis. Everything had stopped, time, the wind, her fingers on the keyboard, her ability to comprehend. The only thing moving was LaCott, frantically pawing through the shirt Ash had just taken off. The sheriff removed a packet of cigarettes, shook one out, and lit it. Then, he, too, finally stopped, staring at Ash splayed-legged on the floor. The only movement in the sepia light was a long, thin wisp of smoke curling from the cigarette.

It was the latex gloves on LaCott's hands that rang alarms into Lexi's head, jarring her thoughts. If he were gloved, then this was planned and who knew what he'd do next? Her brain shouted at her to pick up her cell phone. But who could she call? 911 would direct her to the sheriff's office. No one on duty would believe her. LaCott had made sure they all thought of her as a drama queen.

Movement on the computer screen demanded her attention again. Her brain fogged with no viable options as LaCott flicked his cigarette, bouncing it off Ash's bloody head.

Moments later, tendrils of smoke and a small flame began to rise from the scattered hay. The flames licked the bottom of Ash's new shirt. LaCott tossed the old shirt onto the fire.

Lexi grabbed the edge of her desk, forcing her chair to turn away. Her brain whirled. With no other options, she punched numbers on her phone. Before the operator could say "Emergency Services," she yelled, "Sheriff LaCott just killed a man and set my barn on fire!"

"We will dispatch as quickly as you give us information. Please speak slowly and clearly. Tell me your name."

"Did you hear me?" Lexi yelled.

"Name?"

"Lexi Depriest! Good grief!"

"Your address?"

"I don't have a street address. I live in the country. On a rural route. Seven miles north of Telos. The Depriest Ranch."

The operator asked another question, but Lexi was dredging her mind for landmarks the 911 operator could use to tell the firefighters, ambulance, anybody how to get to her. To keep her eyes off the screen, she turned to focus outside.

A silhouette stood in front of the house.

She slid from the chair, dropping to the floor below the desk. The operator's muffled voice rose from the phone against Lexi's chest.

In a moment, the floorboards of the front porch creaked. The knob rattled. Silence followed. Then a weight slammed against the front door. Lexi held her breath. Another second passed. The porch steps creaked again.

Where had she put the ball bat? Why wasn't that cattle prod around? Her stomach clawed its way to her throat. The side door. She'd forgotten to wedge the chair back under it.

Tearing to the mudroom, she was six feet from the closed door when a man's voice growled outside. He cursed the boot scraper he must've tripped over.

The 911 operator asked, "Lexi, can you answer?"

"Shut up! He's breaking in," she hissed. She slid beneath a stack of coats hanging off a nail in the mudroom. She should cut the phone off, but if LaCott threatened her, she wanted someone to hear it. She buried it against her chest.

The knob rattled and twisted. The door flew open. She scrunched down so her nightgown covered her bare feet.

A step thudded on the linoleum. "Miss Depriest?" A flashlight beam passed through the mudroom and into the house. "It's Sheriff LaCott. You okay? You've had an intruder." He stepped inside.

Lexi's heart thudded in her ears; surely the beat filled the room. LaCott stepped on a boot. He cursed, kicking it out of the way. Keeping his baton-stick flashlight aimed on the floor, he passed her, walking to the light coming from the front room—her computer.

Through gaps in the coats, she could see him standing, staring at the ten frames on the screen. Two of them would show Ash lying face down, smoke fogging the air, yellow flames spreading, rippling, across the tops of the hay toward other bales.

LaCott swung his flashlight. The monitor crashed off the desk. The LEDs in his light blinked out, but the overturned monitor still gleamed, showing Ash next to his bedroll, a puddle of blood under his head. LaCott pulled his sidearm, aimed it at the hard drive under the desk, then hesitated. With quick motions, he holstered it, squatted, and began ripping cords from the tower.

They did not come away easily. Lexi had braided them together to reduce sprawl and tangling her feet in them. He cursed as though fighting snakes. With a gorilla heave, he popped the tower from under the desk.

"I know you're here, Miss Depriest. I saw the computer wasn't on earlier." LaCott called out, then waited. "You got no proof now. It's your word against mine. People know you've got a grudge against Ash. Everyone will believe you killed him when he showed up, threatening you in the middle of the night. Or you could say he passed out, smoking in your barn, and the beams fell and crushed his skull. It's your choice. I can help this go easy on you. But if you don't wanna spend your days doing intimate grinds with the gals at Cain Creek Correctional, you'll keep your mouth shut and let that barn burn to the ground. It's over. You can come outta whatever closet you're cowering in."

He looked around. Hearing nothing, he snatched up the tower and walked toward the door, shouting, "Suit yourself! You're gonna lose it all!"

The heavy cord of the surge protector dragged across the floor, then tightened, jerking the computer from under his arm, banging it to the floor. Cursing, he picked up the tower with both hands, giving it a sideways heave until the cord snapped from the socket.

This was a catastrophic mess. No—worse. He could've claimed Ash set the fire and then passed out, but now he had to deal with a witness. This should've been over and the info given to Vendix weeks ago. But Ash, that total screw-up, had made problems. None of those glitches could've touched his badge—until now.

He stepped out the door, staring at the barn. Still no visible sign of fire. Plenty of time to get ahead of this thing.

A double lightning strike pulled his eyes to the south. One spidery bolt zagged to earth. Another fork streaked in front of it. For a second, it revealed a small figure in a long white nightgown running through the pasture. Then she was gone, blanketed by darkness.

His teeth hurt from clenching them. Cupping his hand around his mouth, he yelled, "Miss Depriest! It's safe now!"

He yelled again, immediately feeling stupid. Years of experience, and here he stood, like a crazed man yelling at the wind. She was worse than Ash, creating more loose ends than he could tie up.

The low roll of thunder rattled the windows. His mind dug for options. He hated improvisation. But surely it would make sense that she'd kill Ash if he'd taken her computer from her house. She'd gotten nutty when the computer in her shop had been wiped. And she'd gotten even crazier when his office had confiscated it. He barked a short laugh. If she knew he'd put a bullet through the hard drive and buried her office computer in a field, she'd go ballistic.

It'd be easy to start the rumor that Ash threatened to keep her home computer until she slept with him. People would believe she killed him, especially since Ash had set her barn on fire.

That meant she'd have to be arrested.

Of course, she'd resist.

LaCott lodged the tower under his arm and hurried to the barn.

37.

Lexi dashed to the barn but discovered the smoke was too thick to get to the ATV. She ran barefooted across the pasture, her toes becoming numb. Stubble-cuts stung the soles of her feet.

Breathless, she glanced behind her and tripped, flying forward, arms out, breaking her fall. Weeds raked her palms. Her face slid through the dirt.

Headlights flashed by her front gate. They had to be LaCott's. She hugged the ground, spitting and wheezing until her lungs could get a full breath.

Rolling onto her back, she stuck her fingers in her mouth and sent a sharp whistle into the air. Spitting grit out of her mouth again, she told the dark heavens, "Please don't throw your lightning now."

She repeated the prayer though she didn't have faith in it. The last time she'd talked to God, she was twelve and her mother was driving away from their house. God never answered that prayer.

The scent of rain hung in the air. Occasional drops splattered her body where she lay. Hoofbeats thumped across the field. Lexi breathed a "Thank you." The paint strolled up and nuzzled her face.

"Help me, Molly." She grabbed the horse's neck as she'd done so many times when she was little and empty and only wanted to ride to the end of her pain.

Lexi hefted herself onto Molly's back. Clamping her knees, she buried her hands in the mane, still gripping the phone, and goading with her heels. Molly jumped forward.

Damp air plastered Lexi's gown against her body as she rode. Six notes sounded from her hand. She startled, unaware she'd disconnected her call as she'd run. Fearful of dropping the phone, she didn't try to answer and hunched against Molly's neck, keeping both hands tangled in the mane.

Along the road, the headlights moved, heading in the same direction. Could LaCott see her? Did he have a rifle trained on her like the hunters who shot deer from their trucks?

Suddenly, Molly skidded on her heels, causing Lexi to slide over. She caught herself before falling off the mare. With a grunt, she wrenched her body upright. The horse had pulled up at the good-neighbor gate. Lexi slammed the latch-bolt out of the way and shoved the gate open with her bare foot. Molly skittered sideways as Lexi flashed her hand up and down in front of the camera's eye.

They had tested the alarm system once. "Please get out of bed, you old coot," she pleaded into the darkness. "Try to remember why the bell is ringing in your house."

She felt doomed. Coot was stubborn and half-deaf. Besides, people always let her down when she really needed them.

Coot's pasture used to be familiar to her, but years had passed since she'd been on this side of the fence. Kicking Molly, they dashed through darkness, Lexi calculating the location of trees and water tanks. Lightning flashed, helping her correct course. She assumed it also helped LaCott because he sped up on the road that ran next to the pasture.

At Coot's barn fence, Lexi pulled the paint up hard. A light was on in the house. Her heart cheered as she breathed another "Thanks." Now all she had to do was get to Coot.

LaCott's truck skidded to a stop at the driveway, cutting its headlights.

A cold panic clutched Lexi's stomach. She hopped off the paint, slapping its hindquarters. "Go! Hide. I'm sorry I made you a target." But Molly U'd her neck, enclosing Lexi close to her withers as the mare had done many times before.

A truck door slammed.

"Go, Molly!" Elbowing out of the hug, Lexi bunched her nightgown in her fist, hurrying to the fence. The rough top boards raked her legs, ripping fabric and skin as she climbed over. She trotted to an old brooder shed, slid down against its weathered wall, and peeked around the corner.

Her phone sang six notes. Lexi froze. She grappled to answer it. "Stop calling! Just send help!" she hissed.

"Lexi Depriest, stay on the line. We need a better address. And—"

The wood exploded four feet above her head, showering her in splinters and wood chunks. On hands and knees, she scrambled several yards before getting her feet under her. A voice on the phone called out, "Was that gunfire? Please confirm!"

"He's shooting at me!" she yelled, disconnecting the call, running and darting behind buildings.

Two gunshots sounded, followed by the ratcheting reloads of a pump shotgun. Nothing around her blew up, so it must be Coot firing at the sheriff. Great! Now she'd gotten her neighbor involved in a shootout. What was the matter with her? What was the matter with the world?

She slipped into the hay shed, squeezing behind the small stack of bales remaining after winter feeding. Too much open space stood between the outbuildings and the house to get to Coot.

In a slow beat that quickly picked up tempo, raindrops plunked the tin roof. A bolt of lightning seared the air. Thunder boomed above her, rattling the old shed, making it impossible to hear anyone coming. With each lightning flash, she stared out, trying to spot movement. She needed to see where LaCott was.

The phone sang again. Quickly, she killed the incoming call and muted the audio. She had more important things to do than talk to 911. Sliding to another screen, she opened the drone app. "No network connection" appeared. Drat. On her belly, she crawled to the front of the shed, wriggling through the dirt until her head and arms stuck out, pelted by rain.

Her hands shook, from fear or cold, she didn't know, but in the open air, she had line-of-sight communication and could call the drone.

In a few moments, it arrived. She tagged the shed's coordinates as its home base, then flew it in a circle around Coot's house. The infrared camera showed someone hiding behind the brooder shed where she'd been. Another person lay next to the house, behind a retaining wall, legs spread wide in sniper position. It had to be Coot; he didn't much believe in going beyond the perimeter. Only one way to find out.

Lexi lowered the drone directly above him. He didn't hear it in the rain, but gave a start like the cattle did when it hovered a few feet beside them. She thumbed the phone screen, but the drone didn't lift. Frantically, she poked the controls, unsure if it was the phone or the drone that wasn't responding. She wriggled back into the hay shed.

Shaking, she lay on her stomach, working the controls. Water ran from her hair into her eyes. Sitting up, she wiped the screen, leaving muddy streaks across the glass. Reaching under her gown, she lodged the phone in her underwear, clasping it against her like a pregnant woman rubbing her stomach, willing what little heat she had in her body to dry it out.

"… Depriest!" LaCott's call floated through a wind gap in the storm. " … got your horse and …" Thunder rolled over the rest of his words.

Wide-eyed, she froze, resisting the adrenaline to run to check on the paint. LaCott couldn't have Molly. Her horse wouldn't go near such a scumball. Thunder boomed—or was it a gunshot? If she could just peek into the pasture, she'd know for sure if—

A shadowy darkness moved in front of the shed. She dropped flat in the dirt. The black drone appeared in the entry, hovering five feet above the ground. She closed her eyes. "Thanks."

The auto-return had kicked in, a safety precaution in the programming in case the drone flew beyond the reach of the transmitter. When the drone hadn't received a signal, it returned to the coordinates she'd entered earlier.

Using hay, she dried the drone as best she could. Each lightning strike jump-started her nerves. Molly or Coot might be hurt. LaCott could pop into the shed at any moment. She needed to know where everyone was. The beat of the rain on the roof had slowed from ear-splitting pounding to annoying drumming. Pulling her phone from her body heat, she activated the app. The drone lifted on command. She let out a long breath.

Elbow-crawling to the front of the shed again, she hunched over the screen, protecting it from the weather and flew a quick reconnaissance lap. Lightning flashed. Angled shadows pulsed on the ground from the silver light as the storm continued moving east.

Molly wasn't in the pasture, but two red figures appeared on-screen near the house. Lexi gasped, scrambled to her feet, and ran into the deluge.

"Coot ... Sull!" she screamed. "He's working his way behind you."

She plastered herself against the well house, raindrops pummeling her back like tiny pistons.

"Shut up, Shorty!" Sull shouted. "You're givin' away your position."

At the sound of their voices, a figure on her screen stopped behind a tree, turned, and began tracking toward her.

"Hey you!" Sull bellowed.

Lexi peeked at the controls sandwiched between her hand and her belly.

A red figure stood and walked from behind the retaining wall. "Stop hidin' in the shadows of that tree. Face me instead of chasing little girls. If I'm bein' shot at, I wanna know why!"

"You don't have to take fire." LaCott remained under the branches.

Lexi pushed buttons on her phone. It had stopped sending signals again. Her last screenshot showed LaCott partially obscured by limbs, and the drone moving toward the hay shed. The auto-return had kicked in again. It didn't matter. She edged around the corner of the well house and pressed her body against the siding. Beneath the narrow eave, she could now watch both men with her own eyes.

Water dripped off Sull's boonie hat, its brim drooping to his eyes. His clothes stuck to his body. His legs looked like sticks. He was skinny and weather-beaten. An old man.

Squeezing even closer against the shed, Lexi quick-rubbed the phone on her chest, trying to friction-dry it. Raindrops peppered her back.

"Looks like a fire at my neighbor's," Sull called out. "You do that?"

LaCott glanced behind him. Flames outlined the building's roof even in the rain. "That's Ash Felway's work," he yelled. "Ash swore he'd get back at Miss Depriest and you. I'm guessing your barn woulda been next, but she clobbered him with a shovel."

"Sounds like she did me a service. 'Course, if you woulda done your job, it wouldn'ta come to that."

"I got to take her in for questioning," LaCott shouted. "You're obstructing the law. You fired on an officer. I'm within my rights to shoot you."

"He killed Ash!" Lexi shrieked. "And set my barn on fire."

"Quiet, Shorty!" Sull barked. "Follow orders. Use your eye. Do what you always do when I talk about 'Nam."

She squinted. Usually, she left when he began reliving his war days. Is that what he was asking her to do?

"Miss Depriest!" LaCott yelled. "Your computer's gone. I'm afraid Ash threw it, and any data you stored on it, into the fire." He moved in her direction.

38.

Lexi saw Sull lift his shotgun to his chest, aiming it at the sheriff as he shouted, "Whup. No ya don't!"

LaCott stopped, his gun waist-high, body motionless.

"We got us a stand-off," the old man said, "so why don't you tell the truth this time. Why's Ash dead?"

Moments passed. Water dripped off the end of the muzzle and streamed from Sull's bent elbows. He raised the shotgun to his shoulder peering down the sights at LaCott. "I'm gonna say it was dark. I had no idea who was sneakin' around my property when I took this shot."

"Okay." LaCott lowered his rifle a few inches. "It was like you said. Getting rid of Ash was a community service. He was a screw up."

"What? Step out here and speak up!" Sull beckoned, slightly waving the end of the gun barrel. "What'd Ash ruin for you?"

"A new life," LaCott yelled, taking a step forward. "Nobody was supposed to get hurt. Ash was paid to get some new technology, but he made it about something else. Her."

"Speak up. I can't hear what you're mumblin'!"

LaCott moved closer, lowering his rifle a few more inches. "I said Ash screwed up, killing to get the drone design. He never found it, but he delayed Celesto, one of the competitors, so there'll be a payout for keeping them out of the race."

"And I suppose you're willing to share that payout since Ash isn't around to claim his part."

"I'm agreeable to that. You two can split Ash's portion. We can *all* walk away now. We'll be very comfortable."

'You shoulda asked Shorty to get the technology for you," Coot said. "She's a lot smarter than that sack of excuses you used."

Lexi tried to clench her mouth shut and stay quiet, but her teeth chattered, the noise clacking inside her head.

LaCott continued, "Reports from my client say she was probably involved with the victim, and uncooperative. We know that last part is true, don't we?"

"What? Speak up!" Sull yelled. "You know what—forget it. I trust you about as much as a naked man offering me a free shirt. The whole thing sounds like a lotta hooey over nuthin'. You've screwed the pooch, and you ain't gonna leave anybody around to talk about it."

"And you … haven't delayed squat!" Lexi yelled in stuttering bursts. "I've already given … the flash drive to Celesto. You aren't going to get … a cent because you delivered *nothing*!"

The sheriff didn't answer. Thunder boomed to the east. Lightning flashed inside clouds. The rain slowed to a steady drizzle, yet the wind still tangled the tops of the trees.

Finally, LaCott called out. "Well, great. Looks like I'll have to continue sheriffing for a while. So, I'll be the one investigating how Ash took his revenge on you two tonight."

"How're you gonna explain your bullets in our bodies?" Sull shouted.

"Hadn't you heard? Ash supposedly stole this Marlin 336 from Miss Depriest's house."

The men stared at each other for several long moments.

"Tell you what—" Sull called out, taking his shotgun off LaCott, pointing the muzzle upward. "I'm wet. I'm cold. My bad arm is shakin', holdin' this gun so long. I don't have anything to live for anyway. Take me, and leave her alone."

"I already made that bargain with her dog," LaCott yelled. "Took the mutt, now I have to take her."

"Steady, Shorty." Sull glanced at Lexi's stricken face pressed against the well house.

LaCott followed his gaze, a smile growing on his lips.

"Don't react," Sull ordered her. "Use your eye. If that don't work, use your legs—run."

"Don't!" She doubted her voice carried over the rain, over the wind and her chattering teeth. Fear flooded her. She stood, unable to make her feet move, frantically scrubbing the phone against her chest.

"All right," Sull turned his focus toward the sheriff. "Do me a favor, LaCott, since I'm a war vet. I been shot at by so many enemies hidin' in the grass, at least do me the honor of stepping out from under that tree so I can see your face. I'd like to see the bullet that's coming to get me, rather than being sniped. I'll even hold my arms up like I used to when I crossed the perimeter." The old man raised his arms like a prisoner surrendering in a war, his body shivering.

"Sure, I'll oblige you, old fella!" LaCott yelled, stepping forward, raising his rifle. "Your problems are all over now, but what a waste. You made a dark mistake defending that girl. And she and her dog made the mistake of interfering with my retirement."

Lightning in the clouds to the east reflected in blue streaks on the rifle's barrel. The rain had slowed to a hard drizzle. LaCott took a breath, set the stock firmly against his shoulder, and looked down the sights. "Thank you for your service, Mr.—"

A dark object smashed into the back of his skull.

LaCott's knees folded. His head cocked sideways, lying on his shoulder. With a *thud*, his body smacked the muddy ground, his arms splayed in an unnatural position. The ten-pound drone flipped across the mud, coming to rest yards away, its four propellers stopped.

Lexi ran from beside the well house, her controller gripped in her hand. She stopped. Raindrops tapped LaCott's still body. She inched forward as though approaching a wounded elephant.

She didn't notice the water running from her hair into her eyes. She didn't feel the cold even though her skin was peaked with goose bumps. She didn't sense the sting and ache of cuts on her feet and gouges on her legs which were streaked with blood.

Sull bent over the body, pulling LaCott's sidearm from its holster and picking up the rifle.

After several long moments, she whispered, "Did I kill him?"

Water beaded on LaCott's face and dripped from the end of his nose. Two of his upturned fingers, quivered.

Lexi stepped back, blinking, shaking rain off her phone. She pried her gaze from the body only long enough to poke the screen, calling 911 again.

Sull knelt and felt for a pulse. "Unfortunately, he's alive."

ϑ

The shower had slowed to a fine mist as Sull Wixly put a blanket around her shoulders. "Why did you do that, you crazy coot?" Lexi pleaded.

" 'Cause you're shivering."

"I meant why'd you offer yourself for me and give him a clear shot at you?"

Sull opened a blue plastic tarp and tossed it over LaCott. "He was always gonna take me out first because I had the gun. That's basic warfare. Then he woulda gone after you, no matter what promises he was making. Your eye-in-the-sky had a chance if I could get him in the open. You like to throw things when I tell 'Nam stories, so I hoped you'd drop it on him. I've seen you drop it right in your hand."

"That was a thin hint. I thought you were telling me to leave. I couldn't drop it on him. He was still under branches. The only thing I could figure out was to come in sideways since you lured him forward. Good grief! The controls were wet. The drone wasn't responding well. It's pure luck you're even alive."

"It wouldn't be the first time, Shorty. War is like that. Makes no sense why bullets hit some people and leave others alive. I've been livin' with that guilt a long time."

"Are you okay?" she asked. For the first time tonight, she looked him in the eye. "You're shivering too."

"C'mon, let's go inside. I'll give you a dry shirt. I'm not sittin' in the rain with that devil."

❧

Lexi drank hot tea at Sull's kitchen table, wearing a green flannel shirt and sweats that smelled as though they'd been in a drawer for years. Her feet were swaddled in Sull's wool-rag socks. She wrapped a dry quilt around her. Sull had changed into a gray flannel shirt over dry camo pants. She told him about the corporate competition gone horribly wrong, Gavin's death, planted evidence, and LaCott's attempt to cover up the whole thing.

"Greed never changes." He shook his head.

Red and blue lights of a fire truck pulsed across the fields and into the kitchen window. Sull peered through the dingy glass, then got up and retrieved his boots. "I don't think they can do much now. Your barn looks gone." He handed her a second pair of boots. "I remember when the Youngs put that building up. Big community barn raising. I was just a sprout. Things were different back then."

They went through the backdoor and down the steps. Outside, the mist had stopped, leaving beaded crystals on every surface.

"Must've been a lotta money in this catastrophe. LaCott sounded like he'd planned it out pretty good. You got proof tying him to any of this?"

"Maybe when they check his bank account. And there's a computer video of him killing Ash and starting the fire in my barn."

"He said all that was gone cuz your computer burned up in the barn fire."

She smiled. "Since the break-in at the shop, everything in my home and business is streamed off-site."

He frowned.

"That means as LaCott was killing and starting the fire, he was being recorded, and that video was immediately saved on a server in eastern Oregon. It's in storage. He can't destroy it. He was beaten by advanced technology."

Sull shook his head. "Yesterday, I was on the front line, defending this country. I could quick-march six miles with a loaded pack. I could take apart and reassemble my M16 in my sleep. Today, I don't understand this new world."

"I don't understand a lot of things either." She gazed at the drone lying on the ground. "I don't get how the man who designed and built this unit was murdered. Then his drone took out one of the murderers." She looked at Sull. "I don't understand why you took such a terrible risk, counting on me to fly that drone. My phone was cutting in and out. I was shivering, trying to make my fingers work. My guts go cold each time I think about it."

"Naaawh, Lexi. I knew you could do it. I've seen you ride bareback on a horse twice as tall as you were. You took care of your dad and ran a ranch and started a business. I've seen what you can do when you decide to do it. Besides, I shoulda died long ago. Maybe bein' here tonight was why I was supposed to live this long."

Water dripped from the tree branches. Runoff gurgled down the rain gutters on the side of his house. In the east, clouds faintly lit up with an occasional flash. Low rumbles of thunder floated over the grasses. The scent of smoke tinged the breeze.

"Sull Wixly, thank you," Lexi said. "I'm glad you were here tonight, and I truly hope you'll be around much longer."

Silence fell, both of them looking away, having come too close to admitting mutual respect.

They stood, staring across the pasture, watching fire ripple up the support posts of her barn. The flames had been dampened by the storm, but still reached above the roofline into the darkness.

39.

"Hey! You trespassing?" Sull Wixly called as he ducked under limbs, walking toward her, his horse trailing behind him.

Lexi untied the rope of the old canvas water bucket from her saddle horn and hefted it to the gravesites. "Nope, I'm ponying water. My third trip from the creek." She tipped the bucket over the shooting stars growing there. "This June has been dry."

"Thanks for doing that. The weather's changin'. I suppose the climate's gettin' mean after we beat up her home for years."

Lexi shook out the last drops and flattened the bucket.

"Shouldn't you be gettin' home? Gettin' ready?"

"Davina's there, welding I-beams."

"You'll miss the wood poles and rafters, won't ya?"

Lexi nodded. "And it'll be smaller."

"Watch out, you're turnin' into a geezer, kickin' up a fuss about change. But tell ya what, just for you, I'll bring over some goats and maybe an old coyote hide and some skunk roadkill. That new barn will be smellin' like your old one in short time."

"You're a prince." She tied the bucket next to the gunny sack and walked Molly from under the trees back into the pasture.

To the north, the rounded crests of the Blues climbed northward. Lone pines stood perpendicular in clearings with Black Angus swatting their backs with their tails. Across the field, at her house, several cars pulled into the driveway.

She scanned the cloudless sky as though the International Space Station would be passing overhead at that very moment. "Celesto got the contract, but I keep wondering if it was worth it. Several lives gone, and LaCott will spend the rest of his time in prison in a wheelchair."

"That's not on you. It's not the fault of progress. It's not even about new inventions. Greed and killin' and jumpin' somebody's claim have been goin' on since Cain killed Abel. At least something helpful came out of it this time. I read where Celesto will be funding your community program for the next five years."

Lexi offered a half-smile. "Yeah. The Gavin Ceeley Progam will provide skills that'll prep Telos kids for new jobs."

"That's good, isn't it?"

"You ever feel like you're on a merry-go-round? Music, lights, noise, speed, but it doesn't change anything? You're just going in circles. Not changing anything?"

"Lexi, you're asking what folks have wondered for centuries—what's it all for?"

"And the answer is …"

"Recursive loop." His eyebrows raised in feigned surprise as though she should've known the answer. "That's what a smart gal once told me."

When she frowned, he pointed at the trucks parking along the road. "You said that input keeps combining with output and becoming input again. Seems to me that you *put* into the community with a program for kids. Now folks are coming out to join you in *putting* up a new barn. The community loop gets stronger. It keeps growing."

"Maybe next, Telos folks will help re-open the old cinema or have a library."

"Little steps, Lexi. How's about instead of tryin' to change the whole world, you just eat the elephant a piece at a time? And when it all gets to be too much, you ride around out here kickin' rocks and lookin' at what'll be here long after you're gone."

"Sometimes when you say something profound, I almost like you."

"I'll try not to do that too often." He glanced at her. "Whatya grinnin' at?"

"That's Mom—coming up the driveway. About thirteen years ago, I asked for that very miracle."

"Yeah, well, we don't get what we want on *our* timeline. Sixteen years ago, I asked for the pain of my daughter's death to go away. Now I've got a new friend that boot kicks me into the future with drones and cameras and gate-dingers. Funny how it works out." They sat on their horses letting the breeze carry their words away.

From Lexi's yard, car doors slammed and people greeted each other. A high-pitched whine of a saw sliced the air as it cut 2x4s. Rooster-tails of sparks fanned from Davina's grinder drill.

Children squealed and played ring-around-the-rosy with PeeWit. More people carrying potluck dishes walked from trucks parked along the road.

Sull smiled. "Those kids will remember this a long time. Everybody will. And I gotta go. There's Pham's pizza truck."

"I thought you hated pizza."

"Yeah, but I love their chicken wings. You tried 'em? I ordered 5 cartons. I better get up there. Without a drill sergeant, people stand around yapping. You comin'?"

"In a bit. I have one more thing to do."

Actually, she had a bunch more to do. She rode the fence, stopping to watch a pair of squirrels chase each other around the bole of a tree. The rapping of a woodpecker called her farther away. She whistled at crows as they watched from branches and alerted others to her passing.

She rode along the creek, the water dwindling to a foot-wide stream in the middle of summer. Molly lowered her head and lipped the water. Under the lighted canopy of the trees, a dragon fly skimmed the edges of the mud, its wings shining in transparent blues.

She unhooked the gunnysack from the horn and dumped it. The roots and seed pods of shooting stars tumbled out.

She worked all of them into the soft soil at the base of a tree. Filling the canvas bag, she watered them in and palmed the dirt, patting it down. She swished her hands in the creek, dried them on the back of her jeans, then leaned against Molly, the paint's neck warming her cheek.

This was the land her father had worked for, the legacy both parents wanted her to have. She would stay here. Nourish it, and let it nourish her into whatever the twenty-first century held for her.

With a last look around, she forked a leg over the paint. They trotted back to the world. She'd make sure the shooting stars would cover this land once again.

ACKNOWLEDGMENTS

Big thank yous go to Ted, David, Ken K., and Brent for UAV Coaching.

I appreciate Go3D and 3D Fast for insights into 3D printing.

To Ken and Alice for your early reading, you were right about sassy characters.

Anne Schroeder, blessings for your listening ear, wise advice, and nudging me to step up.

The Union County Extension Department, no question was too challenging for you. I appreciate your help.

A hearty thanks to NASA Aeronautics Design Competitions, which even helps writers dream of the stars.

Thank you to Iron Stream Media and Kim McCulla for the opportunities. Sarah Hamacker you made my words better. Jennifer Ulharik—Trailblazer Western—hugs and appreciation for your support, encouragement, listening ear, ready humor, and sincere guidance.

Krista Soukup of Blue Cottage Agency, I'm not sure where your untiring optimism comes from, but thanks for sharing it and showing me how to enjoy the marketing process.

To the women of Chrysalis, thank you for critiques and the You-Go-Girl uplift. We started as an eclectic collection of writers but through the years we've become sisters in the trials of life and of many books.

And to Women Writing the West organization, I'm grateful to the writers who've shared their wisdom, time, and grace.

Thanks to my family—for your support and for keeping me tethered to humility.

And always, most of all—thanks, Lord, for the blessings.

If you enjoyed this book, will you consider sharing the message with others?

Let us know your thoughts. You can let the author know by visiting or sharing a photo of the cover on our social media pages or leaving a review at a retailer's site. All of it helps us get the message out!

Email: info@ironstreammedia.com

 @ironstreammedia

---

Brookstone Publishing Group, Iron Stream, Iron Stream Fiction, Iron Stream Harambee, Iron Stream Kids, and Life Bible Study are imprints of Iron Stream Media, which derives its name from Proverbs 27:17, "As iron sharpens iron, so one person sharpens another." This sharpening describes the process of discipleship, one to another. With this in mind, Iron Stream Media provides a variety of solutions for churches, ministry leaders, and nonprofits ranging from in-depth Bible study curriculum and Christian book publishing to custom publishing and consultative services.

For more information on ISM and its imprints, please visit
IronStreamMedia.com